Sexy Beast IV

Also by Kate Douglas:

Wolf Tales

"Chanku Rising" in *Sexy Beast*

Wolf Tales II

"Camille's Dawn" in *Wild Nights*

Wolf Tales III

"Chanku Fallen" in *Sexy Beast II*

Wolf Tales IV

"Chanku Journey" in *Sexy Beast III*

Wolf Tales V

Also by Deanna Lee:

Undressing Mercy

Barenaked Jane

Exposing Casey

Also by Dawn Thompson:

Lord of the Deep

Lord of the Dark

Sexy Beast IV

KATE DOUGLAS
DEANNA LEE
DAWN THOMPSON

APHRODISIA

KENSINGTON PUBLISHING CORP.
http://www.kensingtonbooks.com

CONTENTS

Chanku Destiny

Kate Douglas

1

The morning sun caught his mate and newborn daughter in a flash of light that brought tears to Anton Cheval's eyes. Left weak-kneed by the rush of emotion and a sense of well-being, he grabbed the doorframe for support. It was the feeling that he'd never had so much in his life that was so perfect, that gave him joy.

Nor had he ever had as much to lose.

That insidious thought twisted briefly through his mind, then fled beneath the glare of sunlight as Keisha rolled to one side, cuddling their sleeping daughter against her full breast. Lust, dark and powerful, enveloped Anton. Need grabbed his sac in an iron fist. He sucked in a sharp breath with the rush of blood to his cock. Desire swamped him. It left him feeling at once all powerful, yet uncomfortably unmanned. *His.* These two females, one lush and ripe, the other as pure and innocent as only a newborn can be—both of them, his. Dependent upon him for safety, yet leaving him overwhelmed with an unfamiliar and frightening sense of vulnerability.

Keisha's eyes fluttered open. She blinked slowly, caught

Anton watching her, and smiled. As she brushed the thick tangle of dark hair back from her face, her thoughts floated into his head, as clear as if she spoke them aloud, infused with the intimacy of their mindtalking and the power to raise his arousal even higher.

Lily's out like a light. Do you want to put her in her crib?

He smiled broadly. He couldn't help himself. It had been so long since he'd made love to his mate. *If that means I can finally have Lily's mother to myself, by all means.* Anton walked quietly across the room, carefully lifted the sleeping baby in his arms and carried her to the small portable crib they still used. She felt warm and tiny and so very precious against his chest, but already she was growing. It wouldn't be long before she was too big for the smaller crib.

He'd had no idea how quickly babies grew, nor how much their presence could change a relationship. Anton wrapped a blanket lightly around the tiny bundle and rubbed her tummy until she settled back into a sound sleep. His heart ached with love for her. And, for her mother. He turned around and grinned at Keisha again. His pulse sped with the light from her smile.

Thank goodness for Stefan. Suffering the same fate while his lovely mate healed from the early delivery of little Alexander, Anton's packmate had been a more than willing sexual partner over the past few weeks.

Well, Stefan was on his own today. Shedding his clothing as he crossed the room, Anton was already naked by the time he reached the bed. Keisha held the covers and he slipped in beside her. Damn, he'd wanted her so badly for so long, but now that he lay beside her, Anton realized he was afraid.

I don't want to hurt you.

You won't. I'm healed. I want to touch you. I have to . . .

He nuzzled the soft, creamy skin under her ear. *You're sure? The doctor said at least six weeks. I'm so afraid of . . .*

The doctor isn't Chanku. He had no idea how quickly I

would heal. Shifting seems to have sped things along. Those runs in the afternoon have been very therapeutic . . . and they've left me terribly needy. She kissed the soft skin between his neck and shoulder, ran her tongue along his jawline and then nipped his chin. *Lily won't stay asleep for long, my love. You're wasting time. I need you. Anton . . . my love. I need you so badly and I love you so much.*

Chuckling, Anton rolled over on top of her and found his favorite spot between her thighs. He rested the smooth crown of his erection atop her soft mound of silky curls and sighed with the profound feelings she gave him. "You've convinced me," he whispered. He leaned close and kissed her. His lips slipped over the soft, slick surface of Keisha's mouth, his tongue traced the seam between upper and lower lip, parting her slowly, deliberately. When he fucked her with his tongue, sliding deep inside her mouth and then slowly withdrawing, she groaned. The sound welled up from her throat and vibrated against his lips.

He felt her fingers tracing the length of his hip and lifted when she sought a path between their bodies. It was Keisha who grabbed the pulsing length of his cock, Keisha who directed him to the hot, slick entrance of her sex.

She lifted her hips and seated Anton inside, surging up against him with a powerful thrust that drove his cock deep, and deeper still until he pressed his sensitive tip against the mouth of her womb.

Anton kissed her, long and hard, his body trembling with the need to move, his desire for Keisha a physical, almost painful reminder of how deeply he loved, how easily he feared.

This was the first time since Lily's birth, the first time since almost losing his beloved mate when their plane had gone down on the way to Luc and Tia's wedding. Had it only been a month ago?

He shuddered, suddenly overcome with emotion. His body stilled. Keisha's long fingers spread across his buttocks, pulled him close and directed him to move again. When he hesitated, she rolled him to his back. Taking the uppermost position, she straddled him. Her knees pressed tightly against his hips. She rocked lightly against him.

"I love you," she said, smiling broadly. Her eyes sparkled and Anton knew her tears hovered as closely as his. "How do I convince you I'm not made of spun glass?" She leaned down and kissed him, her tongue boldly slashing between his lips, her hips thrusting forward, driving his cock deep. Her mind opened wide, spilling the sense of Anton sliding through hot, tight flesh.

He groaned at the exquisite pain from so much sensation, so much heat and life wrapped around his cock. He experienced everything Keisha felt, all of her sensations, her feminine arousal doubled over in layers upon his own experience. Her muscles rippled along his cock at the same time he sensed the pressure against *his* womb, the slow scrape of thick muscle sliding over *his* clit.

His breath caught as a bolt of heat flared from the small of his back to the taut sac between his thighs, a roiling, flashing slice of pleasure verging on pain. His muscles locked, his back arched and he exploded upward, filling Keisha with burst after boiling burst of ejaculate.

He groaned and tried to hold it back, but it was too late. He'd not expected to come so soon. Had hoped to make this last for her, but now he felt the grasp of her sex, the tight, rippling clench of those deliciously feminine muscles holding him deep inside. Waves of pleasure, Keisha's pleasure, swept over and around him. He sensed her love—so profound, so powerful, it left him shaken. His hands trembled as he brushed the tangled, sweat-dampened hair away from his true love's face.

She looked down at him with an expression of unimaginable bliss. Tears streaked her dark face. The hand she used to brush the dampness from his cheeks trembled as badly as his own.

"There are no words," she said. "No words to express how I feel. What you do to me. For me."

I know. He pressed her palm over his heart, covering her long, slim fingers with his. Touched her heart with his free hand and knew they raced together, two hearts literally beating as one.

Keisha leaned forward and rested her cheek against his chest. Her body sprawled loose and relaxed and she covered him with her warmth and her delicious feminine scent. Listening to the soft, baby sounds of their daughter in the small crib beside them, Anton put away his worries and gently followed Keisha into sleep.

Stefan Aragat checked the refrigerator first, sighed softly and then shut the door. The cupboards were filled, but there was nothing that didn't require some form of cooking skill if he wanted a meal. He went back to the refrigerator, grabbed a beer and popped the top off the bottle with a practiced flip of his thumb.

Xandi walked out into the kitchen with little Alex snug in a fabric carrier slung over her shoulder and across her breasts. She was absolutely lovely this morning, in spite of the fact neither of them had gotten much sleep. As tiny as he'd been at birth, their son seemed to think he had to nurse nonstop to add the weight everyone wanted him to gain.

Xandi leaned close and kissed Stefan. "Beer for breakfast?"

He laughed. "Nothing else to eat. We're even out of coffee. I can justify it. There's malt, yeast . . ."

Xandi laughed, took the bottle from his hand and poured it in the sink. Stefan merely shook his head and sighed.

"I take it Oliver's not back yet." She tossed the bottle in the recycling bin, opened the refrigerator, stared for a long moment and obviously saw the same empty shelves. "I hate to say it, but if we want to eat today, we really need to make a run into town.

Either that, or one of you mighty hunters needs to shift and go kill something."

"We can always live on love." Stefan pulled her into a loose embrace that included baby Alex. Xandi's dark green caftan shimmered and flowed around her body, hiding the curves left slightly rounded from her pregnancy. The shape of her nipples showed through the fine silk. Stefan leaned down and suckled one through the fabric. "I assume the beast has been fed?"

Xandi pulled away and kissed Stefan hard on the mouth. "Of course he has. He got there first, but if you do that again you're going to get a mouthful of warm milk."

Stefan ran one finger over Xandi's nipple. "At least I won't starve."

She laughed and untied the baby carrier. Then she handed their sleeping son to Stefan. "Sorry, big guy. It's all reserved for the current and future reigning king."

"I never thought I'd be deposed by a five-pound pooping machine." Muttering, Stefan carried his son to the rocker in the corner of the kitchen. There were two of them, placed side by side so the new moms could sit and nurse their babies together. Settling back in the comfortable old oak rocker, Stefan watched Xandi scrounge around the kitchen. She found enough ingredients to make up sausage, biscuits, and gravy for breakfast.

She was right, though. Once Anton and Keisha woke up, they'd really have to make a trip into town. He and Anton could hunt if they had to, but the girls couldn't shift and leave the babies behind, which meant whatever they killed would have to be butchered and prepared for human consumption.

Generally, that was Oliver's job. The little guy was one hell of a cook, and had no problem at all preparing fresh game. Stefan smiled to himself, thinking of the role Anton's personal assistant played in all of their lives. So much had changed since Stefan and Anton had become parents, but one thing remained the same—Oliver'd only been gone for three days on some errand for Anton and his well-organized system was falling apart.

Alex snorted, stretched, and went back to sleep. *Well, not falling apart entirely.* In fact, Stefan thought, settling back with his sleeping son on his chest, he couldn't imagine his life ever feeling more together. He closed his eyes to the sound of his mate humming to herself as she cooked breakfast, and the soft puffs of his son's steady breathing. Awash in a powerful sense of well-being, Stefan slowly rocked, his mind caught in a lazy vortex of memories as he contemplated how far he'd come since his life as a beast.

"There's a nice, clean mattress in the camper. Sure you don't . . . ?"

Adam Wolf shook his head and reached for the door handle. The pickup with its dented camper shell rumbled and smoked. He could have told her the tailpipe was about ready to fall off, but that wasn't his concern.

The buxom blonde in the driver's seat raised an eyebrow. "Well, then . . ." She sighed. "Hope you don't mind if I drop you off here. That's my turnoff. The old man'll be waiting." She nodded toward a narrow side road angling away from the two-lane highway, then reached out and pressed her warm palm against his thigh. Her fingers brushed the line of his partially erect cock. "We coulda had a real good time."

"I'm sure we could have." He smiled and thought, instead, of the woman of his dreams . . . if he could call her a woman. He'd never really had a clear visual of her, but she'd always appeared as something *other*. That was the only way he could describe her, but she'd been there, with him, sharing his nights for so long.

Where was she tonight? He glanced at the dark blue sky. Night was falling and it was damned cold for June. He felt like some kind of fool, turning down what was so freely offered, but . . . not tonight. "Well, thanks. I appreciate the lift . . . and the view." He winked, smiled, and nodded in the direction of her well-exposed cleavage.

The blonde tittered and held her fingers over her ample bosom. Her hand did more to emphasize the dark cleft between her full breasts than hide anything. Adam grabbed his beat-up duffle out of the bed of the truck and stepped back from the road. The blonde waved and the vehicle skidded when she punched the gas. She fishtailed into the turn and disappeared down the narrow country lane, spewing black exhaust out of the damaged pipe.

"Well, fuck." Adam looked both east and west along the empty highway and started walking west, the same direction he'd been traveling. He could have gone either way. He had no destination in mind. If he hadn't figured out the woman was going home to a husband and kids, he might be sleeping in a warm bed between warm thighs, his head pillowed on those exceptionally warm looking breasts. It wouldn't be his first night on an old mattress in the back of a pickup truck, and if the company was right . . . Just his luck to get a ride from a gal with commitments, whether she recognized them or not.

He heard a car coming up behind him and automatically stuck out his thumb without turning around. Appearing anxious for a lift never helped, but he was beginning to shiver beneath his lightweight jacket. Night would be falling soon.

The classic Ford pickup that passed him looked absolutely cherry, but it sounded like shit. Adam recognized the make and model immediately despite the new black paint with the immaculate chrome bumper and darkened windows. It was a 1951 Ford F-1, a beautiful old machine that appeared lovingly restored, but something under the hood knocked and sputtered and then just quietly died. When the vehicle coasted to a stop some fifty yards ahead of him and well off the side of the road,

Adam wasn't sure if the driver had stopped on purpose or not. Just in case someone was offering a ride, he trotted the short distance and reached for the passenger door.

It opened before he grabbed the handle. Adam stopped in his tracks and bit back a grin. The driver certainly wasn't what he'd expected. The man's skin was dark and smooth, his hair slicked down and perfectly combed. He wore an immaculate navy blue suit, a far cry from the typical rough-hewn rancher in this part of the state.

"Good evening." The driver spoke in perfectly clipped English. His voice was soft, a bit high pitched. "I would offer you a ride but my vehicle appears to have chosen this spot to stop working. You're welcome to wait inside where it's dry, however."

"Thank you, but it's dry out here."

The little man nodded and smiled. "Not for long. My name is Oliver. Please, get in."

Before Adam could answer, the first drops of rain caught him. He glanced up. The sky had been cloudless just minutes ago. Now, black clouds roiled overhead. Oliver scooted back to the driver's seat. Adam tossed his bag inside and climbed into the beautiful old truck. "Adam Wolf," he said, holding out his hand.

Oliver took his in a firm grasp and shook hands, but he held on just a bit longer than expected. Adam felt as if the man saw something in him, something even Adam didn't recognize. Stranger things had happened in his thirty-six years but this brief interlude carried a sense of the surreal about it. The odd little man, the vintage truck, the storm that hadn't even been on the horizon—for a moment it left him feeling disoriented and out of sync, almost as if life had conspired to put him in this place at this time.

Maybe there was another reason he'd turned down the buxom blonde. A shiver rolled across his spine as Oliver released his grasp. Adam shook off the simmering unease and leaned back against the rich leather upholstery, his mind spinning lazy circles around the odd sensation of destiny. He glanced at the thick sheets of rain falling outside and relaxed. At least he'd be warm and dry while he waited out the storm and tried to figure out why he was here, now, in this beautiful old truck with this odd little man.

He almost laughed at the convoluted process his thoughts were taking. There was no predestination. There was no determined fate awaiting him. He was nothing more than a man used to living alone, a man who knew how to fix things. Maybe, when the rain ended, he could take a look at the engine and see what was wrong. If it was predestined that he be on this road at this time, his ability to tinker with old motors was probably the reason. Mulling fate versus coincidence and the complex questions such thoughts always produced, he pulled his baseball cap down over his eyes and settled back in his seat to wait out the storm.

The driver's voice intruded. "Did you say your name was Adam Wolf?"

Adam raised his cap and glanced to his left. Once more he felt that shiver along his spine. "Yep. That's me."

"Fascinating."

He paused so long, Adam sat up and stared at the man.

"Mr. Wolf, are you familiar with a young woman named Amanda Smith?"

The question hung in the air between them. Amanda Smith. *Manda?* The same Manda who had haunted his dreams for over twenty years? The woman he'd never met, yet who had directed him with nightly visions, bleak and filled with despair. Visions so compelling, he'd dropped out of college and hit the road in a fruitless search to find her some fifteen years ago.

Couldn't be. The coincidence was too bizarre. The odds this strange little man in the wilds of Montana knew something about the woman who had haunted him for so long . . . impossible."

But what if . . . ? The dreams were gone. They'd disappeared from his life mere days ago, vanishing as quickly as they had first appeared, leaving him with a lifetime of questions.

Adam had nowhere to go for answers. Once again he contemplated coincidence versus the sense of destiny. He'd never been one to believe entirely in acts of fate, but he wasn't an idiot, either.

"I might be," he said, turning around in his seat to stare at Oliver. "What's it to you?"

"I don't know all the details and I've not met the young woman myself, but I recall your name mentioned along with hers." Oliver cocked his head and studied Adam for a long moment. "Many things happen without rhyme or reason, yet their poetry is inescapable. You will come with me."

Adam laughed. "Oh I will, will I?" Hell, where else would he go? It wasn't as if he had any plans, and like the weird little guy had said, things happened. He glanced out the window. The rain boiled now, coming down in dark sheets and blowing back up with powerful gusts of wind. Black, oily clouds hid what little was left of the setting sun. Adam turned back to study the driver for a moment. "From the way this truck sounded," he said, "it doesn't look as if either of us is going anywhere."

"All will work as it should. You carry tools with you, if I'm not mistaken. When the rain stops, you can fix it."

Adam blinked. "How the hell did you know . . . ?"

"Your hands." Oliver gestured with his perfectly manicured fingers. In the fading light, his palms looked ghostly pale. "There is grease under your nails, nicks on your fingers. You are a man who fixes things."

This time Adam laughed out loud. "That I am. I can fix just about anything, except, maybe, my own fucked-up life."

Oliver didn't laugh, but he smiled and nodded. "That is something I help fix. I'm not good with machines. I do people."

Adam studied him for a moment, reassessing the man. Oliver was obviously intelligent and well educated, if his speech and manners were any indication. Almost too pretty to be male, with smooth, dark skin and absolutely beautiful, heavily lashed, dark eyes.

It wasn't the first time Adam found himself sexually attracted to a man, though he didn't sense any interest on Oliver's part. He probably had a wife and children at home, wherever that might be. "Do you live around here?"

Oliver nodded. "Northwest of here. I work for Anton Cheval. I'm his personal assistant."

"Cheval?" The name sounded familiar. "Why would I have heard of him?"

"His name often appears in the financial section."

"Ah. I remember now. He just took over the board for some wolf sanctuary. It was up north of where I grew up."

"Exactly." Oliver turned in his seat and leaned back against the door. The two men faced one another, though there wasn't much to see in the growing darkness.

"What do you mean by that?"

"Only that there is no coincidence."

"You're saying we were fated to meet?" Adam grabbed a water bottle out of his bag, but he knew perfectly well he was merely stalling for time, hoping for an answer. "Just because I know who your boss is and I've maybe heard of Amanda Smith? I find that hard to believe."

"Why do you remember the wolf sanctuary? Mr. Cheval is in the news for many reasons. That was merely a tiny mention in a much longer article."

Shrugging, Adam took a long pull on the water bottle. "I've always liked wolves. Probably because of my name. I feel a kinship with them."

"Amanda Smith's mother manages the High Mountain wolf sanctuary."

That caught his attention. "And your point is?"

"Nothing, really. Probably just coincidence." Oliver laughed. He had a soft, smooth laugh that cried out for a companion.

"Crap." Adam chuckled and leaned his head back against the cold window. "I can't believe I'm having this conversation in a stalled truck in the middle of a Montana monsoon."

Oliver merely shrugged. "Odder things have happened." He grabbed a water bottle out of the space between the seats and took a drink.

The rain beat a powerful tattoo against the truck, but it stayed warm enough inside. If they didn't get a late spring snow, Adam figured they'd at least be fairly comfortable until the storm blew over and he could work on the truck. "Hope your boss isn't worried about you."

Oliver smiled. "Oh, he knows I'm here. With you."

"You got a signal for your phone out here?" Adam had checked his cell earlier and gotten a NO SERVICE message.

"I don't own one. I have no idea if there's a signal or not. Tell me, Adam. What do you do? What kind of work?"

"Whatever I can find." That was weird about the cell phone. How the hell could he tell his boss he wouldn't be home? When had he had the chance to let him know he'd met Adam?

Whatever. "If it's broken, I can fix it. Any make, any model, any kind of machine. I've always had a knack for fixing stuff."

It took Oliver a long time to answer. "If only that applied to people, as well."

Adam watched him, guessing there was much more to Oliver's story than met the eye. He sensed a powerful need in the man to talk. Hardly the first time some stranger had unloaded a tale of misery and woe on him. Adam figured he must have the kind of face that pulled confidences out of people. He took another swallow of water.

Oliver stared into the growing darkness. Adam sensed his thoughts were both years and miles away. There was pain in his eyes, a sad, lost look about him that didn't fit the immaculate appearance.

"What's broken, Oliver? You said you don't fix machines, that you fix people. What do you have that can't be fixed?"

Oliver turned and studied him for so long Adam wondered if he'd erred in asking. The flesh seemed carved over the man's high cheekbones and his eyes glinted with fire.

Amber fire.

How odd. Oliver's eyes were the same strange color as Adam's. A car came toward them, headlights on high. Oliver's eyes gleamed bright green in the slash of light, then returned to dark amber when the car passed by.

Green. The same way his own eyes changed in reflected light. He'd been teased about that for years. For some strange reason, Adam's heart began to race. His head ached, as if he wore his cap too tight.

Oliver finally averted his penetrating gaze. "I am a eunuch," he said at last. "Can you fix that, Mr. Wolf?"

"A what?" He couldn't possibly have heard him correctly.

Oliver sighed. "I'm not sure why I'm telling you this. I've never told anyone before. No one knows, other than my employer." He chuckled, but there was no humor in his laugh. "When I was little more than an infant, my father sold me to a very wealthy man who wanted a playmate for his daughter. I was castrated. The practice was not all that uncommon in my country. I was too young to remember the actual surgery, but it made me a safe playmate for my owner's daughter. As I grew older, I finally realized what a terrible thing had been done to me, that I deserved my freedom. I escaped. I was almost eighteen by then, but obviously the damage to my life was complete. I've never had to shave, my voice did not change and, though I'm small, I'm actually quite a bit taller than many of my people."

Oliver ran his fingers over the steering wheel and appeared lost in old memories and thoughts. "Castration does that," he said. His voice was barely a whisper. "A stallion, for instance, is rarely as tall as a gelding." His voice trailed off.

Rain beat against the truck. Wind buffeted the vehicle. Adam tried to find words but had no idea what to say. Curiosity finally won out. "Did they take off everything? I mean . . . shit, man. That's horrible."

"You have no idea." Oliver actually smiled at Adam. "They took my stones but left my rod. Even so, they took away much more than anyone ever realized."

"Doctors can use hormones, can't they?"

"Probably. Still, it is too late for what matters most."

Oliver turned away, effectively ending the conversation. Adam sat beside him in the darkness, listening to the rain, imagining a life without sexual needs, the constant gnawing arousal that defined so much of his world.

At the same time, he couldn't help but wonder why Oliver had confided such a ghastly secret to him, a complete stranger. And why, when it made absolutely no sense at all, did Adam have the oddest feeling he might actually be able to help?

Leaning back against the warm leather, he closed his eyes and listened to the storm. His body felt tense, expectant. His sense of destiny was more vivid than ever. He'd awakened this morning with a powerful need to reach something, some place unknown to him. Was Montana that place? Did Oliver's story have a part in whatever was to come?

Maybe Manda would return tonight. He missed her in his dreams. Worried about her and wondered where she had gone, what had happened to the ghostly presence who had been his almost constant nighttime companion for so many years. Oddly enough, he thought of her with love but never with lust. In a life ruled by sexual need and almost constant arousal, Manda was a pool of pure love. She needed, she called out to him, but he'd been unable to do more than try to share his own strength, his own sense of purpose.

Did she really exist?

He hoped she was okay. He wanted to think he would know if she'd died, but there was no way to find out. Not unless he stayed with Oliver and discovered what Anton Cheval knew about Amanda Smith and Adam Wolf.

He glanced at the man sitting beside him. Oliver seemed to have curled in upon himself. Probably regretting the terrible secret he'd shared with a stranger.

Adam sighed. Oliver's secret was safe with him. So was Oliver, for that matter. If he didn't think it would frighten the man, Adam would wrap his arms around Oliver and offer him what comfort he could. He'd wanted to do that for Manda for all these years. Hold her, make everything better.

He did that. He fixed things.

The rain beat against the truck. The windows were covered in steam and the sound was almost deafening, but the storm would pass. They always did. No matter. Now he had Oliver to worry about, and Manda, as well as his own pathetic life.

One more lost soul on a lonely Montana highway.

2

Xandi shielded her baby's eyes from the brilliant midday sun while Stefan loaded the last of the groceries into the back of their oversized SUV. She glanced toward the coffee shop just as Anton and Keisha rounded the corner a few paces away with little Lily Milina strapped into her stroller. All their errands were done and they'd planned to meet for lunch.

The voice came from nowhere. It was everywhere. A woman's cry for help, screaming in Xandi's brain. She jerked around and caught Keisha looking at her, wide-eyed. Stefan cursed. Anton calmly surveyed their surroundings, but it was obvious he had a white-knuckled grip on Keisha's shoulders.

"That way." Stefan pointed toward a row of warehouses and a large feed store just up the road. Anton was already in motion, sprinting across the street with the fluid grace of the wolf he was. Stefan glanced back at the women. "You girls stay put," he ordered. Then he took off after Anton.

"Like hell." Xandi glanced at Keisha. She nodded and the two of them followed in the direction their men had gone with Lily sleeping soundly in the stroller as it clattered across the rough asphalt road, and Alex nestled in the fabric carrier holding him against his mother's chest. They might be mothers, but a woman had cried out for help. A woman who might be Chanku.

When they arrived, mere seconds after the men, it was like walking into a cheap buddy-cop flick at the movies—Anton held one man against the brick wall of the feed store, his forearm pressed solidly across the guy's throat while the man flailed helplessly. Stefan knelt over a second man. He had his knee firmly planted in the small of the man's back and a secure two-handed grip on his right arm, which was twisted and pulled tightly up behind his shoulder blades.

Neither Anton nor Stefan looked the least bit rumpled.

A handgun dangled uselessly from the fingers of the man trapped beneath Stefan's knee. Keisha leaned over and carefully took it away, then stepped back and pulled her cell phone out of her purse. Xandi rushed across the parking lot. She knelt down and lightly touched the shoulder of the huddled woman crouching against a garbage can.

The woman raised her head. A filthy gag was tied over her mouth, pulled so tight blood dripped from the corners of her lips. She had a dark bruise over her right eye and another spreading across her left cheekbone. She looked totally shocked and traumatized beyond the obvious injuries.

Fingers trembling, Xandi carefully untied the gag and helped the woman when she made it obvious she wanted to stand. She was as tall as Xandi and painfully thin, but she kept her balance when Xandi helped her to her feet. Thankfully, Alex slept on as Xandi walked with the woman to the steps and helped her sit.

The woman's wide-eyed gaze flickered to the men Stefan and Anton held immobile, then back to Xandi, but she didn't speak. Sirens sounded in the distance. Keisha's voice drifted in and out of the litany of curses from the two men. Xandi grabbed a new water bottle out of her purse, unscrewed the lid and handed it to the woman.

She took it with trembling, bloodied fingers. "Thank you." Her voice was soft . . . barely a whisper and held a hint of the South. Her blond hair hung in rats and snarls, matted with old blood where it had stuck to her face.

"Are you okay? Is anything broken?" Xandi sat down on the steps next to the woman, who shook her head slowly in answer to Xandi's question.

"Who are these men? Do you know them?"

Before the woman had time to answer, two state troopers in sedans and a highway patrolman on a motorcycle screeched into the parking lot with sirens wailing.

Lily woke up and began to cry. Keisha lifted her daughter out of the stroller to comfort her. Alex snuggled closer to Xandi. There was a flurry of activity as the two men were cuffed and secured in separate cars while the officers questioned Stefan and Anton and then retrieved the handgun from Keisha. Within minutes, the frantic pace seemed to slide to a stop. One of the officers turned to the woman who sat trembling between Keisha and Xandi.

His demeanor changed immediately as he crouched down to her level and softly asked if she was all right. She responded in monosyllables. Anton and Stefan stood off to one side.

She was mindtalking, Stefan said. *Her cry for help was telepathic, not verbal. Is she one of us? What color are her eyes?*

Xandi nodded when her mate's words filtered into her head. *I heard her, but her eyes are gray. More like mine.*

We will take her with us. Anton's tone, as usual, projected a sense of strength even without actual sound.

Xandi looked up at him and smiled. *I know.*

Wrapped in a warm blanket, Eve wasn't quite certain how she'd gone from fearing for her life in a filthy motel room to sitting in the opulent comfort of the leather backseat in a luxury SUV. Sitting here in the back with a sleeping baby on either side and four of the most beautiful adults she'd ever seen sitting up ahead was just too weird for words. It didn't feel real.

She'd thought Richard was going to kill her for sure this time. He was no good and his friends were worse, but he'd never beat her quite so badly. Of course, she'd never mouthed off to him quite as much as she had last night. The drugs had made him crazy. She was afraid he'd kill her.

He might have, this morning, if the two men in the front seat of this car hadn't rushed in and beat the shit out of Richard and his idiot partner. They'd been almost courtly when they introduced themselves, with names like the heroes she read about in romance novels. *Anton Cheval . . . Stefan Aragat.* She loved the way their names sort of rolled off the tongue, and she especially liked the way their voices sounded. Musical, but deep and sexy at the same time. Too bad they were both married.

Like they'd be interested in her if they weren't? Who was she trying to kid? They'd saved her, though. Like knights in shining armor. Those two bozos hadn't had a chance. How'd they know she needed help? When Richard gagged her, she figured she was dead meat. *Shit, shit, shit.* Her head wouldn't quit spinning. It ached and her body was a mass of bruises, but Richard and Bob were both in jail. From the outstanding warrants the sheriff's deputy had been able to pull up, it looked like neither man would be out for a long time.

Which left her . . . where? She sat in the backseat with a baby on each side, two gorgeous women in the middle seat and two absolutely drop-dead perfect hunks in the front. No one talked, but she had the strangest feeling they carried on a conversation she couldn't hear. There was a pressure against her skull and a buzzing in her ears. The whole thing was just plain weird.

But the sheriff said he knew them and she was safe. They'd

told her she could stay with them until the police got everything worked out. She didn't have anywhere else to go, anyway. She'd tried living on the streets. Look what that had gotten her?

Richard. Him she could do without. Bob had just showed up out of the blue, looking for some meth and a quick lay. She still hurt from the fucking both men had given her last night. She'd never, not in her wildest dreams, imagined Richard would pass her on to his friend like so much used goods.

But that's all she was, wasn't she? Used goods? The buzzing continued, along with the occasional sympathetic glance from the women. They'd said they would wait to talk until they got home and had the babies down, which made perfect sense to Eve. In fact, it was about the only thing that made sense. Why were they helping her? People like these folks usually walked right past trash like her.

Instead, they'd stood by her at the little clinic in town while a very nice doctor checked her from head to foot, photographed all her injuries and decided she didn't have anything broken, bleeding beyond repair, or worse. The black woman, Keisha? That was such a pretty name . . . she'd gone to a very nice store and purchased clothing so that all of Eve's filthy rags could be saved as evidence, helped her wash the blood and dirt off her battered body and stayed with her while she changed into the softest velvety outfit she'd ever owned.

It was dark gray, exactly the color of her eyes, and it made her feel like a queen to have something so soft and comfortable to wear. Well, she'd be a damned fool to turn down their kindness. Besides, now she needed to figure out a way to pay them back.

How did you pay back people who made you feel like a real person for the first time in your life? Sighing, Eve did the only thing she could. She placed her entire existence in the hands of absolute strangers, settled her aching body back against the leather seat and watched the forest rush by.

* * *

Adam awoke to absolute silence. It was still dark but he had to pee like crazy so he quietly opened the door and got out of the truck. He cringed under the flash of the dome light; he'd not expected it to shine so brightly. Once he'd stretched his aching muscles and relieved himself, he got back inside. Oliver was awake, staring at him warily out of eyes glowing green from reflected light.

"Sorry. I didn't mean to wake you." Adam shut the door. The light winked out.

"I was awake. I'll be back in a minute." Oliver got out of the truck, obviously for the same reason as Adam. He returned a minute later. "The storm's gone. It's almost dawn. Do you think you can get the truck running?"

"Probably. As soon as it's light enough I'll take a look. At least I can figure out why it stopped."

Silence stretched between them. Finally, Adam turned toward Oliver. "Oliver, I . . ."

Oliver held up his hand. "I owe you an apology. I should not have burdened you with my story. I have no idea why I told you."

"No, no apology is necessary." Adam leaned back against the seat. "I have the weirdest feeling about all this. Like I was supposed to be here at this time. I was supposed to meet you and there's still more I have to do. Does that sound crazy?"

"Not at all. Not if you accept that some things are predestined."

Adam laughed. "That's a hard one to swallow, but things seem to be conspiring to make me a believer."

"Possibly." This time it was Oliver turning around. "Have you ever heard the stories of the Chanku?"

"Nope. Can't say that I have."

"We have time to pass until daylight. I'm going to tell you another story, not nearly so gruesome and tragic as my first."

He smiled rather sadly. "In fact, this is one of the stories I will some day tell my employer's children. They're still babies. Not yet ready for the good stuff."

Again, Adam caught himself laughing. He wondered if Oliver even realized how funny he sounded with his precise speech and British accent. "Works for me. Fairy tales are just about all I'm up to this early in the morning, especially without coffee."

Oliver chuckled, then launched into his tale. His voice took on a mesmerizing cadence that quickly had Adam listening with half-closed eyes and a head filled with images.

"Once upon a time," Oliver said, "there was an ancient race of beautiful people who lived on the cold and desolate Himalayan steppe in what is now Tibet." He rolled his head to one side and grinned at Adam. "One must always start a fairy tale with 'once upon a time.' I believe there might even be a rule. Anyway, they were fierce warriors, tall and well formed. Their women were as powerful as the men. In fact, the women ruled in what was a strong matriarchal society. What people outside their society did not know is that all the men and women had an amazing secret, a special ability that no other people in the world, before or since, have had—they could turn themselves into wolves."

"Crap, Oliver." Adam melodramatically slapped his palm over his heart. "You're gonna tell me a scary werewolf story? I thought this was for little kids."

"Pay attention." This time Oliver laughed, but then he continued. "Everything was fine, except the winters were growing harsh and there wasn't enough for them to eat without preying upon their human neighbors, something they would never do. They packed up, as a tribe, and all of them moved on. Eventually the group split up and spread out over Europe and into Asia, but as they moved farther away from their traditional home, something terrible began to happen. The children who were born could no longer become wolves. They were plain old humans, just like everyone else."

"Bummer."

"Big bummer. And, essentially, the end of the Chanku. None of them had remained behind in their native land, yet they were not sophisticated enough to realize what it was they lacked in their new homes that had given them their very special power. As time went on, memories of their shapeshifting forefathers faded into the realm of legend and fable. The Chanku, once a powerful, even mystical people, lived on only in the DNA of the women who had once ruled them. To this day, only the women carry the seed for the Chanku."

"That's it?" Adam felt a strange sense of disappointment. Why would such a silly story resonate so deeply with him? He'd found himself listening to Oliver as if the man were speaking scientific fact, not telling him a fairy tale.

"That's all you get. The sun is coming up. It's time to see if you can fix this truck."

Adam glanced out the window. The sky was indeed growing lighter. He leaned down and unzipped the side of his duffle bag and dug around until he found his leather toolkit. Oliver climbed out of the truck and had the hood propped open by the time Adam joined him.

Damn. The engine was just as clean and tricked out as the rest of the truck. "Oliver, did you do the restoration on this?"

"No. Not me. This was purchased as a gift. I'm merely picking it up and delivering it. Anton Cheval is giving it to his partner, Stefan Aragat. Stefan's birthday is this month."

Adam let out a low whistle. "Nice gift."

Oliver shrugged. "Anton and Stefan are very close. Stefan named his first born son after Anton."

"I've heard of Aragat. The magician?" When Oliver nodded, Adam once again felt a wave of sensation cross his spine. Now he was starting to spook himself!

He tried to imagine having a friend close enough to want to name a child after him. Hell, he'd never known anyone who meant enough to even work at the friendship. So, what did that have to say about his worthless life? He turned his attention back to the truck. "Here's the problem." He pointed to the distributor cap. "Looks like one of the springs came loose." He quickly replaced the cap and readjusted the springs. "It should run fine, now. Go start it up."

The beautiful old truck rumbled to life. "Fantastic! You are definitely a magician." Oliver sat back in the driver's seat while Adam closed the hood and gathered his tools. So much for that. At least he'd earned his ride. He got into the truck beside Oliver and settled back against the warm leather.

For some reason, Oliver's silly story about the Chanku stayed in his mind as they drove through the Montana mountains. One thing was unusually clear, though. Adam realized he felt more comfortable with the little man beside him than he'd felt with any other person for as long as he could remember.

The sense of distance he always felt, the feeling of being outside of normal human interaction, was absent. What existed was a sense of comfort. Of, dare he name it? *Friendship.* Smiling at the convoluted directions of his thoughts, Adam let his mind drift in whatever direction it chose. He'd thrown his lot in with this strange little man. Maybe, just maybe, Oliver could help him find answers to some of the questions bedeviling his life.

He drifted off to sleep, recalling dreams of Manda.

Anton walked swiftly down the long hallway to the guest wing of his home. Stefan and Xandi were putting fresh sheets on the bed while Keisha watched after both the babies as well as Eve, who was probably still soaking in the big bathtub scented with healing oils.

Keisha had shared her view of the poor woman's body with Anton. He winced, even now, at the sight of old and new bruises covering almost every inch of her pale flesh, but it was impossible not to smile when he thought of her. She was

Chanku. He was positive. Her scent, though partially masked by the men she'd been with, had been pure wolf. Her ability to communicate mentally—obviously she'd had no idea her thoughts were broadcasting so clearly to all of them during the ride home from town.

Now, though, even more events were coming together and there'd be a new round of arguments with Stefan over the role of coincidence versus destiny in their lives.

Oliver was bringing home a very special guest. Adam Wolf. Oliver had *chanced* upon Millie West's missing son, hitchhiking outside of Kalispell. Not only had the truck chosen that particular moment to die, but Adam knew how to fix it. Anton wondered how Stefan would argue the side of coincidence when, not only had they suddenly collected two new housemates, both were most likely Chanku. Even better, one was named Adam, the other Eve.

Chuckling, Anton walked into the bedroom. Damn, but he did so love a good argument with Stefan.

Now was not the time for a fight, however. Anton paused in the open doorway without disturbing his packmates. Xandi knelt in front of Stefan, her full lips wrapped around his heavily veined cock. Stefan leaned back, hands braced on the ornately carved dresser, his pants hanging loosely about his knees, his shirt partially unbuttoned and hanging open. His eyes were closed, his expression one of a man on the edge. The casual disarray of his clothing was sexier than hell.

Anton leaned back against the door frame and watched. He was filled with the power of their love, the strength of two people giving and taking pleasure. He knew Xandi's body wasn't quite healed enough for penetration. Alex's birth had not been an easy one, but it was obvious from her body language that she shared and reveled in every sensation Stefan felt.

Stefan's thoughts drifted into Anton's mind. *I thought I*

heard you. Join me. She is magnificent, isn't she? I want to share this with you.

He needed no further invitation. Anton walked across the room and slipped behind Stefan, molding his body to his pack-mate's. Fully dressed, Anton wrapped his arms around Stefan's middle, slipped his hands inside his shirt and brushed his fingers across Stefan's taut nipples.

He experienced the heat of Xandi's mouth on his cock, though she suckled only Stefan. Felt the light tease of his fingertips across Stefan's nipples as if he touched himself, the gentle tug when Xandi wrapped her long fingers around Stefan's sac and kneaded the firm balls inside.

Minds fully linked, both Anton and Stefan shared everything they experienced with the woman kneeling before them. Hers was the power. Her lips and tongue, the sharp edge of her teeth. The hot, wet glove of her mouth, a receptacle, giving pleasure, sharing her love, her desire for Stefan, for Anton.

She let her mind wander to that very first time when Anton had been alone and needy, a man without a mate, without hope of love. She'd taken his hand, led him to her bed and given him everything she could. Without fear, without any reservation or inhibitions, she'd loved him because her mate loved him.

Now, those deep emotions spilled over the three of them, the sense of beginnings, the knowledge they would always have this special link of discovery.

Anton felt the power grow, felt the sharp flash of sensation that rolled out of his spine and through his groin, but it was Stefan's climax he experienced, Stefan's need clawing at his gut. Anton's cock was huge and painfully hard, trapped tightly within his jeans, but he had no intention of spilling his own seed. This was for Stefan. For Xandi.

He pinched Stefan's sensitive nipples tightly, twisting them painfully as Xandi sucked hard at her mate's cock and squeezed his balls in an iron grasp. She opened her mouth wider and swallowed the full length of his erection down her throat.

Stefan cried out. His body went rigid in Anton's firm embrace. Xandi sucked harder, her cheeks hollowing with each draw. When Stefan climaxed, she swallowed his seed, caught up in his orgasm with one of her own.

Finally she released Stefan's cock and leaned her head against his groin. He touched her hair, gently running his fingers through the deep, russet strands. He leaned his head back against Anton's shoulder. Anton kissed Stefan's temple. His fingers still teased the tautly pointed nipples and he ran his fingers through his packmate's mat of chest hair.

Anton had not found his own release. He'd held back, at that precise moment, unwilling to intrude further on Xandi and Stefan's lovemaking.

"Ah, but you made it better. More powerful."

"Thank you. The power, I believe, is Xandi's."

She raised her head and her gray eyes twinkled. "And don't you forget it, either." She stood up and hugged both Stefan and Anton. Then she leaned past her mate to plant a big kiss on Anton's mouth. "I do thank you, Anton. I will never grow tired of the sensation of so many bodies reaching climax . . . But you held back. Why?"

Anton stepped away from Stefan, took Xandi in his arms and kissed her. "Keisha's not here. She's with Eve and the babies. I could not, in all fairness, have too much fun without my mate. Oliver is on his way with Millie West's son. At least we think he's the same Adam West that Millie gave up for adoption. I need my wits about me." He flashed a big grin at Stefan. "It's destiny at work."

Stefan pulled up his jeans, tucked in his shirt and buttoned the fly, but he glanced over his shoulder at Anton. "Purely coincidence, my friend. There is no such thing as fate."

"We shall see. We'll need another bed made up. Xandi, I'll

help Stefan get Adam's room ready. You shouldn't be working so hard."

"Thanks, though I love the fact you men think it's perfectly okay for me to be on my knees with a monstrous penis down my throat, but not okay to spread a clean sheet on a bed." She laughed and irreverently swatted Anton on the butt, then headed out of the room. "I want you to know I'm only leaving because the man who *really* matters is calling."

Anton raised an eyebrow and glanced at Stefan.

"She's referring to Alex. I've been replaced."

Anton patted him on the back. "Not in all things, my friend. C'mon. I want to have the room next to this one ready when Oliver and Adam arrive."

"What do we know about Adam?" Stefan smoothed the comforter on the freshly made bed, then followed Anton out of the room.

"Very little. Oliver said he wants me to meet Adam without any preconceptions, other than the knowledge he is Chanku. It was an unusual contact from Oliver. He sounds unsure, as if something about Adam unsettles him. That is so unlike Oliver. I think of him as virtually unflappable. They should be here in a couple hours."

Stefan stopped by the linen closet with his arms full of fresh sheets. "Where did Oliver go, anyway? I can't recall him being away so long. We actually had to go grocery shopping!"

Anton smiled. "And we rescued Eve." He patted Stefan on the shoulder and offered his most condescending smile. "Would this be a good time to discuss coincidence versus predestination?"

"Probably not." Grumbling, Stefan followed Anton into the next bedroom.

Eve lay back in the warm bath and let the bubbling jets of water do their magic. She'd never known such luxury, had never seen a home as gorgeous as this one. Growing up in the foster care system in Florida hadn't been conducive to learning about the finer things in life.

Keisha wandered back into the bathroom. She'd gone to put both sleeping babies in their cribs. Now she handed Eve a glass of white wine that looked absolutely elegant, put the lid down on the toilet and sat there looking like a Nubian queen in her sapphire-blue caftan with her own wine glass in her hand.

Eve wanted to laugh out loud at the entire situation. Who'd have thought she'd end what had to have been the worst day of her life, relaxing naked in a steaming tub of scented water, drinking fine wine from what might actually be real crystal?

"It is." Keisha's soft voice intruded on her musings.

"Is what?" Eve sat up straighter and took a sip of the wine. The bubbles tickled her noise. She sneezed.

"It's crystal. Anton insists on only the best."

Which is why he had Keisha. She was truly the very best. And so beautiful and sweet, and . . . "Hey! How'd you know I wondered if it was real crystal?"

Keisha took a swallow of her wine. She smiled at Eve. "You were mindtalking. It's a form of mental communication. We all use it, though I'm guessing you're not aware of your abilities."

"Mindtalking? I've never heard of it." Eve sipped her wine, drinking more carefully this time.

"Do you feel as if there's a rubber band around your head? Is there a buzzing in your mind when we're all together?"

Wow! She'd described it perfectly. "How did you know?"

"Because the same thing used to happen to me. Here . . ." Keisha held out her hand. There was an ugly brown capsule in her palm. "This is not a drug, but it's filled with certain kinds of grasses that contain specific nutrients. They'll help you clarify your mind's ability to communicate. It helps with other things, too, but definitely the mindtalking."

Eve eyed the pill warily. She'd seen what drugs could do to a person.

"I took mine, even during my pregnancy. The baby is fine. So did Xandi. The guys take them daily, too. We all do. That's how we were able to save you, Eve. We heard your cry for help."

"I was wearing a gag." She stared at Keisha over the rim of her glass.

"Exactly. We heard you here." Keisha tapped the side of her head with one slim finger. "Here, take the pill. In a few more days you'll be mindtalking as easily as you speak out loud."

Eve took the pill and held it in her hand, staring at it. Keisha was right—it looked like nothing but brown grass in a clear capsule. She held it to her nose. It smelled faintly of fresh hay. With a last glance at Keisha, Eve took the pill with a swallow of wine, then eased back into the tub. "Why?" she asked. "Why are you all so nice to me?"

Keisha shrugged. "Why not? You needed help. You had nowhere to go. Once we responded and realized what was going on, there really was no other choice. You will be welcome here as long as you want to stay. It's a big house."

Eve felt the tears she'd controlled until now welling up in her eyes. It had been so long since she'd had any place she could call home. Never had there been friends, especially women friends. She bit her lip but could only nod once, acknowledging Keisha's generous offer.

"We have another guest arriving shortly. I wanted to let you know so his sudden appearance wouldn't make you nervous. His name is Adam Wolf. I don't know him personally, but we know his mother and sister."

"When will he arrive?"

Keisha shook her head. "I'm not sure. He'll be in the room next to yours, though. If you're not comfortable with a strange man so close, please let me know. I'll make sure you have a room more private."

Eve thought about that for a moment. Just the fact she was going to have her own room was a treat. She could manage a next door neighbor. "Are there locks on the door?"

Keisha smiled. "Of course there are. And a phone with its own line in each room. My private number is on the speed dial. Don't hesitate to call."

Eve slipped back down in the bubbling water with steam rising all around. Soon she would have to get out and let the real world intrude. She would have to think about this thing called *mindtalking* and the fact a man she didn't know would sleep in the room next to hers. Not now, though. Now she would lie here in this warm, bubbling womb and think about the luxury of a room with a lock on the door, and a bed of her own.

3

_____

Xandi held up a pair of almost-new designer jeans and shook her head. "I bet Eve could wear these. I sure can't."

Keisha closed the bedroom door and leaned against it. "Once you shift, you'll run the extra weight off. You'll heal faster, too, but they'll fit you again. I love being a mom, but don't you miss the sex?"

"You're kidding, right?" Xandi plopped down on the bed. "I love being a mom, but it's hard to figure out where I fit in anymore. All my energy goes to Alex. I miss the time Stefan and I had together. I miss touching and hugging and yeah, I really miss the sex."

"Alex is asleep. Oliver's not due here for a couple hours. Get Stefan and go for a run. You'll be surprised how it helps."

"You're sure? What about Eve?"

"She's sleeping, too. Poor kid's exhausted. Go. Now, before the baby wakes up. I'll watch him."

Xandi sent a silent call to Stefan, hugged Keisha and headed for the door. "Thank you. I'm gonna owe you big time."

"Of course you will. Why do you think I offered?"

Xandi was still laughing when she met Stefan in the woods behind the house.

"What's up? Is something wrong?"

Xandi stripped off her sweats. "Nope. It's right. Keisha's watching Alex and you and I are going to run." Naked, she looked back over her shoulder. "I've missed you so much. Missed this."

Then she shifted and left Stefan struggling out of his clothes.

Keisha was right. This body was strong and lean and already aroused. Though she still wanted sex and her orgasm today with Stefan and Anton had been wonderful, she'd wondered where her usually rampant libido had gone, if it was mostly wrapped up and stored away while she cared for their child. Now she wanted. She needed.

Stefan caught up to her and they raced together, bodies and minds totally in sync, hearts racing, feet tearing up the soft earth. The sun was warm on her back, the scents of the forest ripe with life. They found a narrow track and followed it deeper until they burst into a meadow barely touched by sunlight.

This time Xandi was the aggressor. She turned, teeth bared, and nipped Stefan's shoulder. He didn't hesitate. Pawing her back, he turned Xandi and mounted her, driving deep and hard, his cock slipping between her welcoming folds. The knot at the base of his penis formed quickly and he tied with her almost immediately. She growled, but it was a sound torn from pleasure, not pain. Her body opened for Stefan, welcomed him.

He took her, there in the deep woods, their minds linked as tightly as their bodies. Xandi reveled in the feminine power of the wolf, this familiar, yet soul-searing sense of unity. Their minds connected, thoughts melding one upon the other until the bond was everything, the sensations each experienced, shared completely. She and Stefan were one, a single entity, linked now and forever.

She'd feared this in her human form, feared the pain of entry after all the indignities of a difficult birth had left her bruised and torn. Now, though, there was no pain, nothing but unbelievable pleasure as he thrust into her. His claws dug into her shoulders, his panting breath was a harsh blast against her ear. She shivered with the powerful sensation of hard, fast bestial sex.

Stefan grunted and climaxed just as she slipped over the edge, her sex rippling and clenching his cock in lush waves of pleasure. Both of them tumbled to the ground, mouths agape and panting. Before she could talk herself out of it, Xandi shifted.

She'd feared pain. There was none. Her human body held Stefan's wolven cock deep inside and she reveled in the feelings, the pure animal pleasure of the act. He panted, licked her cheek, and shifted, but he stayed inside her, his human cock still pulsing with the power of his orgasm.

It had been so long. Too long. Xandi touched his cheek and felt the tears he'd shed. "Stefan? Are you all right?"

He kissed her fingertips, her palm, the sensitive skin of her wrist. "Better than all right. I've missed you. Missed our time alone." He leaned close and kissed her on the mouth, his lips molding to hers, his tongue barely teasing the sensitive inner flesh. "I had no idea how much our lives would change when we had a baby. In some ways, so much better. In others . . ." He pressed his forehead against Xandi's. "Dear Goddess, I love you so much."

Xandi wrapped her arms around Stefan and held him tight. So often he was the jokester, the one who loved to tease Anton and Keisha, always the lightest spirit among them. She wondered if the others really knew the depths to her mate, the power of his love, his devotion, not only to his wife and son, but to the pack.

Stefan raised his head. His eyes narrowed and he stared back toward the cabin. Xandi's first thought was the baby. "Is Alex okay?"

Stefan blinked, then kissed the tip of her nose. "I imagine

he's still asleep. However, Oliver is back. And he's brought Adam Wolf." Stefan sat up and pulled Xandi with him. "It's weird. I sense Adam's presence. He's not shifted yet. I shouldn't feel him as strongly as I do."

"We'd better go back." Xandi disentangled herself from Stefan's long legs.

He flung one leg back over her hips, trapping her. "Soon. We'll go back soon." Then he kissed her, and teased the greedy mouth of her sex with his reawakened cock. When he found her clit, swollen and slippery with arousal, with the fluids from her climax, Xandi had to agree. They still had plenty of time.

Adam had to consciously shut his mouth when they rounded a long, sweeping curve and Anton Cheval's home came into sight. Made of wood, glass, and stone, it seemed hewn out of the very earth, a massive yet aesthetically perfect structure framed with wide stairs and towering cedars alongside. A covered deck stretched across the front and around both visible sides.

"Good God, Oliver. You didn't tell me he had a mansion out here in the middle of nowhere! This is unreal."

Oliver nodded, smiling as he parked the truck in front of the entry. "It's huge. It's also surprisingly comfortable, even casual inside."

Adam just shook his head. "I find that hard to believe. I'm suddenly picturing you as the butler."

As the two of them got out of the truck, a tall, dark haired man raced down the front steps. "Oliver. This is perfect. Quick! Put the truck in your garage and throw a tarp over it. Stefan's out for a bit and I was wondering how we'd keep this secret until his birthday. You must be Adam. Grab your things so Oliver can go. Stefan could return any minute."

He paused, laughed out loud and held out his hand to Adam. "Welcome to my home, Adam. I'm Anton Cheval, and I'm not usually so bossy."

"Yes, he is. Hello, Adam. I'm Keisha Rialto, Anton's mate."

"And the woman who's really in charge." Anton shook Adam's hand and then grabbed his heavy duffle as if it weighed nothing at all. With Keisha beside him, Anton led Adam up the stairs as Oliver drove away.

The inside of the home was as beautiful as the outside, all light and glass and warm, polished wood. Cheval led them into a large room with comfortable leather furniture scattered about. There were newspapers on the floor near one of the chairs and a pair of worn slippers by a door that led outside to another deck. For all its size, the home appeared comfortable and, as Oliver had said, very casual.

Adam sat where Cheval indicated, but his curiosity had him ready to explode. Who were these people? Why did they know of him, and what?

"You're right to wonder."

"What?" Adam jerked his head around to stare at Cheval.

"First of all, yes. I do know what you're thinking. There is so much I want to tell you, yet I don't even know where to start." Cheval had remained standing. Now he paced nervously. The woman who referred to herself as his mate had disappeared down another hallway. Adam thought he'd heard a baby crying.

"The beginning might help," he said. "Why did Oliver bring me here? How can you read my mind? How do you know who I am?"

"I know your mother."

"She's not my mother." Adam's stomach suddenly knotted. It always did when he thought of the lies and half truths he'd lived with most of his life.

"Your real mother. Your birth mother."

Thank goodness he was sitting or he would have ended up on his ass. "How? Who is she? I didn't find out I was adopted until I was in college."

"I wondered if that's why you dropped out."

Adam shook his head. How much did these people know about him? "Partly. I grew up in an abusive home. Then my parents went through a nasty divorce when I was about twenty." The memories poured into him. His mother, drunk as usual, screaming at his father and accusing him of stupidity for buying Adam when he was an infant so he could have a son. His father, just as drunk, calling it a waste of money and a mistake, as big a mistake as their marriage.

Adam lurched to his feet. He didn't know this man, wasn't sure if he wanted to know the details. What kind of mother sold her own child?

Cheval was suddenly beside him, his hand warm and comforting on Adam's shoulder. "Your mother wasn't married, but she loved you. She wanted you very much. Her uncle arranged the adoptions without telling her. When she awoke after giving birth, both you and your sister were gone."

"My sister?" So many things suddenly fell into place. Still, his hands were shaking and he felt lightheaded. "A twin?"

"Yes. Amanda Smith. Oliver said you know her as Manda."

Adam's breath caught in his throat. The woman he'd searched for all those years, his sister? Suddenly it all began coming together. Finally making sense. "She was in my dreams. Horrible nightmares. She's the reason I left college. I wanted to find her. I had to know if she was real because I wanted to save her. I saw brutal, terrible things, but it was always from her point of view, as if I were the person these things happened to. I never saw her but I sensed there was something different about her. Something that set her apart. People called her Manda. Is it true?"

He felt physically ill, remembering, reliving the images he'd not been able to hide from. Rapes, beatings, and worse. Treatment so foul . . .

Cheval nodded. "Unfortunately, what you dreamed really happened to her. She's okay now, and Keisha has called to let her know you've been found. We've contacted your mother as well. I expect everyone will be here by tomorrow evening."

The air left his lungs and once again Adam sat. It was too much, all of this so unbelievable. Cheval sat next to him on the couch. "There is more and it's even more amazing."

Adam laughed. "Well, I certainly can't imagine anything more mind-boggling than what you've already told me. So far you've found a mother and a sister for me that I didn't know existed. It's going to be hard to top that."

Cheval laughed. "Trust me. I'm definitely topping it." He got up, walked to the glass door that opened to a back deck, slid it open and whistled. Two huge wolves bounded across the back meadow, raced across the deck and into the room. The smaller of the two continued on down a long hallway, but the other stayed.

Speechless, Adam could only sit and stare. The animal stared back at him out of amazingly intelligent eyes. Eyes that looked oddly familiar. Adam heard the door slide shut behind him and glanced toward Cheval.

"Watch him very carefully," he said. "There is no easy way to explain this. It's easier just to show you." Cheval stood next to the wolf with one hand resting on the animal's broad head. "You are not exactly who you've always thought yourself to be, Adam Leyton Wolf. Your mother bequeathed you with an amazing genetic code that exists only in a very small part of the population, a code that all of us in this room share."

Adam frowned. Obviously Cheval included the wolf in his conversation. What the hell was he talking about? He studied the wolf. The animal was obviously well trained, but there was something unusual about him, something that raised a shiver along Adam's spine. He glanced up at Cheval, then back at the wolf.

Suddenly, the animal seemed to waver. He didn't actually see how or what happened, but in place of the wolf, a tall, slim, naked man faced Adam.

"Holy shit." Adam sat back hard. "Holy fuckin' shit."

"Nice to meet you, too. I'm Stefan Aragat." He held out his hand.

Adam took it, moving as if through water. A memory clicked into place. "You're the magician. I caught your act in Las Vegas about ten years ago. Shit. That's one hell of a trick."

Stefan grinned, shook Adam's hand, but glanced at Cheval. "See? Told you I was famous." He looked back at Adam. "It's not a trick. Believe me. If I'd done that on stage when I was still entertaining, I'd be a star. For now, I think I'm going to get some pants on. I'm feeling a bit underdressed." He turned away and headed down the hall in the same direction the other wolf had run.

Stunned, Adam watched him walk away. He realized he was concentrating on the smooth bunch and flow of the magician's perfect ass, and caught himself. When he glanced back at Cheval, the man grinned at him.

"He does have a perfect ass, doesn't he?"

"What?" Adam shook his head. "You do read minds, don't you? Are you going to explain what the fuck I just saw?"

"You mean beyond Stefan's ass?" Laughing, Cheval sat in a chair across from Adam.

Adam let out a breath. "Shit. Sorry. I can't seem to form words beyond four letters. What did I just see?"

"You saw what is called Chanku. A shapeshifter. I am one. Your mother, your sister, and you as well, are all Chanku."

"Chanku?" Oliver's fairy tale suddenly popped into his head. "The shapeshifters from Tibet. Oliver said it was a fairy tale. He told me a story about werewolves but I thought it was make believe."

"We are the stuff of legend, but we're most decidedly not

werewolves. We don't bite our victims to pass on a curse, and the full moon is no more important than something to howl at. And yes, we do communicate nonverbally. We call it mindtalking."

"I'd think you were nuts if I hadn't just seen him shift." Adam shook his head. "Of course, he is a famous magician, but shifting from wolf to human? That's pushing it."

When he looked up, Anton was holding a jar of pills in one hand. "He is a magician and I am a wizard. Our abilities in the realm of magic are completely separate from the fact we are Chanku. That is its very own special magic, and something you share. Okay. Here's the way this works. You'll need to take one of these every day. I imagine you'll be able to shift as easily as Stefan in less than a week. The capsules contain the nutrients our species need in order to shift. Your mental abilities are already surprisingly strong, so it's hard to say exactly how long it will actually take you."

Before Adam could answer, Oliver walked into the room. "I've done as you asked," he said, addressing Cheval. "The truck is well hidden. The keys are under the mat." Then he turned toward Adam. "Welcome, Adam. I see Anton has told you the next chapter of my fairy tale."

Stefan returned before Adam had a chance to answer. It was too much. Stefan appeared perfectly casual, dressed in worn jeans and an old sweatshirt with the sleeves cut off. Adam felt his world spinning. Definitely too much, too soon, and none of it believable. He was still trying to process the whole bit about the wolves when a voice slipped into his mind. Soft, pleading, precisely British.

Only you and Anton know my secret. Please, do not tell Stefan or anyone else.

Adam raised his head and looked at Oliver. The other man wouldn't meet his eye. He couldn't help but wonder just what in the hell he'd gotten himself into this time.

* * *

Eve crawled out of the tub, dried off and wrapped herself in the thick terry robe she'd found hanging on a hook on the back of the bathroom door. Totally relaxed for the first time in forever, she walked into her bedroom. A huge dog stood next to her bed. Keisha wandered in, glanced at the beast and laughed.

Eve frowned. "Is he yours? What kind of dog is he?"

The animal raised its head and yipped. Keisha took Eve's arm and led her to a comfortable chair. "Sit."

Eve sat. "What's going on?"

"First of all, that's not a dog, it's a wolf. And it's not a he, it's a she, and while this is a little difficult to explain, it's not always a wolf. Sometimes it's Xandi. Just as I am sometimes a wolf."

Eve stared at Keisha for a long moment, then finally gave up. No way did any of that make sense. "I don't get it."

"Xandi? You want to show her?"

Eve glanced back at the wolf just in time to see it shimmer, fade, and suddenly disappear altogether. In its place was Xandi. Naked, her auburn hair tousled, her smile as bright as ever.

"Oh. My. God." Eve turned slowly and looked at Keisha. Keisha shrugged her shoulders, slipped out of her blue caftan, and before Eve had time to process the fact another naked woman was standing beside her, Keisha became, instead, a wolf.

Mouth dry, heart pounding in her chest, Eve could only stare at the Keisha-wolf. Then, as quickly as she'd shifted from human to animal, Keisha was once again standing beside Eve. She picked her caftan up off the floor and slipped it over her head.

"It's easier showing you than trying to explain." Keisha touched Eve's shoulder. "Remember the pill I gave you? Those nutrients I mentioned? They help with things beyond mind-talking." She shrugged. "They also sort of activate abilities you already have."

Xandi stood on the other side of her. She'd slipped on a robe similar to Eve's. "We share the same genetics, Eve. I think of us as sisters of the heart. You are Chanku. We suspected it when you first called for help using the powers of your mind, but there's more."

"Your scent, for one," Keisha added.

"I smell?"

"In a good way," Keisha said, laughing. "The scent of the men you were with masked yours in the beginning, so at first, we weren't positive. Our ability to pick up various smells and identify them is quite powerful. Once you bathed, we had no doubt."

This was way too much to take in at once. Eve thought of the dreams she'd had for as long as she could remember, the nights where she'd raced through the forest on four legs, howled at the moon and hunted. All imaginary, or were they? "You're saying I can do that? Change into a wolf?"

"Not right away. It takes the pills anywhere from three days to a week, with women. It can take even longer with men."

"I've had dreams." She looked down at her hands and re-membered paws. "They were so real. Does that mean I've al-ready shifted before?"

"No," Xandi said, "but we've all experienced really powerful dreams. We think it's like a genetic memory, but they're very real."

Keisha agreed. "You'll know you're getting close to being able to shift when you start noticing a crawling sensation on your arms."

"It itches like mad," Xandi said. "Feels like your bones want to crawl out of your skin."

"Probably because they do." Keisha laughed. "And no, we don't know how the mechanics of the shift actually work. Anton's tried filming it and slowing the film way down, and we still can't tell. One minute you're human, then you appear all shimmery and suddenly you're on four legs."

"And what it does to your libido is scary." Xandi fanned her fingers in front of her face. "In a good way."

"A very good way," Keisha said. "Do you like sex?"

Eve nodded, laughing. Following these two in a conversation was mind-boggling. Talk about your non sequiturs! "Yes, I love sex, but you're telling me I'm going to want more?"

"Most likely. Lots of times when Xandi and I run, if we get back and the guys aren't here we just jump each other's bones . . ."

"Keisha, my dear. We jump each other even when the guys are here." Xandi grinned at Eve. "Hope you're okay with that. Which reminds me. Keisha, thanks for watching the beast. Stefan and I took full advantage of our run in the woods."

"Did it hurt?"

"Nope. You were right. The shift made me feel much better." Xandi turned back to Eve. "I was still sore after having the baby and a little afraid to try sex with my mate, but once I shifted all my parts felt better." She sighed. "Much better. Damn, that man knows what buttons to push."

"Are you saying you have sex when you're wolves?" Eve tried to imagine the logistics. "Isn't that just a little bit weird?" For that matter, this entire conversation was weird. She couldn't believe she was calmly talking to women who could turn into animals.

But she'd seen them. With her own eyes.

"Just wait. You'll be pleasantly surprised." Keisha stopped and tilted her head. "Oops . . . there goes Lily. I'll be back in a while."

Eve watched her go, but her mind was spinning and nothing seemed to make sense. She turned and looked at Xandi. "Keisha said that as if it's a given. That I'll be able to turn into a wolf and there will be a man just like me who loves me." Eve felt the tears gathering, felt the thickness in her throat. Damn, there'd just been way too much going on today, some of it horrible, some wonderful, but this was totally unbelievable.

Xandi plopped down next to her on the bed. "Hon, this is, without a doubt, going to be the biggest day of your life. Forget the bad stuff. It's over. What's going to come your way from now on will amaze you. It will change your life forever, but it's all good. Really. You should have seen me when I met Stefan. Hell, for that matter, you should have seen Stefan!"

"He's gorgeous. Both he and Anton look like models. They're perfect."

"Not always." Xandi brushed Eve's hair back from her eyes. "The night I met Stefan, I was running away from a horrible engagement. I'd caught my fiancé having sex with another woman. Then I had a car accident in a blizzard. Stefan saved my life, but I was unconscious when he found me. I awoke in darkness, in his bed, and ended up having the most amazing sex I'd ever had in my life. What I didn't know until the next day is that I hadn't had sex with a normal man. He'd been caught in the midst of a shift for almost five years. The man I thought had made love to me was really half wolf, but I still fell in love with him. In fact, I loved him from the very beginning. Stefan says it's coincidence, not fate that we met that night, but I know it was our destiny. I couldn't believe it when he turned into the most gorgeous man I'd ever seen."

"This is way too bizarre." Eve leaned back against the pillows on the bed and Xandi scooted up next to her. "I feel as if I'm caught in a dream." She laughed. "I'd call it a nightmare but you guys are just too nice."

"Thank you. I know what you're saying, but it'll all make sense. Trust me." Xandi flipped her fingers in the air in a helpless gesture. "What's really funny is that Anton and Stefan have had this ongoing argument about whether or not things are predestined or just happen. We found you today. Oliver, Anton's personal assistant, found Adam. He's Chanku, like you, and we've all been searching for him. There are very few of us that we know of, and the odds are just . . . well, astronomical!" She covered her mouth to stop the giggles. "I think Anton's going to win this round. It must be fate. The coincidence is too bizarre."

"So are our names," Eve said. "Why were you looking for Adam?"

"We know his mother and his sister. Millie, the mom, had her twin babies taken from her at birth. Another Chanku, Baylor Quinn, found and rescued her daughter, Manda. She was like Stefan, trapped halfway between wolf and woman, but she's okay now. They'll be here tomorrow."

Xandi suddenly stopped talking, tilted her head and looked as if she was concentrating. Eve felt the tightness around her skull and heard the faint buzzing in her ears, so she wasn't at all surprised when Xandi looked at her and smiled.

"That was Anton. Dinner's ready. Here—I've brought you some clothes. We're the same height and I used to be as skinny as you." She opened the closet and pulled out a dark blue velour jogging suit. "I put the underclothes we bought for you in the top drawer of the dresser. There're some jeans and shirts, too, but this will be more comfortable. You're still so bruised! We'll make a trip to town when you feel up to it and get some more clothes for you, but this'll do for now."

Then she was gone and Eve was alone in the room. *Her* room, and her head was spinning from all she'd learned. She wondered if anything would ever seem normal again. She'd taken one of those pills already, so if this wasn't a dream, if it was all real, she'd be able to turn into a wolf within a few days.

Unless she got caught in the middle of the shift. Xandi'd mentioned that happening to Stefan and that other woman, too. Why? What had gone wrong? What if it happened to her?

Crap. One more thing to worry about.

This certainly wasn't how she'd expected to spend her week. Eve shuddered. Her injured body wouldn't let her forget Richard's fists or Bob's brutal sex. This new reality was a lot better, and at least didn't hurt as much. She slipped out of the warm robe and put on the soft, velour suit Xandi had given her. There was a brand new comb and brush in the bathroom. She brushed all her hair back from her face and used a clip she found to fasten it at the base of her neck.

There was no hiding the bruises. For some reason, she didn't care if the people here saw her as she was. They already seemed to know her better than she knew herself. She looked in the bathroom drawers anyway. As she suspected—no makeup to cover them. At least the marks would heal. She closed the drawer and realized her hands were shaking. Had to be shock. There'd been one too many surprises today, but damn it all, she was a survivor. She'd made it through seventeen years of foster care and managed to survive since getting kicked out of the system at eighteen.

Xandi'd said she had a whole new life ahead of her. It was like a fresh slate. One where she was in charge of her own future.

As a wolf? Well, first she had to figure out the woman. She was obviously still a work in progress. One step at a time . . . and her first step was finding the dining room. Holding her head high, Eve opened the bedroom door and hoped she wouldn't get lost along the way.

Adam showered and shaved and put on the one clean set of clothes from his duffle, a pair of faded blue jeans and a dark green V-neck sweater. His hair was a little too long, so he tied it back in a short queue with a rubber band he found in the bathroom. It might have felt a bit pretentious, but he'd noticed that both Stefan and Anton wore their hair long. Only Oliver had really short hair.

This was just so damned weird. The room was perfect. He had a king-size bed to himself, his own bathroom, and there were clothes in the closet that actually looked as if they'd fit. He'd heard some movement in the room next to his and guessed it must be Eve, the woman they'd told him was staying there.

Eve. Shit. You'd think she could have at least had a different name. He hadn't seen her yet, but oddly enough, he'd sensed her. Felt her presence, almost as if she'd hovered over his shoulder. His head hurt. He sensed voices, but couldn't make them out. Sensed people, yet hadn't seen them. This place was just flat-out weird.

He stared at himself in the mirror. Same face. Same overlong dark blond hair, same small scar on his chin. Yep . . . the same guy as yesterday, but suddenly he felt as if he saw a stranger. In just a short time, he might actually have answers. Might know things he'd never thought to ask. Okay. For answers like that he could handle weird.

He turned away from the mirror and left the room. As he stepped out into the well-lit hallway, the door next to his opened. Damn. It was definitely a cliché, but in that one heartbeat, Adam almost forgot how to breathe.

She stood in the doorway, tall and slim and absolutely gorgeous. Gray eyes, blond hair, a dark bruise across her cheek, she paused like a startled deer when she saw him standing there, watching her.

"You must be Eve," he said.

She held perfectly still, then raised her chin and looked him in the eye. "Adam?"

He nodded.

She smiled. His heart sort of caught, stopped, then started beating much faster than it should have.

She sighed, then, and some of the tension seemed to flow out of her. "They told me you'd have the room next to mine." She looked along the hallway and shrugged. "I'm not really sure where the dining room is. This place is huge."

It was that simple. He took her hand. She wrapped her long, slim fingers in his and the two of them walked down the long hallway to dinner. And all the while, Oliver's comments about fate and coincidence kept up a steady litany in his mind.

4

Oliver cleared away the last of the plates. Dinner had been absolutely delicious, and much more relaxed than Adam would have expected. Eve was delightful company and the two of them had had more than enough questions about shapeshifting to keep the conversation flowing. On top of that new reality, he would finally meet his mother and his sister tomorrow. That thought alone was completely overwhelming.

But what of Eve? Orphaned as an infant, she'd never really known her mother and her father's name wasn't on her birth certificate. Raised in a series of foster homes, she had no one. Adam hardly knew her, but already she mattered to him. He glanced at Eve sitting quietly beside him and felt a tightness in his chest, a need so powerful he feared everyone at the table sensed his desire.

"Anton, why don't you and Keisha run tonight?" Stefan set his napkin on the table and smiled at his mate. "Xandi and I can stay and watch Lily."

"Do you mean run as wolves?" Eve's slight Southern accent flowed like honey over Adam's mind.

"Yeah. We used to go every night, but that was before the babies." Xandi laughed. "Things changed a lot after Lily and Alex showed up."

"Eve and I can watch your children, can't we, Eve?" At least if he had to watch babies, Adam figured it would be easier to control his libido around the gray-eyed witch. He couldn't keep from watching her, had to fight the need to touch her.

"We can't . . ."

Eve cut off Anton's denial. "If you're worried, Oliver will be here with us." She glanced at Adam. "I don't know about Adam, but I've spent lots of time caring for new babies. Growing up in foster care . . . well, there was always a little one around. How long would you be gone? Not more than a couple hours, I imagine."

"Eve's right." Oliver had stepped back into the dining room. "I'll be here, there is plenty of breast milk stored in the freezer and no reason for you to worry."

It was almost comical, how quickly the four adults stripped out of their clothing, shifted, and raced off into the woods. The silence in the room after they left was broken by the loud wail of one of the babies.

Laughing, Adam stood up and took Eve's hand. "I wonder if I'll ever get used to that," he said, staring in the direction the four wolves had run. He shook his head and answered his own question. "Nope. Probably not." Then he called to Oliver, "C'mon, Ollie. You volunteered, too."

"Ollie?" Oliver stood in the doorway. "Did you just call me 'Ollie'?"

Grinning like a fool, Adam grabbed Oliver's hand on the way past, and dragged the two of them down the hall to the nursery.

Oliver tried to remember the last time he'd been treated as someone's friend. He couldn't recall. As a child he'd been more of a pet, as a young man, mostly lost and confused in a sexual world where he'd never fit. Once he'd come under Anton's care, he'd been a valued employee, a confidant, never truly a friend. Not an equal.

Adam didn't seem to care about any of that. Maybe he cared too much. Oliver realized he was grinning broadly, following both Adam and Eve down the hallway.

Alex merely needed a new diaper and was asleep again before Eve had his little nightshirt changed. Lily slept on. Anton, Keisha, Stefan, and Xandi were merely a thought away, so the three of them returned to the kitchen and the dishes from the night's dinner.

Usually this was Oliver's job. Adam grabbed an apron. Eve sat on a stool at the bar. "Hey," she said, "I changed the diaper. It's only fair."

Adam began rinsing plates and stowing them in the dishwasher. "I've done more than my share of dishes. Take a break, Ollie."

"It's Oliver," he said, but there was something familiar, even fun about being called Ollie. When the kitchen was cleaned, he opened a bottle of wine. The three of them sat at the kitchen table. Eve and Adam both had so many questions about the Chanku. Oliver answered what he could and watched the body language between the man and the woman.

There was so much sexual tension you could cut it with a knife. He'd always been aware of the Chanku sensuality, though he'd never actually experienced it. Now though, for some unknown reason, Oliver felt the physical tug of arousal. It wasn't precisely Adam's sensations, or even Eve's. More a combination of the two.

Eve took a sip of her wine. Oliver felt her studying him and knew there was another question coming. "Do they just run when they go out as wolves? What do they do out there? I mean, it's dark and kind of scary."

"Not if you're a wolf." He took another swallow of wine. It was one of Anton's better cabernets. The wizard definitely knew his wine. "Wolves fear no one. They own the forest. They will make love, they might hunt. Later, I imagine we'll hear them howling. As wolves they run free, unhindered by human concerns. Their minds are linked, their thoughts, and even their arousal, shared."

Eve laughed. "I can't wrap my head around the sex as wolves thing. That's just too weird."

Adam sipped his wine. "Not if you're a horny wolf. I imagine it's just fine, then." He winked at Eve over the rim of his goblet.

Oliver leaned back in his chair and studied the dynamics of the man and woman. "It's beyond pure sex, whether you're human or wolf," he said. "There's that powerful mental link. Whatever one person feels, they all feel. That is the Chanku way. Four people in the bed . . . each one shares what the other three are feeling. Think of how good the sex is and multiply it by however many partners you are with."

"I've only been with one at a time." Eve shuddered delicately. "Sometimes even that was one too many."

"You've obviously not had very good partners."

Adam's soft comment raised a shiver along Oliver's spine. He sensed Eve's growing arousal, knew Adam was hard as a post and highly aroused. Oliver felt his skin flush and shifted in his chair. He never got an erection. Never.

He had one now. *Impossible.* His castration had been complete. There'd been drugs, other things done to him to prohibit any sexual development. His penis had been good for aiming piss and nothing more. Now it swelled within his cotton briefs, pressed against the seam of his pants.

He shifted in his chair and frowned, concentrating on the waves of pleasure coming from that spot between his legs where he'd felt nothing all his life. He sensed Adam's eyes on him. Raised his head.

Adam nodded. His lips barely curved in a small smile. Eve watched both of them with unabashed curiosity. He couldn't let her know. Not about this.

"Oliver, are you Chanku?" Eve's question, coming on top of the new sensations coursing through his groin, caught Oliver unprepared.

"No," he said. "Yes, kind of, but . . ." He looked helplessly at Adam.

"Oliver has a medical condition that doesn't allow him to shift. Right, Ollie?"

That was safe enough. "Yes. I take the pills every day because it maintains my ability to mindtalk. I can actually communicate over very long distances with Anton, but much of that is due to his power. Shifting, however, has been nothing more than a dream."

A powerful dream. One that haunted him. Would always haunt him. He clenched his jaw, willing that covetous, needy side of his nature into the background where it belonged.

There was a small commotion on the front deck, the sound of claws on wood, a yip and laughter. The kitchen door swung open. Anton, Stefan, and both women entered, all of them naked, each one obviously surprised to find their guests and employee in the kitchen, sipping wine.

Eve slapped her hand over her eyes. Adam laughed and obviously enjoyed the view. Oliver wasn't sure if Adam preferred the women or the men—he seemed to watch all of them with equal interest.

"It's okay, Eve. We're not real big on modesty around here." Keisha swept by them, leaned over and kissed Oliver's cheek and ran down the hallway leading to their wing of the house.

Anton paused by the table, lifted the wine bottle and one

dark eyebrow. He studied Oliver for a long, solemn moment. Then he nodded. "Excellent vintage, Oliver." He smiled and winked and followed his mate.

Stefan and Xandi trailed after Anton. "Thanks, guys, for watching the babies. We all needed the break."

The kitchen felt strangely empty when they'd gone. Oliver let out a deep breath. He was still erect. He wondered what his cock looked like, how big it was. Wondered if it would ever happen again.

He had to get out of here. Needed time alone, time to figure out what was happening to him. Why it was happening. He practically leapt to his feet. "I'm exhausted. If you'll excuse me . . ."

Adam stood as well. "Me, too. It's been a pretty wild day."

Oliver closed the door behind him. Both Eve and Adam were still in the kitchen when he left.

"That was odd." Eve stared at the door. "I wonder what got into him?"

"I don't know."

But he did know. He'd had no right to do what he'd done, but Adam couldn't help himself. There was that damned need to fix what was broken, and he was getting the hang of this sharing, mindtalking thing. Eve might not even realize it, but she'd been turned on all evening, sending out the most amazing messages of lust and heat and need. Adam certainly hadn't been immune, but Oliver hadn't noticed.

At least, he hadn't noticed until Adam began to share. It was a simple thing, really, taking Eve's arousal and mixing it in with his own, then sending the message on to Oliver. Sharing it with the little man, making it a seamless joining of Oliver's arousal to Adam's.

At least now he knew it worked. And who was to say it wouldn't work enough to help Oliver shift? He held out a hand to Eve. "C'mon. I'll walk you to your room. Wouldn't want you to get lost now, would we?"

There was something about this house, these people, that seemed to magnify all her needs, her fantasies. She'd been looking at Adam and imagining him in her bed. She'd added Oliver to the mix when they'd mentioned sex with multiple partners, letting her mind go places she'd never dreamed of before. Now her body, as beaten and bruised as it was, thrummed with waves of lust, a pulsing, rhythmic pounding like an ocean against the shore, each wave higher and harder than the one before.

When Adam took her hand and led her down the hall, she imagined the touch of his fingers between her legs. Her nipples drew up tight and hard and the soft fabric of her jogging suit abraded the tender tips.

They reached her room first and she paused with one hand on the door. Should she kiss him good night? She hardly knew the man. No matter. She wanted him, now. Her need was a growing, growling, live thing coiling in her womb.

Adam answered Eve's question for her. He leaned over and kissed her lightly on the lips. Mouth closed, lips together, but when he drew back and looked at her, it was obvious he wanted more. So obvious.

She still hurt from Richard's beating. Her pussy ached from Bob's rough sex. Still, she wanted, but it wouldn't be pleasurable. It couldn't be, as battered as her body felt.

Adam kissed her again. This time his palm held the back of her head and his lips moved over her mouth. His tongue licked the seam between her lips and she parted for him, groaned against the sweet invasion of his tongue, the warm, wet mouth suckling hers.

"Let me taste you. Just my mouth, tasting your body. I know you're hurting. I feel it, there in your thoughts. I only want to taste."

She groaned again, imagining that mobile tongue moving over her bruised flesh. Soothing her. Arousing her even more than she was now. She wanted him. Wanted to see him naked. His body was long and lean and hard. No sign of dissipation, not like Richard with his beer belly or Bob with the disgusting flab and the even more disgusting little cock. How he'd managed to hurt her so much with a weapon so small, she'd not figured out, but . . .

Adam kissed her throat and his hands slipped up her back, beneath the soft top she wore. His fingers played along her spine and she arched against his body.

"I'm afraid . . ." Her whisper stopped him and he pulled away. She whimpered, lost without the warmth of his body against hers.

"Not of me," he said. "Never of me. I promise never to hurt you."

Eve closed her eyes and heard the need in his voice. Felt it singing through her own body and knew she matched his song. She didn't answer. Instead, she opened the door with one hand, pulled him through the opening with the other. When they were both inside, he pressed it shut with his hip and took Eve in his arms once again.

Before she realized what he was planning, he'd lifted her against his chest and carried her to the bed. She was a tall woman, but he made her feel feminine, protected. He kissed her as he lowered her to the thick comforter. She heard his shoes hit the floor as he followed her down, kissing her with teasing little nips and licks that turned her skin to fire and covered her with goose bumps at the same time.

She didn't feel her shirt come off, but there he was, lying beside her, suckling her naked breast. He rolled the nipple of her right breast between his fingers, rolled the left against the roof of his mouth.

She arched her back with each flick of his tongue, each sweep of his fingers. She whimpered once more when he kissed his way to her waistband, slowly tugged both her pants and panties down over her bruised and battered hips, kissing each mark along the way. He was gentle, so very gentle that she wanted to weep. No one had treated her with such care, not for as long as she could remember. Sex had always been something taken, something hard and fast that left her even more needy when it ended.

Now, she felt desire building, felt the clenching in her sex and the thick cream between her thighs. Maybe it wouldn't hurt . . . maybe, if he was really careful and not too big . . .

She heard his laughter in her mind. He was there, listening to her thoughts! If only she could understand his words.

He must have sensed her inability to mindtalk yet. He raised his head and rested his chin on her navel. "I'm much too big and you're still too sore. I've got a better idea."

Before she could answer, he'd scooted lower and parted her thighs. She felt the warm sweep of his tongue, the soft touch of his lips sucking and nipping the folds of her labia. The bridge of his nose nudged her clit and another rush of fluids had him licking deep, feasting on her taste and scent. She'd gone down on so many men. Never, not once had a single man taken the time to give her so much pleasure.

She felt her climax building with each sweep of his tongue. His fingers trailed in the slick heat between her buttocks and he pressed her there, finding a rhythm with his mouth and probing finger that took her closer, ever closer to the edge.

Her fingers twisted in the soft, down comforter. She anchored herself and raised her hips to his mouth.

He suckled her clit, pressing against it with his tongue, sucking hard and driving a finger deep inside her bottom at the same time. Eve arched her back and screamed. Waves of sensation boiled from spine to womb to clit. He sucked harder, probed deeper with his tongue and finger and she climaxed again, harder this time.

Adam brought her down slowly, licking, touching, tasting. He moved up along her body and kissed her tears, then pressed his mouth to hers. She tasted the salty, almost bitter flavor of her own fluids on his lips.

He kissed her again and then eased away from the bed. She felt limp, boneless, as if her body would melt and flow away like hot wax. He rolled her beneath the covers and kissed her once again.

"Good night, sweet Eve. Sleep well. I'll see you in the morning." He brushed the damp tangles of hair back from her face, kissed her forehead this time, and quietly left the room.

It wasn't until the door shut behind him that she realized he'd given her the most amazing orgasms of her life, and not done a thing to ease his own needs.

What kind of man was he? Caring. Unselfish. She'd not believed anyone like Adam actually existed beyond romance novels. She stretched and snuggled deeper into the covers, thought of Adam, and smiled as her eyes grew heavy.

Amazing. The man was utterly amazing.

He stood outside Eve's door, grinning broadly. She was everything he'd ever imagined in a woman. Everything, and so much more it was scary. *Chanku.* He was one. She was one.

Oliver was one. At least he had the potential to be one.

The house was quiet. Oliver had gone to his own home, a small cottage across the broad expanse of lawn. He might not appreciate the visit, but Adam was wound too tightly to go to bed. Besides, it was a good thing, this pulsing, aching sexual need. If his theory was right, he might need all this energy to work a miracle.

Oliver met him at the door, wearing nothing but a towel

around his lean hips. Obviously, he'd been expecting Adam. "You know what happened. But how?"

He stepped aside and Adam entered his home. Immaculate. Just like Oliver. It was also surprisingly warm and comfortable inside. Adam shook his head. "I'm not sure. I only know that, somehow, I have a feeling I can help you. I don't know how or why, but I've felt this way since last night when we talked."

Oliver sat on an oak stool at a long bar in the kitchen. "You fix machines." He waved his hand dismissively.

"I do." Adam went to the refrigerator as if he owned the place, opened the door and looked for a beer. He found one, offered Oliver one of his own bottles, and grabbed a second.

"Make yourself at home, why don't you?" Oliver took the beer, flipped the lid off with his thumb and took a swallow. Adam sat on the stool next to him.

"I will, thank you. Look, I fix things that are broken. I've never tried people. Not sure why." He tilted his head and stared at Oliver. "You still got a hard-on?"

Oliver shook his head and smiled sadly. "No. I came home to look at it, but of course it was gone."

"Will you let me try something?"

Oliver took a long swallow of beer. "I don't know. Depends. Right now I feel no sexual desire. Not like I did earlier."

Adam nodded. Then he let his mind wander back to Eve's room, to the smooth underside of her breast, the taut nipple against his tongue. He remembered the taste of her fluids and the musky scent in the air. The way her sex had rippled and contracted around his tongue, the smooth nub of her clitoris swelling with desire. When he'd penetrated her anally, her muscles had clamped his finger in their tight, hot grasp.

His cock swelled and his balls ached and still he let the memories invade his mind.

"How do you do that?" Oliver's voice broke on a harsh whisper. He grabbed Adam's arm. "I'm hard again." He whipped the towel off and reached down with his hand. His fingers barely encircled the diameter of his cock. He was uncut, his foreskin rolled back behind the crown. The smooth tip glistened. Distended veins traced darker lines along the thick shaft. There was nothing beneath his cock beyond an empty sac. No testicles. His cock stood out, not overly long, but thick and hard, and obviously lonely.

Adam raised his head and caught the look of pure, animal need in Oliver's eyes. "This is the first step. The first thing we need to do. Is it okay?"

Confusion clouded Oliver's face. "I don't know what you're asking."

"I want to give you an orgasm. You have no testicles, so I imagine there won't be much ejaculate, but I want you to know what it feels like. You're going to help me reach one at the same time. I'll share the sensations, like I did just a minute ago. You're hard because I am. I'm with you on this one, Ollie. It's your turn."

"Whatever you want me to do. Anything."

Adam laughed. "Just touch me. I'm that close. C'mon." He grabbed Oliver's hand and led him to the big couch in the living room. He had him lie down and knelt beside the couch. Then he took Oliver's cock in his hand and stroked it, carefully using the man's foreskin to stimulate the crown.

Oliver scooted over on the couch and made room for Adam. It took a bit of maneuvering, but the two of them managed to lie side by side, head to toe, arms and legs all tangled and awkward. Adam took Oliver's cock in his mouth and stroked the base with his palm, squeezing him firmly.

He felt the warmth of Oliver's mouth, the soft play of an inexperienced tongue and questing lips over his own cock, and he shared the sensations, the heat, the wet slide of flesh, the pulsing in his balls and the ache that transferred itself from pain to pleasure.

He shared all the nuances of arousal, the emotional as well as the physical. Opened his mind with this new ability that seemed to grow by the hour, this ability to transfer his feelings, his experiences, to another.

It felt so strange to stroke Oliver's cock, to search for the heavy ball sac below and find only a small, shriveled pouch beneath the shaft. He touched it anyway, sharing the feeling of Oliver's fingers on his own sac, the firm shape of his own balls.

Oliver moaned against his cock and his lips tightened around the crown. Adam felt the jerk and twitch of Oliver's hips and knew he was close to coming. Licking, sucking, and swallowing him as deep as he could, sharing the sensations, the flavors and feelings with Oliver, Adam let his arousal climb, let the inhibitions dissipate.

He thought of Eve. Thought of her gentle touch, her warm lips, the tantalizing flavors of her sex. For one brief moment in time, he forgot Oliver, forgot his plan altogether.

He thought of Eve and his body reacted. A coil of heat and need, of pure lust spiraling from spine to balls to cock. He sucked hard on Oliver, felt his partner's shocked response as his own orgasm took hold.

Oliver swallowed what he could of Adam's burst of seed, but he stopped, suddenly, threw back his head and cried out. His hips thrust forward, his muscles locked tightly, and he climaxed.

Adam swallowed what little ejaculate there was. Sucking hard and licking, using his lips and tongue, he gave Oliver whatever pleasure he could. At the same time, Adam shared his own powerful orgasm, the deep throbbing in his balls, the surge of arousal that washed over his entire body.

The two of them hung there, suspended in sensation, their bodies shaking with the power of their shared climax. Finally, after what felt like forever, Adam relaxed against Oliver's groin. He gave his cock one final lick and slowly pivoted and sat up.

Panting, his breath coming in quick gasps, he waited for Oliver to get himself back under control.

Oliver lay back on the couch, his face a study in mixed emotions. He reached out for Adam, touched his arm, closed his eyes. Tears trailed wet streaks across his dark face. "I've always wondered. Always wanted to know what it was that drove Anton, drove Stefan forward. Why they needed their women beyond the mere fact of friendship or procreation. I read about love, read about sex, but I never knew. Never understood. *Never.*" He looked at Adam, his eyes shimmering with tears. "Thank you. For showing me, I thank you."

Adam rolled his head to one side and looked directly at Oliver. "I'm not just showing you, my friend. I'm telling you what will be. Listening to Anton and Stefan tonight, hearing the women talk about recovering from childbirth. It gave me an idea. Look, here's what I think. If we can somehow get that Chanku part of your brain to develop, we can help you shift. Will you be a neutered wolf when you shift, or will you have balls? And, if you have them as a wolf, where will they go when you come back to your human form?"

Oliver stared at him for the longest time. Then he started to laugh. He lay back on the couch, his hands over his eyes and laughed until Adam wondered if he was losing it. "Ollie? You okay?"

It took him a minute to regain his composure. He rolled his head to one side, and there was a twinkle in his amber eyes. "Only you, my friend. Anton, with all his powers, has never even considered anything like this. You, an untried Chanku, have come up with what might be a solution. I have wanted to be the wolf as much, if not more, than I have wanted to be a whole man. Your idea can't hurt. It might work." He closed his eyes for a long moment. When he opened them, he was once again the serious, precise employee of Anton Cheval.

"Thank you. Whether it is successful or not, thank you. You are the first to have cared enough to try."

Much later, Adam wandered back to the house. He slipped quietly inside and headed down the hallway to his room. Anton met him halfway.

"Adam? Wait a moment. Please."

Adam felt the weight of Anton's hand on his shoulder. "What? Is something wrong?"

Anton shook his head. "No, unless you count me feeling like a fool. I was letting my thoughts wander tonight. I tried to contact Oliver. You were there. In his mind, in his heart."

His hand fell away from Adam's shoulder. He gazed off in the distance in the direction of Oliver's house. "At first, I was jealous. I have loved Oliver for so many years. He is my son, my brother, my very dear friend. Not once did I consider a way to help him. Not once did I wonder how his condition affected his life. He seemed to accept his state. Ergo, I accepted."

He turned away and Adam felt his shame. This time, it was Adam's hand on Anton's shoulder. "Sometimes," Adam said, "those who are closest miss the most obvious. You can't blame yourself. We don't even know if my idea will work."

"True. But you've given Oliver hope where none existed. I know he tried drugs years ago, hormones to replace what he'd lost, but they were not successful. This may have a chance. Even if it fails, you've given him more than I ever imagined possible. Thank you."

He turned away before Adam could answer. Tall, lithe, moving like a panther in the dark, he headed back to his own rooms. To his lovely mate, Keisha. To his daughter.

Adam watched him leave and his heart felt heavy. He thought of Oliver, alone in his cottage. Thought of Eve sleeping in her beautiful room, the very first room all her own. Then he headed back to his own room, and thought how lonely it felt without a partner. Without either Eve or Oliver. He'd been alone for so long, liked his status as the lone wolf, yet now he missed the warmth of another body, the sound of another heart beating. He crawled between the crisp sheets and thought of the connections he'd made tonight.

Those memories were all he had to comfort him. Tomorrow would bring him a mother he'd never known, a sister he'd known all too intimately. *Manda.* What was she like now? What had she really been like then . . . ? Damn, a lifetime of misery and he'd not been able to help her. She might hate him, knowing how worthless he'd been. Nothing to be done about it now. Nothing at all.

Putting those concerns out of his mind, instead he thought of Eve. Dreaming of her willing body, her warm breasts, her sweet kisses, Adam drifted off to sleep.

5

Adam wandered out to the kitchen around six in the morning and found Stefan grumbling about making his own coffee. He'd found a note from Oliver on the counter saying he'd not felt well. He wasn't coming in.

Anton showed up about the same time as Adam, gave him a knowing nod and proceeded to take over the coffee-making duties. Adam found a seat at the kitchen table, took a section of the morning paper and kept his mouth shut. It wasn't his place to tell Oliver's story.

Over the next hour or so, Xandi stopped in to say good morning, and Keisha brought Lily down to Anton so she could take a shower. It was all so domestic, so normal. Then Anton handed Adam another of those big pills. Both he and Stefan took theirs.

"It's real, isn't it? I really am going to be able to turn into a wolf?"

Anton patted Adam's shoulder in a fatherly way. "I'm afraid so. Do you mind?"

"You're kidding, right? All the years of dreams, the fascination with wolves. It's finally starting to make sense."

"It will make more sense when your mother and sister arrive."

Adam shook his head. "It's hard to realize I have a mother I've never met, a sister. All those dreams over so many years. Will Manda ever forgive me?"

Anton seemed to withdraw for a moment. "She loves you. She credits you with keeping her sane."

"How? All I did was have horrible nightmares. I could never find her."

"You sent her strength. You cared. You were the only one, for all those years, who cared. She couldn't link to you as we do, with mindtalking, but she felt your concern, knew you prayed for her safety. She mattered to you. You, to her."

Anton's words carried him through the day. Eve was gone for most of it, off on a shopping trip with Keisha and Xandi. They'd commandeered the SUV and headed back to town to buy necessities for Eve and things for the babies. The house seemed large and empty without their presence.

But he wasn't alone. No, he felt Manda hovering at the edge of his mind all through the day. Felt her strength, her utter sweetness. It helped him prepare for the most intense meeting of all.

He would finally meet the woman who had given him life. Since learning he was adopted, hearing his parents discuss buying him, he'd felt nothing but distaste for his birth mother. Now, to find out she'd been as much a victim as he—and Manda—left him with a gaping hole in his heart, a sense that nothing was as it seemed.

What was she like? How would he react when he finally saw her? Finally saw Manda? He wished Eve were here. Though she was a stranger, she understood. He'd felt her compassion, her encouragement. She cared.

Oliver showed up early in the afternoon to prepare dinner. He was quiet, but according to Stefan, that was nothing unusual.

Oliver nodded, acknowledging Adam as he left the room, but they didn't speak. Adam wondered what the man thought, how he felt about their shared climax from the night before. It must have been a powerful experience for Oliver.

It still lingered with Adam. He'd been on edge all day long and the feeling only grew worse as the afternoon progressed. When he showered and dressed, he sensed Manda growing nearer. After so many years dreaming her thoughts, Adam realized they still had a connection.

It grew stronger as the minutes ticked by. He looked down at his hands. His damned fingers were trembling! His palms felt sweaty and he rubbed them along his pants. At this rate he'd be an absolute mess by the time everyone got here. Ulrich Mason. Adam's mother, Millie West. Baylor Quinn . . . and Manda. Amanda Smith.

He didn't care about the men. They were Chanku, they were mates to the women who mattered. Adam knew their approval was a necessary evil. He stared at himself in the mirror and wondered how he would be judged.

College dropout. Wanderer. Itinerant mechanic. Son, brother . . . *Chanku.* At least they had that common link. He glanced at the clock beside the bed and realized they wouldn't arrive for over an hour. He'd go nuts by then.

A door nearby opened and closed. He sensed Eve.

His heart rate slowed. His breathing calmed. Without giving himself time to reconsider, Adam opened his bedroom door and stepped out into the hallway. He knocked softly on Eve's door.

She'd half expected Adam and opened the door immediately. He stood there with his fist raised, prepared to knock again.

Eve opened the door wide and stepped back. "I knew it was you. Come see what I bought today!" He had to be a wreck, waiting on his mother and sister. She'd felt terrible leaving him, but Xandi and Keisha had been so excited about taking her shopping.

Now, though, looking at the desperate gleam in his eye, she wished she'd stayed here with Adam. He needed her. This day must have been hell for him.

He stepped into the room and shut the door. Eve grabbed the first big bag of outfits, turned and caught him watching her.

Clothing appeared to be the furthest thing from his mind. He reached for her, and she knew his desperation was over-whelming, knew his need was all caught up in the evening ahead. It didn't matter that all he looked for was release. He might only want to take his mind off the emotional morass of meeting a mother and sister for the first time, but it was Eve he turned to now.

The bag fell from her fingers and she moved into Adam's arms. He caught her mouth with his, lifting her as he kissed her and carried her to the bed covered in bags and parcels. He swept them all to the floor and stretched her out on the cover-let. His need was great and it spilled over on to Eve.

Her mind opened to his, her heart pounded the same desperate song as Adam's. She touched him with fingers that flittered across his high cheekbones, through his long, dark blond hair. The sun had streaked it gold and his skin was weathered from the elements. She'd thought him rugged and sexy the first time she saw him.

He reminded her of the quintessential man of the west, all raw, rangy strength and sharp, gleaming eyes. His hands were big, the fingers long and covered in scars, the hands of a me-chanic, a farmer, a cowboy.

He'd said he fixed things.

Who fixes you, Adam? Who was there for him?

He whispered her name and trailed small, hot kisses along her jaw. She arched her back and pressed her body against his. He groaned and his kisses grew more desperate, his hands sweeping the length of her body, tugging at her clothing, baring her body regardless of the cost to fabric and buttons. She knew his gentleness, but she'd not experienced his need, his powerful desire to bury himself in her warm body.

"I don't want to hurt you. God, Eve, I need you tonight but I'm afraid I'll . . ."

She put her fingertip over his lips. "I'm okay. Anything. Whatever you want from me, I'm here. I want it too. You make me feel. Make me want. I want you."

Her words unlocked something powerful in him. She sensed the change, the sudden burst of desire no longer managed or controlled. He stripped off his clothing. Something compelling, an almost visceral sense of indomitable strength tugged at her heart when she saw him naked. His beautiful body was tense and shaking, his muscles hard. A fine sheen of sweat covered his chest.

She lay in the center of the big bed and stared at him, drinking her fill of what had to be the most perfect male she'd ever seen. Powerful muscles rippled over his chest and arms, along the tops of his hair-roughened thighs. His belly was flat with perfectly defined muscles, the trail of dark blond hair growing darker, following a line from between his perfect, copper-colored nipples, down the center of that gorgeous belly, leading the eye to the biggest erection she'd ever seen.

Her mouth watered as she looked him over, imagined the slide of that thick cock between her lips. He stood, unmoving, and at first she thought he posed for her. Then she realized he was waiting for permission. For Eve to invite him to her bed.

She smiled and reached for him. His fingers touched hers. She tugged. He leaned close. Placed one knee on the bed. She touched his shoulder, and with the slightest pressure of fingertips brought him closer. Kissed him lightly, then leaned her head back against the pillow, laughing.

"I can't believe what's happening to us. Adam, love me. Last night you made my body sing. Tonight I want a duet."

Her stupid joke took the nervous look off his face. He lay down beside her, trailed his fingers along her thigh, found the damp center between her legs. She whimpered and arched her back to meet his touch, shivered when he breached her opening, slipped his fingers deep inside.

Nothing . . . nothing was more intimate than this touch. A cock speared and drove deep, a tongue tasted . . . fingers . . . fingers felt her deep inside. Felt her heat, curled against her inner walls and trailed along a part of herself she would never see. He stroked her with infinite care, but his gently controlled touch belied the tension contained within that perfect, male body. She felt his need, accepted it, relished it.

"Just a minute." He leaned away, and his fingers left her body. She felt bereft, abandoned, but he returned within the beat of her heart and held up a condom, still neatly contained within the wrapper. "Hang on. Just take me a minute."

He tore the wrapper with his teeth and sheathed himself. She felt her emotions welling up inside, threatening to spill over. She was on the pill, but he'd taken the initiative. He'd protected her. No one did that. Not ever.

So why did that frighten her so? Why did his act of consideration, on top of his generous loving last night, change everything? When he moved over her, kissed her sweetly and nuzzled her breasts, she trembled. It wasn't all desire. Some unknown fear coursed through her, a sense of *too much, too soon.*

Already her body was changing. Her skin itched and twitched and she knew the pills were doing something to her. She wanted Adam. Wanted his heat and hard, thrusting cock, wanted his mouth on her breasts, his tongue in her sex.

But did she want *him?* Was she ready for the bonding Keisha and Xandi talked about? The lifelong link with a mate, tied forever to one man? Everything Eve was, linked forever to Adam? Right now it was all *need* and *want* and *desire. That* she understood. What would happen when it was more than her own pleasure? More than just Eve? For the first time in her life, she had no one to think of beyond herself. She wanted to get to know the woman she was meant to be. Wanted to know her as she changed, like a butterfly emerging from the twisted chrysalis of her totally screwed up life. Everything had always been on someone else's terms, someone else's rules. From her foster families and their constantly changing dynamics as she was shuttled from home to home, to the men who had kept her throughout her adult years.

Always an object. Always at the whim of someone else's desires. Now, for the first time, she had a chance to be her own woman. A woman with powers beyond human, a predator. Her body shuddered. Her arms itched and a wave of arousal spread from breasts to womb to that fiery point between her legs.

Adam's thick cock pressed against her sex and, just that easily, Eve forgot her own path. Forgot her needs and worried only about his. He paused there for a moment. His breath was a harsh crescendo in her ear, his heartbeat pounding in sync with her own. She had time to consider each sensation, each separate feeling. The heat of living flesh, the broad, smooth crown pausing at her entrance, the sleek yet steady pressure as he slowly but surely moved forward.

Tonight. Eve sighed and opened completely for him. Her body seemed to clutch at his cock, compressing, relaxing, pulling him deeper. She would take what she could, give Adam what he needed.

Tonight, and only tonight.

She was growing stronger, her body healing, her heart sensing freedom. There was no time for love. Not now. Maybe never, not if love meant giving up her one chance for freedom.

Xandi and Keisha didn't see it the same way she did. They hadn't understood when she'd tried to explain that linking with anyone, Adam or any other man, meant giving up part of herself.

A part she'd never wholly owned.

Adam thrust deep and hard and she grasped his buttocks and pulled him close. The hard muscles rippled beneath her palms and she stroked him. Loved him with her body, if not her heart.

A few more days, maybe less, but soon. Eve knew the day was close when she would have the strength to find her own way. To finally live her own life.

She would not fall in love. No matter how perfect he seemed, no matter how tempting the path. She had to do something, anything, on her own. Even if it was merely to leave.

I do not need him. No matter how much I want him, I do not need him. The words spun in her mind, a mantra reinforcing her decision. She would let the pills work their magic. She would learn the world of the wolf, the mysteries of the forest.

And then she would go away.

Adam lay beside Eve, his chest heaving like a bellows, heart pounding, skin shivering. Sex with her was amazing. Overwhelming. Better than anything he'd ever experienced in his life.

So why did he feel so empty? And why did she lie beside him, her face turned away, her body still trembling from climax but the doors to her mind firmly shut?

He'd have to find out later. There was just enough time to clean up before his sister and mother arrived. He leaned over and kissed Eve's forehead. He sensed the distance between them as he got off the bed and headed for the door. He'd shower in his own room. For now, he needed time away to think about the walls between them. Walls Eve held in place. He had no idea why . . . it was obvious she was absolutely perfect.

And it was just as obvious, Eve refused to see.

He felt Manda's presence before he reached the main room. Adam walked faster. He was practically running by the time he opened the big door and stopped. She stood in the middle of the room, caught in a sunbeam, all sleek blond hair and gleaming smile.

He knew her immediately, just as he also knew the older woman standing beside her. "Manda?" He tore his gaze away from the younger woman to study his mother. "Mother? Mom?"

He might have been ten years old or a hundred. He moved slowly, his world tumbling out of sync. Both Manda and his mother raced toward him, one the younger image of the older. They might have been alone in the room, so focused was he on the women who were his family.

His blood. He didn't remember hugging them both against his chest, couldn't recall the last time he'd wept like a child. He stood there, holding Manda and his mother in his arms, crying like a baby, and knew. He'd been reborn.

The others, if they'd even been in the room, had gone. The three of them remained, huddled together as if attempting to reestablish links broken long ago. Long moments later, Adam led both women to a large, leather couch. He sat in a chair opposite them. He picked up a box of tissues someone had thoughtfully left beside the chair, grabbed one for himself and handed the box to his mother. Both she and Manda grabbed tissues, laughing as they dried their eyes.

"I need to look at you," he said. "Both of you. I can't believe you're real."

"I feel the same way." His mother reached for him, took his hand. "So many times I dreamed of finding you, both of you, but it was only that, a dream. You're real. You look just like your father, the way I remember him. Too handsome for his own good." She scrubbed her eyes once more. "For my own good, too. Obviously. Oh, Adam . . ."

"I've always wanted to thank you." Manda's voice wobbled. "All those years . . ."

"But I couldn't find you. I couldn't help." Adam took her hand, linking the three of them. His mother squeezed his.

"You did help. I was always aware of you. I had no idea who you were, whether or not you were real, but I never felt entirely alone, no matter how bad things were."

"I need to know." Adam looked from his mother to his sister. "I need to know what happened. Why we were separated, why you were tortured all those years. Tell me, please."

Anton walked in and sat beside Eve at the kitchen table. He handed her one of the big, brown capsules. She swallowed it down with a glass of water, her second pill. Stefan, Xandi, and Keisha had eaten earlier and gone back to their rooms. Oliver had taken a light meal in for Adam and Manda and their mother, then quietly departed to give them their privacy. Baylor and Ulrich had shifted. They ran tonight, to give their women time with Adam.

Eve couldn't contain herself any longer. "Adam told me he was sold when he was an infant. How can he sit in there with that woman and . . ."

Anton shook his head. "It wasn't like that at all. When Millie gave birth without any idea where the father was, her uncle had the babies taken from her before she even saw them. They were turned over to their church for immediate adoption. Millie's not sure if her uncle knew the pastor sold the babies rather than going through a legal process, but she's searched for them all their lives."

"Oh. That changes . . ." She gazed toward the closed door and opened her thoughts to Adam, just as he'd taught her. Nothing.

"Manda went with a missionary couple to Tibet. She must have eaten just enough of the local vegetation that, when her adoptive parents were killed, she went through an involuntary shift. Because of her young age and the fact she'd probably not had enough of the nutrients her body needed, she was caught midway through the shift. The man who rescued her . . ." Anton paused, then sighed. "If you could call it that, used her like a lab animal until just recently. Baylor found her. He helped her through the process, helped her find her true heritage as Chanku."

"Is that why they bonded? Because she felt she owed him?"

Anton stared at her as if she'd grown three heads. There was an odd sensation, a pressure in her mind that made her wonder if the wizard searched her thoughts as carefully as he appeared to search her face. No matter how much the others seemed to love him, he gave her the creeps. There was such a sense of power about him. Barely controlled power.

"No," he said, finally, shaking his head. He smiled at her, but it was sort of a sad looking smile and Eve wished she could read his mind as easily as he appeared to read hers. "Manda bonded with Bay because she loves him. Without love, there can be no bond. It can't happen. Not a true, complete bond. You have nothing to worry about, Eve. You won't be forced to take a mate. You'll know when you're ready. Obviously, that time is not now."

She heard Adam's door open, then close as the first rays of sunlight filtered through her window. He must have stayed up all night, talking with his mother and sister. She wondered what it would be like to finally meet family after so long. Wondered what it felt like to actually have family.

Her bed was huge. It was definitely designed for more than one person. She'd been so thrilled to have a room to herself. It made no sense, this disappointment that Adam hadn't come to her. Her skin itched, her muscles twitched and her *sense* of Adam was much stronger than it had been the night before. She clenched the muscles between her legs and knew she'd grown damp just thinking of him, of the way he'd loved her.

Without thinking of the consequences, she crawled out of her warm bed. Completely naked, Eve left her room and stood in front of Adam's. She paused for a moment, one hand raised, took a deep breath and knocked on the door.

It opened immediately. He wore nothing but blue jeans. The top snap was undone, the zipper still up. His feet were bare, his chest covered only in a mat of dark gold hair. Dark circles edged Adam's eyes, but he didn't hesitate. Smiling broadly, he grabbed Eve's arm and dragged her through the doorway. "I almost went to your room, but I didn't want to wake you."

Before she could answer, he kissed her, his lips moving over hers, his tongue probing and entering. She shivered. His hands swept up and down her sides and she wrapped one leg around his waist, stretching upward on her toes, pressing her mound against the rough fabric of his jeans. He was hard beneath the zipper and she rubbed against him like a bitch in heat.

Needy. She was so damned needy and he tasted so good. Adam moaned into her mouth, reached down between them and freed his cock. She felt the heat and power in his erection. Lifting her body away from his, straining on the toes of one foot she opened for him.

Adam's cock found her center and speared deep. She arched against him, wrapped her other leg around his hips and clung to his body. His jeans slipped down his hips as he walked her to the bed.

By the time he laid her down on the soft covers, they were both laughing, both gasping for air, groaning with the exquisite pleasure of their joining. The bed was high and her legs draped over the edge, perfectly placed for Adam to stand there and pump hard and fast into her willing body. He leaned over and took one sensitive nipple between his lips, sucking until she cried out.

He moved to the next one, biting and sucking as he thrust inside her willing flesh. Eve slipped her hands along his back, stroked the sleek muscles along the curve of his absolutely perfect ass, raking him with her fingernails, pulling him even closer, deeper, harder.

"Lord, Eve, this is so damned good." He kissed her and she felt his tension grow, felt her own body tighten. Adam's thoughts slipped into her mind, his sensual power, the pure eroticism of fucking hard and fast without any foreplay, with a partner who was so new to him, yet so amazingly connected.

Her own arousal spiraled up, higher, tighter, the sensations growing, her body quivering with each powerful thrust of his hips. Suddenly she sensed Adam's climax, felt the tightening at the base of his spine, the coil of heat spiking through his groin straight to his balls. A rush of fire caught her, took her to the top and over.

He shouted, an incoherent cry of pure lust mingling with Eve's own cries of completion. Muscles clenching, spasming around the heat of his cock, she felt the hot burst of his seed, the powerful tightening of her own climax as she held him close.

Breathing hard and fast, Adam slipped his cock from her sex, kicked his pants off and crawled into bed. She lay there, body pulsing with the aftereffects of the most powerful climax she'd ever experienced. Adam stroked the length of her body, cupped her breast in his palm, then trailed along the sensitive flesh to her belly. He swirled one finger in her navel and laughed when she shrieked and drew her knees up to her chest.

"Eve." He sighed. "Eve, what are we going to do? I hardly know you. I need you. You're like a drug and I'm a hopeless addict."

He slipped his fingers lower as she thought of his words. Already she felt the same way about Adam. She didn't want to. Not yet. Not until she had time to be free, to be herself without any responsibilities, without ties of any kind.

He dragged his fingers slowly over her clit and she parted her legs on a moaning sigh. Her sex was all wet and slippery from her fluids and his. Suddenly Eve realized he'd not used a condom. She'd not taken her birth control pills for two days.

Keisha said the Chanku had total control of reproduction. Eve wondered if the process worked before she'd started shifting, but that worry fled when Adam dipped two fingers deep inside her channel and slowly began to fuck her. His thumb rode over her sensitive clit and she knew it was too soon. It had to be. She'd not recovered from the first orgasm, but her body didn't seem to understand the need to take a break.

Whimpering, clinging to his arms and arching her back to meet each thrust of his fingers, Eve let sensation sweep her away. She was pure desire, her body aroused to a feverish pitch and he kept her there, riding the wave of sensation without going over the edge.

He added another finger. His hand was big, the pressure inexorable, unbelievable. Screaming, Eve clamped her thighs tightly around his wrist, arched high against his thrusting fingers. Ripples of pleasure, immeasurable pleasure verging on pain, raced in pulsing waves through her body.

Finally she peaked, cried out once more and went limp. His hand stayed buried inside her heat, unmoving now, but connecting them. He held her close, buried his face in her full breasts and simply, without any words or another kiss, fell asleep.

She felt his body relax against her, felt the soft puffs of his breath against her distended nipple. Her inner muscles still rippled over his fingers. His thumb pressed enticingly against her clit.

She'd had a full night's sleep, but still she grew drowsy, lying here wrapped in Adam's warmth, the heady perfume of their passion filling the room. He was a fascinating man. An amazing man. The best lover she'd ever known.

There'd been more than enough lovers—of both sexes.

She'd not asked him about his mother. Not wondered about his meeting with his sister. She'd merely known he needed her.

She'd had no idea how much she needed him.

Not good, Eve. Not good at all.

With that thought uppermost in her mind, she slowly drifted into an uneasy sleep.

6

_____

"So, what you're saying is that Xandi's car crashing and my finding her was predestined? That we had no choice in the matter, right?"

"Exactly." Anton sipped his wine, yet still managed a wink in Adam's direction. "You don't honestly think she would have mated with you if she'd had a choice, do you?"

"Yes, I would have." Xandi patted Stefan's hand and smiled sweetly, as if talking to a four-year-old. "He was just too cute for words."

Everyone at the table, including Anton, laughed.

Stefan kissed Xandi on the nose before continuing the argument. "Then Oliver's picking up Adam was predestined, just as our rescuing Eve was planned by fate?"

"Of course."

Adam felt Eve's tension clear across the table. He'd not seen much of her all day, but he'd been so involved with his mother and sister during their brief overnight visit, he'd not really noticed Eve's distance. Now, though, with Millie, Ulrich, Manda, and Baylor headed for their respective homes, Adam realized she'd been avoiding him all day.

"What do you think, Adam?"

Stefan's question caught him by surprise. "About?"

"You and Eve. The fact you're both Chanku, the fact you both ended up coming here at the same time. Destiny or coincidence?"

"Definitely destiny." He smiled at Eve. She looked away. How could she, after what they'd shared? He shook his head. "That doesn't mean I know how it will all play out."

The argument went on around him, good-natured as always. Eve stayed quiet, but she was rubbing her arms. He'd noticed the same itchy, twitchy sensation, though obviously not as powerfully as Eve. She must be growing closer to her time to shift. Anton said it happened faster in women.

There was something about her that felt different this evening. Would she shift tonight? Suddenly, Eve stood up. "How will I know?" She looked about her, frantically. "How will I know when it's time to shift?"

Anton set his wine down and stood as well. He tilted his head and smiled at her. "You'll know when you leap to your feet and ask us when. I think you're ready, Eve. Do you want to try?"

Adam sensed Oliver's presence. He stood in the doorway, watching Eve. Then he glanced at Adam and nodded. Keisha and Anton followed Eve out to the porch. Xandi agreed to stay with the babies. Stefan chose to stay with her. Adam followed Eve outside. He had to consciously tamp down the surge of jealousy, that she would experience this amazing change without him.

She was already stripping out of her clothes, ignoring Adam, totally caught up in her body, in the strange sensations that must be coursing through her.

Anton shifted first. Eve stared at the big wolf for a moment, then stared at Keisha. It happened so quickly, Adam couldn't pinpoint the exact instant they changed, but where two women had stood together on the porch, wolves now paced.

Eve's coat was pale, more gray than brown. Under the porch light she glistened with streaks of silver and gold. She turned once and looked at him, her eyes glowing gray instead of amber like Anton and Keisha's. Then she turned away and raced down the steps. The other two wolves followed close behind.

Adam and Oliver remained on the deck. Oliver touched Adam's shoulder, nodded toward the house and both men went back inside. Before closing the door, Oliver glanced back toward the dark forest. "When she returns," he said, "she will need more than just you for sex. One man will not be enough. That first run . . . it fuels the libido. She will be highly aroused, insatiable. Desperate, even. You need to know this."

Adam laughed, but he didn't really see much humor in the situation. "Thanks for the warning, Ollie. I'll be ready. Make sure you are, too."

Nothing. Nothing in her entire life could have prepared Eve for this. Racing down narrow, brush-clogged trails, eyes wide to the ambient illumination of the night, she marveled at the pure poetry of running on four legs. And her *tail!* A beautiful plume, part of her body, a signal to all of her moods.

Her own, personal banner.

Ears pricked forward, she followed close behind the Keisha-wolf, aware of the scent that was so uniquely hers, the mental signature that identified Anton's mate.

Anton remained a few paces behind. She wondered if he protected them or deferred to his wife's lead. There was so much to learn, though much about this body seemed to flood her mind with knowledge. She *knew* how to control her breeding. *Knew* how to shift, how to be a wolf. To kill. To fight.

She wished Adam were here sharing this most amazing time. Then she realized she was glad he'd not shifted, not yet. She needed to do this on her own. Needed the confidence, the sense of freedom.

Would he want to mate immediately? Would she have to bond with him? Anton said no one could force a bond. She'd make sure Adam knew that. Knew how she felt.

Tonight, though . . . tonight she ran with the wolves. She hunted, and when the rabbit she'd brought down was consumed, she stood atop a rocky promontory with Keisha on one side, Anton on the other, and howled. There was no freedom greater than this. No power stronger than the wolf.

No hesitation at all in Eve Reynolds. She embraced her new self. Reveled in it. Gloried in her first taste of freedom and power. Howling into the night, part of the pack, a victim no more.

Adam sensed Eve's return before he saw her. Her gray eyes glowed with blue fire when she finally broke out of the woods. He watched her race to the front porch, look quickly around, and shift.

She didn't see him, or Oliver, either. She stood there like a pale goddess in the reflected light from the house. Her body glistened, bathed in a soft, golden glow. Her breasts were high and firm, the nipples dark points against their smooth surface. The two men waited in the shadows, watching. Adam finally spoke, but he used mindtalking so he wouldn't startle her. She carried the scent of the forest about her, and something more. The musky scent of her arousal, ripe and rich, tickled his nostrils.

Eve? How was it? Was it everything you hoped for?

Adam? She glanced around and he knew the moment she spotted him. Her smile spread across her face and his heart lurched in his chest.

I'm right here.

He loved her. It was that simple. He loved her, but he knew she didn't love him. Or, if she did, she fought it. Right now, though, she definitely wanted him. He wondered how she'd feel about adding Oliver to the evening's entertainment.

He and Oliver stood up. He heard Oliver's heart pounding in his chest, knew the other man was terrified of sharing his secret, but at the same time so enthralled by the idea of actually having sex with a woman he was willing to try anything.

"Oliver?" Eve glanced at Adam, smiled at Oliver and shivered. Her nipples ruched into tight little beads, moisture glistened between her thighs and her clitoris peeked out from its protective hood. Adam knew she didn't care if Oliver joined them, wouldn't care who made love to her, so long as she found a way to ease the desperate need swamping her body.

He took her hand and led her into the house and down the long hallway to his room. Oliver followed. His need flowed into Adam's mind, every bit as pressing as Eve's. So confusing, the myriad sensations. It was Adam's desire that fueled Oliver's, Adam's mental link to Eve and her powerful Chanku libido that drove both men to the edge. Eve turned to Adam and kissed him hard on the mouth. Then she held her hand out to Oliver and pulled him forward.

"I want you. Both of you." She laughed, the sound harsh, so unlike Eve. "As horny as I am right now, one man wouldn't be enough. Even you, Adam, as good as you are. It's more than I imagined. The whole fucking experience." Her breath came in harsh gasps and her eyes held a wild, feverish light. She pinched at her left nipple, pulling and twisting it between her fingers. Adam scooped her up in his arms and laid her on the bed. He nodded to Oliver.

Oliver needed no further instructions. He shucked his clothing, crawled up on the bed and then lay down on his back. Eve immediately straddled him. She hovered over his cock. Her eyes were closed and Adam didn't think she'd even noticed what Oliver lacked. Oliver's erection stood high and hard against his belly and he caught it in his fist, pressed it against Eve's sex and thrust forward as she came down on him.

Adam sighed, so tightly linked to both Eve and Oliver that he felt the thick head spearing her silky walls, experienced Oliver's first sexual penetration of any woman. He struggled to contain both his and Oliver's orgasms.

Oliver groaned. Adam cut back on the sensations he shared. The little guy gave him a quick nod of thanks, lifted his hips and pressed harder and deeper. Eve screamed and climaxed, her peak coming so tight and fast she caught Adam by surprise.

He sheathed himself with a condom and knelt between Oliver's outspread legs. Eve raised and lowered herself, sliding almost delicately now, up and down Oliver's shaft. Adam slipped his fingers inside her swollen sex, right alongside Oliver's cock. At the same time, he pressed his thumb against her tight anus. Eve shuddered and wriggled against his thumb. Her thoughts spilled over Adam and his own sphincter clenched at the intense sensation, the welcome violation of yet another nerve-rich part of Eve's body. He pressed harder, penetrated slightly, and rubbed slow circles around the sensitive ring of muscle.

She moaned and leaned forward, baring herself to his touch. He grabbed a jar of lubricant from the bedside table and rubbed the slick gel along the cleft between her round cheeks. His fingers slipped in easily and he fucked her with two of them, softening her, preparing her for the broad head of his cock.

Her muscles tightened against his fingers, clenching and releasing in rhythmic need. Adam's body responded, keeping time.

He pressed against her. She groaned. So did Oliver. Adam adjusted his stance, held his sheathed cock in his hand and pushed harder. He felt Eve's taut sphincter soften, then slowly clasp just the head of his cock. He slipped through. She tightened around his shaft and she was so damned hot inside.

Hot and wet and tight. Fighting for control, his own and Oliver's, Adam carefully slipped his cock in all the way. He felt the tip slide the length of Oliver's shaft, deeper until he'd buried himself completely in Eve's pulsing heat. He paused there for a moment and let the sensations fill him. Eve's hot, moist channel clasping his cock. The solid length of Oliver's shaft inside her tight sex, so close to his. The subtle pulse and quiver of life as feminine muscles rippled around both men.

Joined so intimately, minds and bodies tightly linked, Adam struggled for control. His thoughts churned and seethed, a veritable kaleidoscope of images and sensations as Eve's arousal tangled with his. He shared it all with Oliver.

Slowly, Adam eased his way out of Eve. Carefully, he pressed forward again, preternaturally aware, when he filled her, how his balls rested just at the base of Oliver's cock. Close against the small, empty sac between Oliver's legs.

She'd never felt so stuffed full before, never needed sex so much or wanted it as badly. Oliver's cock, surprisingly large for such a slightly built man, seemed to touch all the right spots with practiced ease. She'd never enjoyed anal sex, but her body shivered with greedy delight when Adam entered her. She wriggled her bottom just so, and he slipped in even deeper.

His thoughts were in her mind and she sensed Oliver's need, his silent litany of desire. Since shifting her mindtalking skills were amplified. She understood more of what she heard, caught thoughts sent between the two men that were probably not meant for her.

The reality of what they were doing suddenly slammed into her. This was Oliver's first time with a woman? He didn't want her to know, so she buried the knowledge and concentrated on the act. Two men fucked her, both of them more intent on her pleasure than their own.

So why did it make her so sad? Why did the obvious love she felt from Adam, the almost pathetic gratitude from Oliver, leave her feeling depressed and despairing?

It made no sense. She made no sense, but her body had needs she'd never experienced, her sex throbbed and her muscles contracted greedily around the two cocks that filled her. Oliver reached tentatively for her breasts and rolled her nipples between his fingers and thumbs. She arched and cried out from the sweet pain. Adam thrust harder, as if laying claim to her body with each powerful penetration.

Once more, she flew over the edge, but this time Eve wasn't alone. Oliver tensed beneath her. She felt his cock surge deeper as his climax overtook him. Adam was right there with them. He speared her deep and hard and his groan blended into her whimpering sigh.

She heard his thoughts in her mind. Words she willed him not to say. Words that trapped her, held her when she couldn't be held. Wouldn't be held.

I love you. Eve, I know it's too soon and my timing sucks, but I love you.

Sated, trembling, terrified . . . she dropped all loose-limbed and weak to Oliver's chest. He wrapped his arms around her and wept. Adam came down gently, holding both Oliver and Eve in his strong embrace. He loved her. She'd heard him. He was right. It was too soon and his timing sucked.

She'd barely discovered the wolf. She hardly knew the woman. She'd held on to a few extra pills, enough, she hoped, until she could find out what was in them, get some made for herself. She didn't want to lose the wolf. Even more important, though, she didn't want to lose herself.

Sandwiched between two men, her muscles still clenched in the age-old rhythm after climax. Oliver's cock was planted against her womb and Adam was still hard, still deep inside her bottom. Eve felt Adam coming back to life, fought the desire beginning to blossom within her once more. Fought the primal needs rising inside, the hollow ache in her womb that begged once again to be filled.

She didn't need this. Didn't want this. She didn't feel loved. Not at all. Shivering between two very hot, sexy male bodies, her own filled with surging need, Eve merely felt trapped.

She slipped out of bed before dawn and used the shower in her room, gathered up a few of the items Keisha and Xandi had purchased for her, and tried to figure out how she was going to get away without anyone finding out. They were in the middle of nowhere. These people had been so wonderful to her, but she had to go, now, before Adam shifted, before he wanted her as his mate and she'd not have the strength of will to refuse.

She loved him. In spite of herself, she was almost certain she loved Adam Wolf.

Quietly, carrying her boots and walking in thick socks, Eve slipped down the hallway and started through the kitchen. Anton Cheval sat at the kitchen table, barely visible in the predawn light. "Cup of coffee before you go?"

Eve felt the tension fall away. It was actually a relief someone knew. A bigger relief that someone was Anton.

She pulled out a chair across from him. "I've probably got time for one."

Anton poured her a cup and she sat down. He handed her a jar full of pills. "This should be enough for a month. I imagine you'll know by then if you want to come back or not."

She looked at the pills in her hand, then at Anton. He smiled at her. "But why? I've taken terrible advantage of you. I'm sneaking out and running away. Why are you helping me?"

"Because you are Chanku. Because you will come back, but

it must be of your own accord. You are a strong woman, Eve, but until you recognize and learn to love your own strength, you can't love another. It wouldn't be fair to you, nor would it be fair to your mate, whoever he is."

"What if it's not Adam?"

"Do you love him?"

She shook her head. "No. Yes. I'm not sure. But I could. I will, I think. Someday."

Anton smiled and nodded his head. "Exactly. If Adam is your destiny, you will find him again."

She thought about that a minute. Thought about the man she'd barely begun to know. He'd told her he fixed things. Unfortunately, Eve understood all too well, she had to fix herself. Adam couldn't do it for her.

She raised her head and smiled at Anton. "I hope you're right. I really, really hope you're right."

Anton put a small wallet on the table. "Some cash, a credit card. I've taken the liberty of adding your name to the account." He smiled at her. "Your driver's license is there as well. The sheriff dropped it off yesterday." Then Anton grabbed her hand, spread her fingers open and put a key in her palm. "The vehicle is old, but it will take you where you need to go. Be careful with it. It's very special. I'd really like to have it back by the twentieth of next month."

"The twentieth?" She glanced at the key. It was definitely old-fashioned.

"It's Stefan's birthday. The vehicle is a gift to him."

"You'd let me take it?"

"You'll be back, or you'll find a way to return it. I trust you. Now go, before the rest awaken. I will tell them you had to leave." He leaned close and kissed her. His lips brushed her mouth and she felt a tingle, a reawakening of sexual need. No one had underestimated the changes in her libido.

"One thing you must remember." Anton sat back in his chair. "Our identity as Chanku is a closely guarded secret. Take care no one learns what you are."

Anton's words stuck in her head, a steady refrain as she drove down the long road to the highway. *Take care no one learns what you are.* Just what the hell was she? Who was she? And would she ever figure it out?

Stefan wandered out to the kitchen just as a beautifully restored classic Ford pickup truck backed out of Oliver's garage, made a smooth turn around the curved driveway and headed out the road. "Holy shit, Anton! What a gorgeous old truck. Who the hell is that?"

"Do you like it?" Anton threw an arm around Stefan's shoulders.

"What? The truck? Of course. You know I've always wanted one of those." He watched with longing as the taillights disappeared around the first bend in the road.

Anton laughed. "Well, with any luck, I'll be handing you the keys to that one on your birthday. That was my gift to you. We merely need to hope, now, that Eve finds a reason to return."

"My truck?" Stefan stared at Anton. "She's leaving? You gave my truck to Eve?"

Anton shrugged. "Merely a coincidence, my friend. She needed a vehicle for the next month. Yours was available. She'll bring it back. I hope."

"My truck . . ." Sighing, Stefan turned away from the window and poured himself a cup of coffee. *Coincidence, hell.*

Adam lay in bed long after the sound of the departing truck had faded. He scratched at his arms and felt as if his bones wanted to pop right through the skin. He glanced at Oliver, still sleeping soundly beside him, and noticed he'd scratched the skin on his arms raw as well.

Maybe at least one plan he'd put into motion was working.

He'd certainly screwed up the main one. He'd been so sure when they made love last night that Eve would realize they had to be together. He loved her. She loved him. It was right there in her thoughts, not blocked, not hidden at all.

So why the hell did she leave? More important, where did she go?

No matter. He'd find her. Once he got things right with Oliver, he'd hunt for Eve. When he found her, he'd make sure she wanted to come back. She had to. It was her destiny. *He* was her destiny.

With that thought in mind, Adam climbed out of bed and headed for the shower.

Mid-July, three weeks later . . .

Are you thinking of going after her?

Adam glanced at the black wolf standing beside him on the hilltop. *Always. I think of looking for her day and night, but the time isn't right. We'll know, Oliver. We'll know when it's time to go.*

I hope you know what you're doing. I don't want to lose her. She's been gone now for three weeks. Oliver paused, cocked his head and his long, pink tongue lolled from between sharp canines. *Thank goodness you were right about me.* He trotted over to a large tree and raised one leg to pee. From this angle, his balls were visible beneath his huge plume of a tail. Two perfect orbs, positioned between his rear legs.

If Adam had been in his human form he would have laughed out loud. Anton trotted up and sat beside him. *I see Oliver's showing off the family jewels again.*

Oliver scratched at the dirt and wandered back to sit beside Anton. *Wouldn't you?*

You certainly seemed to enjoy displaying them to Keisha and Xandi last night.

They enjoyed the show just as much . . . almost as much as you did, Mr. Cheval. He cocked his head and there was laughter in his mental voice. *My ass is still sore.*

If I'd known you were going to keep your balls when you shifted back to human, I might have reconsidered encouraging Adam to help you. I think he's created a monster.

I have a lot of time to make up for.

That you do, my friend. That you do. Amber eyes twinkling with wolven glee, Anton turned and trotted down the trail. Oliver and Adam followed along behind. Almost as if it were an afterthought, Anton glanced back over his shoulder. *Adam, Keisha got a call from Eve. She's in Florida. She said she's having trouble with the truck. Personally, I think she's getting lonely.*

Adam stopped in the middle of the trail and nipped Oliver on the shoulder. He'd never felt so sure of himself before.

It's time, he said. Then, with Oliver following close behind, Adam turned and raced Anton back to the house.

Abundance

Deanna Lee

1

Darkness. Heat. Stale air. Kayla reached out blindly and gasped when she encountered a smooth metal surface. Her mind raced, and then quieted as memories of going into a stasis pod surfaced. She pushed both hands out in front of her, slid them down the sides of the pod searching for the emergency release, and then paused. If she released the lid and she was in the vacuum of space . . . shuddering, she closed her eyes.

Finally, her fingers brushed over the two release levers. The rapidly thinning air, the heat, and the fear of what lay beyond the confines of the pod would likely drive her insane. How much air did she have left? How long had the pod's environmental system been offline? What exactly did she have to live for? Death or a life sentence awaited her on the other side of the stasis pod lid. Her hands fell away from the levers and she lay there in the pitch dark, her breathing suddenly labored.

How long had she been in stasis? Was she already on Fourth Colony? Maybe no one knew her pod had malfunctioned and it was sitting on a loading dock waiting for General Philippe Marceau to come collect the wife he'd purchased. Her father had made all kinds of excuses and had spent hours explaining to her what an honor it was to be chosen for such a profitable marriage.

The fact that Marceau had wanted her at all was a relief to everyone but her, considering both her age and her unaltered appearance. With no cosmetic surgeries, Kayla was ordinary and somewhat plain among her thoroughly *enhanced* sisters. No fake breasts, cheek implants, lip injections, or body shaping procedures of any kind; not even the common labia restructuring that would have pushed her clit out and upward for display.

The fact remained that her own father, General Augusta Michaels, had sold her to a stranger in exchange for a few trade routes and a private cargo ship so that he could *retire*. She bit down on her lip to stifle a cry of frustration. Her desire to survive warred inwardly with the knowledge of the completely, utterly miserable life that would soon be hers.

No! Lying there and waiting to die or worse was simply not an option. She slipped her fingers around the levers and took a deep breath. At least if the pod was in space, death would come quickly. She pulled hard and moaned with relief at the fresh fragrant air that swooshed inside. Not space, but certainly not a docking station on Fourth Colony either. The pod lid lifted away and she blinked in the inky darkness that surrounded her.

The call of birds greeted her as she sat up and slipped from the pod. The sensory input monitors attached to her forehead and hands snapped away under the tension. As her eyes adjusted, she realized that she was surrounded by dense jungle. *Great. Just great.*

She pushed back her hair from her face and glanced over the pod as her eyes began to adjust to the darkness. She made a mental note to get her ocular implants updated as she blinked several times to hurry the adjustment. The pod's condition was startling and frightening. It's once gleaming silver surface was blackened and covered with blast and pockmarks. Had the *Nobilis* been attacked and her pod ejected?

She went to the end and jerked open the control panel. The screen was blank and the locator beacon wasn't blinking. Her knees weakened at the implication and she dropped the lid on the panel with numb fingers. General Marceau had sent a first-class vehicle to collect everything he'd purchased from New Earth. There had been forty people on the cargo ship that had been chosen to take her to Fourth Colony. Were they all dead?

Bending down she plucked a small bag she'd insisted on having with her in the pod free, and hugged it to her chest. The thin white dress and barely there sandals were not going to be much protection in the situation she found herself. She looked upward and frowned at the large pale blue and white planet that dominated the night sky. Its luminous surface blocked out much of the stars surrounding it. She turned around and sighed heavily at the sight of two moonlike objects.

Jungle plus giant water planet plus two small moons equaled only one thing in this quadrant. She was on the jungle moon Abundance—uninhabited and toxic to humans, or so she'd always been told. The fresh and amazingly pleasant-smelling air around her didn't appear to be life threatening. The calls of birds and other animals she was sure she couldn't identify spoke of a healthy ecosystem.

Yet, there was no doubting that she was on a small moon orbiting the water planet known as Hydra. Hydra had several large water-collection facilities but no colonies. The weather on the planet that was ninety-five percent water was entirely too violent for a large population to endure.

What did she know about Abundance? There were no human outposts on the moon and no research probes. The name had always been viewed as a sarcastic joke because it had been reported that the moon could not sustain human life. The jungle plants were aggressive and poisonous. No sentient life. Nothing. Nothing but her.

Jude Aroca stretched out in the tree and rested his large head on the branch in front of him. The black fur that stretched out over his body allowed him to blend into the night and remain shielded from the woman's discovery. She was beautiful in a strictly human sort of way. Long pale blond hair fell down her back in curls; the thin clothing she wore accented high firm breasts, a slim waist, and full hips. Small, perhaps just a little over five feet tall, but certainly curvy.

The stasis pod was heavily damaged; he realized that she was lucky to even be alive. The fine woven material of her dress and the smooth healthy glow of her skin spoke of privilege and wealth. Someone was going to miss this pretty little thing and they would come looking for her.

He frowned at that and inched closer, the heavy weight of his *Yaw* cat form caused the branch he crouched on to bend gently. Her smell was sweet, intoxicating, and entirely female. If the woman had a man, she hadn't been with him in several weeks. Jude had met few human females, and only had scant memories of his mother before her death. Humans weren't allowed and their presence on the small moon he called home could be considered an act of war.

Yet, this tiny woman was no invading army. She was a lost, and certainly in distress, female. She would never survive on her own. He wasn't entirely sure she would survive anyway. His home had never been kind to females and human females were far more delicate than the *Yaw* women. She turned then and looked right at him. He knew she couldn't see him, yet her face tightened with fear. *Good instincts.*

Jude stood and leapt from the tree to the ground in front of her in one graceful leap. Her bag fell abruptly from her hands and flopped between them as he started to shift. Sleek black fur receded quickly, leaving behind only smooth honey-brown skin in its wake. Bones slipped and muscles condensed, seconds later he stood before her on two legs. Tall, broad shouldered, and naked as the day he'd been born.

It had been several years since he'd had cause to speak the *common tongue*, but he knew it well enough to communicate with her. "I am Jude Aroca."

She blinked and took a step backward. "You-you . . ." She paused, her hands tightened into fists at her sides. "You can't be real."

"What?" He frowned at her.

"Abundance is uninhabited," she snapped, her voice cracking with desperation.

Jude watched in stunned silence as she picked up her bag and turned to walk away from him. He hadn't thought her crazed. She took several steps before he caught up with her. She gasped the moment he touched her, the sound of her breathing filled the damp night air around them. Slowly, he pulled her back and turned her to face him.

"Woman, you are in a dangerous place. Now is not the time to lose your mind."

"You can't be real," she whispered, tears dampened her eyes and her voice broke. "I'm all alone."

He took her hand in his with care, pressed her palm against his chest over his heart, and held it there. "I am Jude Aroca, and yes you are on the moon the humans call Abundance. My people are the *Yaw*, we have two forms—this humanoid shape, and the cat shape you saw first. I am most certainly real and you are not *alone*."

The heat of her body teased his blood in a way he'd never known before. Her scent, stronger now that they were close, overwhelmed him. His cock lengthened and hardened against his thigh. How could he want this slight human female? She was nothing like the women he had sought in the past.

Kayla closed her eyes. "Everyone says that the air and soil are toxic here. Life cannot be supported."

"The air is perfect, and has been carefully monitored by my people for centuries. The soil produces the sweetest of fruits, rich vegetation, and supports a large animal population."

The relief that she was not alone was only dampened by the knowledge that everything she'd ever been told about the moon Abundance was a wrong. Knowledge had always been her ally in life. It had been her companion in childhood, her haven through most of her adulthood. While her sisters had prepared and altered themselves for a profitable marriage, she had immersed herself in learning all that she could.

She'd studied alien species, learned everything she could about every single documented encounter and scientific study, and nowhere had there ever been any mention of a species of shifters.

This man or cat, depending on his preference apparently, stood at least six-foot-five and was probably close to two hundred pounds. Dark brown skin covered a trim, muscled body. Kayla bit down on her lip and dropped her gaze. Her breath caught in her throat at the sight of the erection he was making no effort to hide. She was certainly no stranger to the sight of an aroused male, but she'd never seen one quite like Jude Aroca. Wetness rushed against her bare labia, soaking the thin silk of her underwear, and her nipples tightened painfully.

Kayla glanced upward at his sudden intake of breath. His lips were pressed tightly together, she wondered if he could smell her arousal. Did he want her? Would she be beautiful among his people or would she stand out in her unaltered, unadorned state as she had among her own?

She shook herself free from that ridiculous thought and cleared her throat. "What is the standard date?"

"I haven't been keeping up. I'm three days from finishing a

yearlong period of *solace*. The point of which is to remove oneself from the constraints of society."

How long had she been missing? Had they searched for her
or given her up for dead? She pulled at her arm and then took a
deep breath. "Please release me."

"You cannot run off into the dark, not alone. My world is
too harsh for someone so delicate and female." Jude loosened
his grip on her arm and used his free hand to tilt her chin up.
When their eyes met, he continued. "I'm in my final days of *solace*. My men will come to retrieve me in three days. You will
stay with me until that time."

Her stomach dropped at the command in his voice. This
man/beast was not used to anyone disobeying him and she
wondered briefly what her punishment would be if she refused
to stay with him. What would he do if she ran? "Will you return me to my people unharmed?"

His black eyes seemed to go even darker in that moment.
"What is your name?"

"Kayla Michaels, daughter of Augusta." She swallowed
hard, her whole body tense.

"Kayla, daughter of Augusta, your presence on Abundance
is a violation of a peace treaty that has existed between your
people and mine for nearly thirty-five years. You can be assured that you will be returned to your people in due course."

"Due course?" she repeated. "What does that mean?"

"We are far from the city."

"I know nothing about a peace treaty with your people.
None of this makes any sense." Kayla forced herself to take
several deep breaths. She could simply not afford to indulge in
the fit of temper that was already brewing inside her.

"Come, it will be darker soon and it will be far more dangerous for you then."

She watched him in silence as he reached down, retrieved

her bag, and started to lead her away from the pod. She hesitated for several seconds, her gaze fixed on the thing that connected her with everything she'd ever known.

"It's done all it can to serve you. The fact that you are alive at all is somewhat extraordinary."

She glared briefly at her captor and nodded. "You have a dwelling nearby?"

"Of a sort." His hand slid down her arm to grasp her hand as they moved along a narrow path. "You're not dressed for travel."

"I'm dressed just like I should be for the kind of travel I was doing," Kayla muttered. "I was to sleep the entire trip to Fourth Colony . . . how was I to know that I'd wake up in the middle of a bloody jungle?"

"So, this is what human females sleep in?" He looked back over her shoulder and looked her thin gown over. "And the shoes? Do you wear shoes to sleep as well? Seems like all that is just designed to get in a man's way."

"Who says I want to make it easy for a man?" No way in hell was she going to admit that her future husband had sent her the ridiculous outfit to wear. She pulled briefly, trying to dislodge her hand. "Look, I'm not going to run. I'm small, unarmed, and out of my element. I might have a few moments of lunacy here or there for the next few days, because quite frankly I'm sure I deserve the right to them, but I'm not going to run off into the night and get eaten by a big alien monster."

He turned abruptly and jerked her close. "You're looking at the biggest predator on this moon, and if I get it in my head to have a taste of you I seriously doubt you're going to do much complaining."

Kayla gasped and jerked back as his still-erect cock brushed against her belly. "As if I'd let a man . . . a beast . . . whatever you are, touch me."

Jude pulled her closer, until her breasts pressed against the muscled wall of his chest. "I can smell you, woman." He pushed his free hand between them to cup her pussy and allowed his fingers to drift over the damp material that covered her.

She groaned and for a moment pressed back against his fingers. A fragrant spicy scent swept in the humid air around them and her whole body weakened. Her nipples tightened further as his fingers pressed against the silk. A shudder ripped down her back and she closed her eyes.

"I could rip off this ridiculous covering, bend you over right here, and fuck you. You'd take every inch of my cock and beg for more."

Kayla stilled against his hand and pushed at his shoulders. "An involuntary physical reaction does not grant you leave to abuse me."

His hand fell away and she bit back a moan.

"I've never abused a woman in my life," he ground out through clenched teeth. "If I were that kind of man I'd be balls deep in you already." Jude released her completely, picked up her bag from the ground where he'd dropped it, and shoved it in her direction. "Just keep up, I'm tired and don't feel like having to search for you if you fall behind."

"Just stay on two legs and we'll be fine."

He turned on his heel and walked away leaving her standing there for a few seconds before she rushed after him.

"Hey, am I prisoner?"

"Of your own reality, perhaps."

She frowned at his back and picked up her pace. "That's pretty deep for a panther-man living in the jungle."

"Panther?"

"Yeah, you look like a panther from Old Earth in your other shape. I've seen the vids on the animals." She arranged the straps of her bag on her shoulders as she moved forward after him. "Only bigger . . . you're much bigger. Are your people from here?"

"No, we colonized this moon nearly four hundred years ago because our planet was dying. The jungle itself suits our more primitive side, but since we spend nearly all of our time in humanoid form we built an underground city to see to our other needs." He glanced back at her. "You really thought it was uninhabited?"

"Yeah, I only babbled about it like an idiot. Of course, I thought it. The last probe that was sent here reported foul air and soil then promptly malfunctioned. We never sent another. That was probably a hundred years ago."

"Humans landed on this moon forty years ago."

"They did not. We decided against a manned mission to Abundance."

"An expedition of humans landed here forty years ago. There were eight humans in the party. At first, it seemed that our people and yours could broker some kind of peace and co-exist. My father realized quickly that it wasn't possible. Humans are greedy and wasteful. They saw our home as a place to be harvested, stripped of everything that makes it what it is."

Kayla stopped on the path, her vision blurry. "No."

As if he sensed her distress, he turned and walked back to her. "My mother was one of those human travelers; she stayed here with my father and gave birth to me before she was killed in an accident. I was still quite young, perhaps not five years."

"And you don't know the specific date? Do you know the standard year?" She met his gaze as she pressed her lips together to keep from screaming.

"3157."

"No." She shook her head. "That's not possible."

"I have isolated myself from my people for my period of *solace* but I am aware of the year." He glared at her.

"I couldn't have just laid there in that fucking pod for forty years!"

"This part of the moon is rarely traveled by my people. In

fact, the last person to seek *solace* here was my father and that was shortly after the death of my mother. If your stasis pod landed here that many years ago, the communications array was damaged on impact, otherwise my people would have picked up a signal."

"The jungle would have swallowed the pod in that time," she whispered, her voice weak with grief.

"Abundance is a volatile and dangerous place as I mentioned. There are times when wild fires cover twenty to thirty percent of the surface. It kills off most of the vegetation and any animal life that doesn't escape it. We are barely six months from the last event in his area." His tone was gentle, as if he was trying to soothe her and push away the insanity that was edging against her mind. "If it has been forty years since you left New Earth, no one is looking for you."

"No." She bit down on her lip. "No one is."

Jude watched, leery, as she shrugged her bag off and dropped it on the path. Her shoulders sagged and she slid to her knees in defeat. "Now is not the time to grieve what you've lost," he said gently.

She slapped his hand away when he tried to help her up from the ground. "I can't do this."

With a sigh, he picked up her bag and shouldered it. He really wasn't in the mood to carry anything, much less a woman, an hour back to his cave, but he couldn't very well leave her on the path to rot. Beautiful or not, the woman was turning out to be a pain in the ass. Forgoing the desire to toss her over one shoulder, he urged her to her feet and picked her up. She looped one arm around his neck and buried her damp face against his neck.

Her slim body shook as he held her. Her scent, a combination of some fragrance he couldn't identify and sexual arousal, surrounded him. Jude knew little of human women, and what he did know worried him a great deal. His home was not kind to such delicate creatures. He held her tighter to his chest, and bit back a curse. Touching her had been a mistake, he'd known it the moment he'd grabbed her arm.

Kayla awoke on a sleeping platform in the back of a large cave. It figured. Panther-man, jungle, and cave all sort of merged together to complete her nightmare. Her captor was sitting at a desk, *still* naked, in front of a compu-screen, his chin propped on one hand. "The date?" she asked.

Jude turned and looked her, his gaze raking over her in interest. "It's interesting seeing a woman in my bed."

She pursed her lips, slid purposefully to the edge of the bed, and stood. The last thing she needed to do was remind him of the sex he'd all but promised her hours ago. "Date?"

"The standard date is 3157-122."

Forty-one years. "I left New Earth on the trade ship bound for Fourth Colony on 3117-151." She rubbed her mouth and closed her eyes to keep the tears from coming.

Had anyone even searched for her? She turned away from him and took a deep breath. How long had she drifted in space before landing on Abundance? She remembered those last moments before she'd been sealed in the pod, her sisters crowded around her, all three of them in tears, while her father had appeared indifferent to the fact that he was sending his oldest child into a life of basic sexual servitude for his own personal gain.

She'd known for a year she was to be sent to Fourth Colony to marry a near stranger; with a shudder she pushed the mental picture of the man that had *purchased* her out of her head. Kayla had grieved for the life she'd been forced to give up long before she'd been put in stasis and shoved into a cargo hold bound for the only thriving human space station colony. The fourth and largest of all of the stations, it was a success while the first three had become sanctuaries of the roughest kind of people and alien life she'd rarely been given the opportunity to fully explore. Her gaze moved to the real live alien she'd been left to deal with.

"What is this *solace* you keep talking about?"

"Ah, yes. It is a ritual of passage, a time of reflection when a man must decide the path of his future."

"And what decisions must you make?"

"None really. My path in life is pretty clear. It's an ancient practice that I made use of to stave off a few husband-hunting politicians and my uncle." He grinned when she raised an eyebrow. "I may be a weird alien animal to you, but among my people I'm very desirable."

She didn't doubt it for a second. His strong, sleek body, beautiful smooth skin, and impressive cock must make women fall at his feet. Her gaze unwillingly dropped to his lap and she sucked in a breath at the sight of his thick erection. "Do you stay that way?"

"Not normally." He spread his legs, and grinned when she wet her lips with a sweep of her tongue. His cock shifted slightly as it jutted unhindered from his body, and the tip dampened with pre-come. "But having you sprawled out on my bed in that bit-of-nothing gown, smelling amazing, has made it difficult to be anything but hard."

"You can't actually find me attractive. First, I'm nothing like you." She crossed her arms over her breasts and winced at the way her nipples tingled at the pressure. "Second, I'm not even attractive by human standards. I'm too short, too pale, and unaltered."

Jude stood and walked to stand in front of her, his gaze narrowed as he took in the details of her face. "Unaltered?"

"I don't have lip injections, or cheek implants."

"What is wrong with your face that you would need such things done?" He reached out and ran one finger along her jaw.

"Your face is quite nice actually; the women of my people often have stronger, more angular faces not unlike the males. But you are soft and your features delicate. It is very appealing."

"It's nice of you to say." She looked away from him in disbelief. She'd been told all her life how unfortunate she was in the appearance department.

"And your mouth?" His finger slid until he could trace the fullness of her bottom lip. "Quite amazing, I've never seen lips so pink and inviting. The last hour all I've thought about is how it would look if you were sucking my cock."

She felt her face heat as his hand dropped away; if she allowed herself to think about it she could imagine sucking his thick dark cock, too. "Do you try to seduce every woman you find in the jungle?"

"You are the only woman I've ever found in the jungle," he admitted softly. "What else would your people see altered so that you would be beautiful by their standards?"

"My breasts are too small. My father tried to give me implants for my seventeenth birthday but I refused them."

"Why?"

"Because I didn't want to be made into something I'm not." She frowned at him. "You agree that they are too small?"

"No. I don't agree. I'm pleased that you did not let anyone alter you. I had no idea humans mutilated themselves in such ways." He smoothed both of his hands over her shoulders and pushed the straps of the gown downward until the whole thing loosened and slid off her body. "Your breasts are perfect."

His fingers slipped over her hard nipples and her womb clenched in response.

"I shouldn't let you touch me." She bit down her bottom lip when he pinched her nipple, wet heat flooded against her labia, and her clit started to pulse. How long had it been since she'd known a man?

"I smell your need."

Forty-one years. The knowledge echoed through her mind as Jude stepped closer, his cock brushed against her stomach and a soft moan escaped her lips. Had she really escaped the marriage? Had everyone really given her up for dead? Would she be sent off to marry another when Jude arranged her return to her family? Was her father even alive? His hands drifted over her rib cage and then upward to cup her breasts.

"Three days?" she wondered aloud. Could she have enough passion and pleasure with this man to last her a lifetime in just three days?

"I could contact them now." He sighed and moved away from her. "But, honestly I'm not looking forward to returning."

Kayla reached out and grabbed his arm, her fingers clenching against his smooth, dark skin. "No. Don't."

Jude paused, stunned by the fear in her eyes. "I promised I would not hurt you."

"My marriage was arranged. I met him twice and the second time he stripped me naked and looked me over like I was some *thing* that he'd just have to get used to having around. I don't know why he wanted me. As I told you, most men of his station would prefer an enhanced and altered woman." Her nails bit into the flesh of his arm as his hand covered hers. "If he's still alive, he'll expect me to be delivered to him. He paid my father well."

"Paid?" Jude demanded, his voice rough with disgust. "What will three days give you, Kayla?"

"You want me."

"Of course." He touched her face and gently turned her head so she could meet his gaze. "You're beautiful, but no matter my current physical state and the far more basic instincts I'm barely controlling, I don't misuse women."

"No man has ever honestly wanted me." She laid her hand on his chest. "Education and appearance made me an unattractive match for most of the men in the colony. The men who were interested in me, really only wanted my father's favor. While not of the ruling class, his standing in the Colonial Army afforded me and my sisters opportunities. If I had agreed to be altered, not pursued my degree, and pretended to be the arm ornament material most men wanted I could have married any-one."

Her hand drifted downward and Jude growled as her slim pale fingers wrapped around his cock. "I'm not a civilized man, woman. You are playing with fire."

She stroked him with gentle but sure fingers and let her thumb drift over the head of his cock, playing in the pre-come she found there. "Fire?" Kayla laughed. "No, I'm fairly certain I'm playing with the biggest cock I've ever seen."

Jude fisted both hands against his thighs as her fingers slid over him again and again. Letting her touch, explore . . . the gentleness of her hands was a heady lesson in a different kind of pleasure. "What do you want from me?"

"Every woman wants to be desired."

"Human women are delicate."

"You said your mother was human." Her tongue drifted over her bottom lip as he moved closer to her, pressing his cock into the steady stroke of her fingers. "You're half human."

"Yes, but I'm all animal."

Kayla looked up, her gaze taking in the taut features of his face, and she smiled. "I'm looking forward to it."

"Woman."

The warning in his tone should have made her pause and re-consider, but all she could think was that this man wanted her. His body was tight with the anticipation of what was to come between them and as much as it startled her, it aroused her more.

"It'll be hard."

"I can handle it."

His eyes were wild and dark. "Are you wet?"

"Can't you smell me?" she asked softly, her fingers suddenly still on his cock. The spicy musk of his own arousal thickened in the air around them and she dampened further.

"Yes." He traced the sides of her face with the tips of his fingers gently as if he were prepared to ignore the violent need that brewed between them. "Lay down on the bed."

Kayla released him and went to the sleeping platform. The thin blanket that had covered her lay crumpled to one side. She crawled onto the surface, and turned to look at him as she rested backward on her arms. "Like this?"

2

Jude walked to the end of the bed, his dark gaze taking in the lush curves of her body. This was exactly what he wanted, her willing and ready for him. "Spread your legs, so I can see your pussy."

He bit back a groan as she met his demand, the dark pink flesh of her sex was so inviting that he couldn't help but slide onto the bed between her prone legs. He ran two hesitant fingers over her bare labia and cleared his throat. "Human women don't have hair here?"

"Some do. I had mine removed a long time ago." She blushed when he glanced up in surprise. "I guess even I have a few vanity issues."

He let both hands drift over her silky smooth legs. "Here as well?"

"Yes." She bit down on her bottom lip as he spread her legs further apart exposing her sex completely to his gaze. "Do you want to taste me, Jude?"

Of course, he thought. He'd wanted to know how she tasted since he set eyes on her. Watching her face for any sign of fear, he moved upward on the bed and lowered his mouth to place a soft open-mouthed kiss on her inner thigh. She took in a ragged breath and her eyes drifted shut. Her trust in him was astounding.

Jude groaned softly as he moved downward, the heady scent of her aroused sex made his balls tighten painfully. He spread his legs and rubbed the head of his cock against the blanket beneath them. As much as he wanted to slam into her and ride her hard, he wanted more. The desire to know everything she wanted . . . the need to truly satisfy the woman who had spread herself out before him for his pleasure was overwhelming.

He slipped his tongue into her slit, allowing himself to dip briefly into her clenching channel before moving upward to draw her throbbing clit into his mouth. Her sweet taste assaulted his senses in a wave of awareness that shocked him. Jude swirled his tongue around her clit and sucked hard, drawing a series of broken, harsh cries from her lips.

His. She belonged to him. He'd known it since he'd set eyes on her. It didn't shock him so much as it confused him. Never before had he ever felt such a thing for a woman. A part of him had always thought that maybe his human half would stave off the natural *Yaw* urge to claim a mate.

Pushing two large fingers into her, he lifted away from her so he could watch her body rock and thrust against his hand. Her pussy tightened in demand and pulsed around his fingers. She lifted her hips as he looked upward and met her gaze. Her dark green eyes were bright with need as she bore down on his fingers again and again.

Her desire was compelling and so alluring that he could no longer deny himself the pleasure of her. Jude pulled his fingers free and moved upward, stopping briefly to lick and suckle each nipple. Her body arched beneath him and she spread her legs wide to make room for his large body.

Clenching his teeth, Jude pressed the wide head of his cock

against her entrance and thrust forward. He urged her legs around his waist and buried his face against her neck as he surged upward into her, until he was seated to the hilt. He stilled completely when he realized that she was tense beneath him.

He lifted his head and brushed her hair from her forehead. "Are you all right?"

"Yes." Kayla ran her hands down his back and slowly relaxed beneath him. "I've never been so full. It's perfect."

He brushed his mouth over hers, and slipped his tongue in when her lips immediately parted. Unable to remain still, Jude slowly began to move within her. The wet, silken pull of her body pushed at his beast and demanded things from him that he had not expected. The urge to mate with her was so strong that he lifted up and braced his hands on the mattress to remove himself from the temptation of sinking his teeth into her flesh.

He would not give into the animal that lurked under his skin; this soft beautiful human woman was for the man in him not the beast.

Kayla closed her eyes and dug her fingers into him, her nails bit into him harder with each heavy push of his body against hers. The thick press of his cock into her was the most pleasure she'd ever known. Her clit pulsed between her spread labia as waves of pleasure swept over her in time with each invading thrust of his cock.

"More." She dragged her nails down his back and pressed up against him. "Please, Jude, more."

He leaned down and kissed her mouth with a gentleness that belied the near violence of their blending bodies. Slowing his practically brutal pace, he ran one hand up over her leg as he lifted his mouth away from hers. "I don't want to hurt you."

She barely had time to recognize his plan before he rolled them over and she sank fully down on his cock. He cupped both of her breasts, his thumbs rolling the hardened nipples in a lazy circular motion. Kayla shook back her hair and rocked on him carefully, taking the measure of him with unsure motions. She bit down on her lip at the slick pleasure/pain that slid along her back with each movement of her body.

His hands moved downward to grasp her hips, and he lifted beneath her. She hissed at the movement and her head fell back. "Yes, that's perfect."

"That's it, little one." Jude sucked in a ragged breath. "You're the one that wanted to play with this big cock."

She laughed softly and nodded. "I did."

"Now, work this like it belongs to you."

The thought of him being hers . . . claiming this big beautiful man forever, made her whole body hum with pleasure. His fingers tightened on her hips as she started to move up and then down, taking him as deeply as she could with each downward motion. When he picked up her rhythm and started to thrust upward against her, orgasm edged in and burst open. She came in a sweet, quick rush, her whole body shuddering at the pure pleasure of having him. This was the kind of passion she'd spent years looking for, the kind of passion she would risk anything to keep.

He rolled her abruptly beneath him and started to pump steadily into her, penetrating deep and hard. "Tell me you can handle this."

Kayla nodded, lifted her legs, and wrapped them high around his waist. "Yes. Yes."

His body covered her completely, sheltering her from everything but his presence. The spicy scent of his arousal, the heaviness of his breath against her neck as he slid one arm underneath her, and the steady unbelievable push of his cock into her combined so that all she could think about was him. Jude lifted his head and met her gaze. His black eyes were bright, but focused. The skin on his face tightened and she gasped, her fingers digging into his shoulder blades.

"No. Don't shift."

He shook his head. "Relax little human, I couldn't shift right now if I wanted to." Brushing his mouth over hers in a series of soft kisses, he rotated his hips slowly in a small circle while she twisted beneath him. "*Yaw* women have a place inside. . . ."

"Yes." Kayla nodded abruptly and stiffened when the head of his cock rubbed up against her G-spot. "Fuck."

"Ah." He shortened his stroke and tilted his hips slightly causing the head of his cock to brush over her G-spot with every stroke. "This is yours, yes?"

"Jude, please." She lifted her hips against him. "I can't . . ."

"Of course you can. Come again for me, woman." His mouth covered hers, his tongue slipping in and rubbing over hers in unison with the penetration of his cock.

Kayla relaxed beneath him, let her legs drop from his waist, and clutched at his back as another orgasm rushed over her. Her pussy clenched around him and in that moment he slammed into her, his body bowing. Jude moaned into her mouth, he thrust into her several more times before stilling completely. He rested against her briefly before he pulled from her and rolled onto his back beside her.

"Once isn't going to be enough."

She laughed softly; amazed by the little waves of pleasure that still ebbed over her. "No, not nearly enough."

He moved to his side and propped his head on one hand. "I know little of humans, but I know that you don't treat sex as casually as my people do."

"No." She bit down on her lip. "Well, some certainly do. My sisters had more sexual partners in a year than I'd had in my entire life." What had the years done to her sisters? Had they married well?

"You are frowning." He slid one finger down her between her breasts, making a path across her damp stomach, and then downward to slide between her labia.

"I don't want to go back."

He stilled beside her. "You'd stay here?"

"I'm a coward," she admitted softly. "I would love to see my sisters again, to know what has happened with them in the years . . . but General Marceau is there as well. I can't count on the fact that he might have died." She frowned at that. "It's horrible to wish another person dead."

"He purchased a woman like he would a ship or a crate of food." Jude sighed. "Such a man does not deserve respect, nor does he deserve your concern."

"My father would have had to return the ship he gained from the marriage."

"There was a ceremony?" Jude asked carefully as he pulled his hand away from her. "Did you promise yourself to that man, Kayla?"

"No." She met his gaze quickly and saw the anger that he'd successfully kept from his voice, burning in his dark eyes. "He insisted that we would marry on Fourth Colony with his family. I frankly assumed that I would never get the benefit of legal marriage, that I was to be nothing more than a possession for him."

The tension slipped out of his body and he rolled onto his back as if the anger had shocked him as much as it had shocked her. "I see."

"You said your men would return for you in three days?"

"Yes. I've pushed my uncle as far as I dare on this *solace* issue."

She sat up and glanced around the cave. "At least the ritual doesn't require you to live primitively."

Jude laughed softly and ran one hand down her back. "You're very sexy. I never thought I'd find human women attractive."

"Are all *Yaw* as dark as you?"

"No, but we are all shades of brown and black." He kissed

the small of her back and then ran the tip of his tongue upward until he encountered her shoulder blades. "Does the color of my skin displease you?"

"No." Kayla gasped as his teeth grazed the top of one shoulder. "You're beautiful."

He kissed her neck and moved closer, wrapping his arms around her so that he could cup her breasts. Thumbs drifted over her nipples and she pressed back against his chest. "I love how you respond to me. You've been with men of your species, obviously. None of them wanted to be in your life permanently?"

She flushed. "As I said, I'm not highly desirable on New Earth. A woman so unwilling to seek perfection through enhancement is considered somewhat old-fashioned. Hardly the sort that most men would want to marry."

"They were all very foolish men." He pinched her nipples and chuckled when she arched in his arms. "Did I tell you how much I enjoyed licking your cunt?"

Kayla shuddered and pressed her thighs together in an effort to appease the sudden unbearable ache his words had created. "No, you didn't."

"I could lick and suck you for hours." He pressed an open-mouthed kiss on her neck. "Just thinking about putting my tongue in your slit again has me so hard I can barely think."

"Are you trying to make me crazy?" she demanded in a hushed tone as he pressed his cock against her ass and slid one hand downward to cup her pussy.

His fingers delved between her labia to rub her clit. "Humans do not mate for life?"

"It is rare for a couple to stay together for that long." Kayla pushed back against him as she started to rotate her hips against the pressure of his fingers. "Why?"

"The *Yaw* mate for life." His teeth grazed the top of her shoulder near her neck as he spoke. "The male of our species bites the woman of his choice on this very spot, releasing a chemical into her blood that creates a bond that links them mentally and physically until one of them dies."

She shuddered. "His choice? Does she not get a choice of her own?"

"It is considered highly offensive for a male to force a bond on a woman and the intimacy of the bond would make the situation undesirable for the male as well. He would be exposed to her anger and her resentment for life," Jude whispered, as he maneuvered her in front of him on her knees. "I need more."

Kayla shuddered as he ran his large warm hands down her back to her hips, he spread her legs wide, and pressed two fingers into her pussy. It was rare that she let a man move her into such a submissive position but with Jude, it felt right, perfect. He grabbed several pillows, shoved them under her, and tilted her hips into position with his free hand.

She rocked back against his fingers, moaning with each thrust inward. Fisting her hands into the bedding beneath her, she turned and looked at him. He had his cock in one hand, casually stroking it in time with the press of his fingers into her. When he met her gaze, she realized just how much effort he was putting into controlling himself.

"Remember that hard fuck I promised you?"

"Yes." She bit down her bottom lip and moaned when he pulled his fingers free.

"You're about to get it." He gripped her hips and rubbed his cock against her labia. "You'll have to tell me to stop if I hurt you."

She lowered her forehead to the mattress in front of her and closed her eyes. "I want to be everything you need."

Jude's fingers bit into her hips as he thrust forward burying his cock into her with one single hard push. A low harsh sound burst from her mouth as he started to move, each heavy thrust of his body into hers a reminder of his strength. Her body rocked against his as if driven by some primitive need that she didn't understand, taking every pounding inch of his cock as if it were her due. The head of his cock met with the mouth of her womb every time their bodies slapped together, causing a mixture of pleasure and pain to rip over her until she could do nothing but moan his name and plead for more. She felt absolutely owned, and for the first time ever that didn't seem like a death sentence.

Jude closed his eyes briefly, but the image of his cock sliding into her soft pale flesh time after time was branded in his mind. In just a few hours, one woman had turned his entire world upside down. He wondered if she understood he meant to keep her. He lowered his body full against hers, pulling the pillows beneath her away, and pressing her into the mattress.

Fisting his hands into the blankets on either side of her head, he slowed the pace of their bodies and started to rotate his hips. The need to pleasure her warred with the demand of his body for release. She cried out, the walls of her pussy clenched around his cock so hard that he pressed deep into her and came without even thinking to stop himself. They were both still for a minute and then a soft sob slipped from her lips.

He pulled from her immediately, and turned her with gentle but firm hands. "Kayla?"

Tears slid down her cheeks, her eyes bright with some emotion he didn't understand. "I'm all right."

Jude brushed the tears from her face with shaking hands. "You're crying. I hurt you?"

"No!" She grabbed his hands and pulled him close. "You didn't hurt me." Kayla rested her face against his chest and closed her eyes. "At least not in a bad way. It was just so . . . perfect. I didn't mean to cry."

He relaxed and wrapped his arms around her in relief. "Woman, you'll be the death of me."

Lying back on the bed, he clutched her still-shaking body to his and swallowed hard. His position among his people was a solid one, and his half-human blood made mating with another human seem almost natural in some respects. Regardless, no one would question the connection that was building between them. Did she feel it? Were humans open enough mentally and emotionally to grasp the concept of soul bonding? Her response, her submission to his desire, might confuse her but she hadn't shied away from him or their mutual need.

A part of him had never wanted to surrender to the weakness of a mating bond. His father had done it and in the end, he'd died just a few years after his mate had been killed. Jude had found himself an orphan and the heir to the throne of his people at the age of seven. He'd been raised by his father's brother, Remus Aroca. Remus had acted as regent since that time, but their people had called on Jude to assume his place as their leader more than a year ago. He'd immediately sought *solace* to prepare himself, he'd told everyone, to be a leader and to select a mate.

He'd spent most of the last year in his cat form, unwilling to deal with what was to come, yet now that he'd found Kayla, what was ahead of him didn't seem overwhelming.

"What were you doing when you found me?"

Jude glanced down and found her staring at him, her tears gone. "I was hunting and I must admit I'm quite pleased with what I caught." He ran his hand down her back and over her ass as she laughed. "With only three days left and much expected of me upon my return to *Atelier*, I was quite determined to spend the rest of my time running around the jungle on four legs."

"*Atelier.* That is the name of your city?"

"Yes. When my people came here, they found the surface surprisingly resilient to our terraforming programs. After fifty years of trying to fight back the jungle, they started to build below ground. They found a large cave system that stretched well beneath the surface and developed our city in it."

"How large is the population?"

"On this moon, our numbers are small . . . perhaps fifty thousand."

"There are other *Yaw* colonies?"

"Yes, of course. When our home world started to die, our people built thousands of ships. This is our only settlement in this sector of the galaxy, but it is central to all of the others."

"Why?"

"Because Abundance is where the ruling family settled. The other ships spread out from here, settling planets and moons that would best serve our people."

Kayla frowned and sat up. "And your treaty with the humans?"

"They landed on the surface and immediately set up an encampment for scientific study. That, of course, was unacceptable. They made no effort to control their pollution of the surface and our people approached them. There was misunderstanding on both sides, and one human was killed and my father gravely injured. My mother protected him from her own people and in the end stayed with him after the treaty was brokered. Once a year we send the humans a supply of plants that they deem important, token gifts of technology, and in exchange we receive the material comforts my people find amusing."

"I can't believe my people are content with that." Kayla frowned. "My government is full of people who thrive on the use and misuse of everything and everyone around them. We aren't a people who learn from our mistakes . . . if we did, we would certainly treat New Earth better than we did where we originally came from. Who comes to trade with you?"

"A scientist or two, and normally an ambassador from Fourth Colony. They always try to renegotiate the treaty." Jude sighed. "A total waste of their time."

"No military?"

"Arrival of military personnel here would be a treaty violation and could lead to war."

"And could your people survive such a war?"

He almost laughed, but her sincere worry prevented it. "Little one, most of the technology we exchange with the humans is several hundred years old and while our number on Abundance might be small . . . my people number in the tens of millions. An attack on us would lead to the extinction of humans in this sector."

"*Your* people." She repeated softly. "Your father negotiated the peace treaty . . ." Kayla cleared her throat. "Who exactly are you, Jude?"

Her tone was cautious, her body suddenly tense. How would she react? Most of the women of his people were actually pleased to gain his attention but Kayla was in a difficult situation already. Yet, he knew he couldn't afford to lie to her.

"I am the regent-apparent to the throne of the *Yaw*." Jude took hold of her arm when she pulled away. "I'm also the man that was balls deep in you less than twenty minutes ago so don't turn away from me."

"King? You lead this settlement?" Fear drifted over her features and he regretted it.

"No, currently my uncle leads our people in my place but when I take the throne, as I've been asked to do in three days, I will lead it all. Not just this colony, but all one hundred and twenty-two settlements. And while this moon will remain my home, I will be compelled to travel and see to the needs of all of my people." Fear turned into a mixture of horror and fascination, the combination did not soothe the ache that had formed in his gut. He'd wanted more time with her before revealing everything, but now he felt he had no choice. "You were in that pod for a long time and I realize that everything around you is so very different than what you expected."

"Yes." She bit down on her lip.

"But I will keep you safe, you have my word."

"Is there a *Yaw* ambassador on New Earth?"

"New Earth is seven months of travel from Abundance and we've always communicated directly with the Fourth Colony space station as our treaty dictates. In the past three years, the humans have started to request advanced weapon design."

She paled. "Did you supply them with weapons?"

"No. We would never give a potential enemy the means to fight us. We only provide medical and standard of living technology, and as far as I'm concerned that is all they will ever get."

Kayla relaxed slightly. "How did your mother die, Jude?"

He released her arm and slid from the bed. "She was a scientist, as I stated. Her field of study happened to be botany."

"Makes sense." She shrugged when he glanced her way. "If I were building an expedition team to study a moon like Abundance, a botanist would be pretty high on my list."

"She was brilliant, my people considered her an asset to the settlement. Her knowledge of plant life and ecosystem development made her an ideal addition to our scientific community. When she wasn't traveling to the other settlements with my father on the *Cittade*, she would be working with our scientists here . . ." He turned and looked toward her then. "You said you were too educated for the men of your people?"

"I have degrees in exobiology and psychology." She bit down on her lip when he raised one eyebrow. "So, I'm perfectly suited to handle a crazy alien-shifter-man."

"Indeed," he murmured and then walked toward his desk. "My mother was killed in the jungle by one of the native plant species. Her death was quick but painful."

"I'm very sorry."

"I barely remember her but my father never recovered from his loss." He sat down at the desk and then turned in the chair to look at her. "Their soul-bond was unique and strong. Most assumed that a human and a *Yaw* could not form such a bond."

"He died of a broken heart?"

"A broken spirit," Jude corrected. "He was simply incomplete without her and the loss was too much for him to bear. When he grew ill, he came here to die instead of seeking the help he needed."

"What is a soul-bond?"

He was silent for a few moments, as he considered how to answer her question. "It begins long before the physical mating." He glanced up and watched her hand drift over her shoulder and upward to the spot near her neck he'd told her about. Before their three days were done, he knew he would sink his teeth in her there and mark her for life as his. "There is a blending of needs, thoughts. Oftentimes it can start without either party being fully aware of what is to come. The couple will seek to touch each other almost immediately upon meeting, as if their souls have known each other forever. The attraction will be sexual and emotional on such a profound level that once it's fully realized they will seek to physically mate as quickly as possible."

"How long does this take?"

"I've seen couples meet, bond, and mate in mere hours."

3

Kayla slipped from the bed and picked up the thin dress from the floor. It offered little protection but it was better than nothing. She pulled it over her head with amazingly steady hands and started to run her fingers through her hair. She'd gone into that stasis pod with no hope of a better future and had come out of it forty years later to face an entirely different situation than she'd forced herself to prepare for.

Jude had returned his gaze to the compu-station and was silently filtering through what looked like a series of communications. The king of an entire species of people—the prospect was mind-blowing. Would he keep her for a lover until he found a *Yaw* woman to mate with? The thought of him fucking another woman, of mating with another woman, had her blood boiling.

"Are the *Yaw* monogamous?"

He immediately turned and looked at her; if he realized she was angry he didn't acknowledge it. "Yes and no."

She frowned. "Explain."

"We mate for life but it is far more than a sexual mating. It is a mental and emotional mating. Once that mating bond is created, neither party will ever mate fully with another. That does not mean that they will never have another lover. Many couples chose to have a third party in their bed."

"Oh." She frowned at him. "Would you?"

He laughed. "Well, I have no interest in other males and I've always been content with one female, so I doubt it. I have a large appetite for sex; but my mixed blood keeps me from being truly hedonistic like some of my people." Jude tilted his head and looked her over. "Would you want me to bring another into our bed?"

"Our bed?" she asked softly.

"Hypothetically," he murmured with a grin.

"No, I believe I would prefer to be the only one." She turned from him, unwilling to allow herself to dwell on such a fantasy, and gave herself a few minutes to truly inspect the large cave they were in. A narrow passageway near the front appeared to be the only exit. The walls were dry, but the chamber only had essential furnishings. "Is there a place to bathe?"

"I have a bathing unit in the next chamber." He stood and stretched his arms over his head. "Would it be all right if I joined you?"

"Of course."

The bathing unit was the one thing he'd absolutely insisted on bringing along. The rest had been his uncle's doing. He would have been fine without a bed and certainly without the compu-station, but going without hot fresh water for a bath was absolutely unacceptable. The unit took up the small chamber almost completely; its glass and metal frame no longer seemed entirely out of place to him. It would be a shame to leave the home he'd made in the small cave for the confines of the city, and eventually the ship that would carry him from world to world.

Jude glanced at Kayla as he programmed the unit. She'd pulled the thin gown over her head and tossed it aside again. He'd tried to hint to her what was to come between them but he wasn't entirely sure she'd caught his meaning. He opened the door and offered her his hand. "There is a step down."

She slipped her fingers into his hand without pause and let him guide her into the unit and shut the glass door behind them. Water fell over them from nine nozzles, in streams of hot and cool. The difference in temperatures had always been a pleasurable experience for him, and the way she smiled and her eyes lit up told him she felt the same.

He found her so beautiful in that moment, that it took his breath. Her small hands drifted over his chest and upward to anchor around his neck as she pressed herself completely against him. Jude wrapped his arms around her and buried his face in her damp hair. Suddenly, three days alone with her wasn't nearly enough.

He lifted his head and touched her face with gentle fingers. "It's been a long time since any woman has interested me the way that you do."

"Not hard to do when you've been alone for a year." She grinned when he laughed. "Am I very different from the women you've known?"

"You are softer." He cupped one breast, and used his thumb to worry the nipple. "I understand why my father kept my mother."

"You didn't before?"

"No," he admitted softly. "And he was not around for me to ask. My Uncle Remus resented my mother and her death only heightened that resentment. He and my father were of the same birth and were very close. He did the best he could for me as a child and has served in my place all of these years."

"Is he ready to give up the throne?"

"I don't know if he's ready but he's prepared to do it. He's lead us for a long time, but my people are fairly insistent that I take up the role that is my right by blood. Also, the humans have become increasingly interested in securing technology we do not want them to have." He reached out and brushed his fingers across a touch panel and a thin narrow tray slid out from the wall with a soaping cloth on it. "I could turn on the sanitizer jets, but I prefer the tactile experience of soap."

She nodded and took the cloth from his hand. "Allow me."

Jude sucked in a breath as she placed a soft kiss on his chest above his heart before she ran the cloth from his neck downward to his navel. Intent on her task, she washed his chest and arms before moving downward. On her knees, she skipped over the rapidly hardening flesh of his cock and soaped his legs slowly. It was the sweetest bit of agony he'd ever known.

Pale, delicate fingers grazed his balls as she wrapped the cloth around his cock and covered him with the slippery soap. Jude fisted his hands against his thighs and took several deep breaths as she cleaned him; each brush of the cloth brought him closer and closer to release. No woman had ever aroused him so thoroughly.

"You're going to pay for this."

She glanced up and laughed, her eyes bright with desire and amusement. "I sincerely hope so. Turn around."

He held out a hand to help her stand and then turned as instructed. Pressing his hands flat against the wall, he lowered his head as she washed his back with slow circles of the cloth. Her breasts brushed against his back as she moved closer to reach his shoulders. Exactly how much of this torture was he supposed to take?

Her hands slid down his back, nails scoring skin gently as she brought the cloth across his lower back and then downward to press between the cheeks of his ass. Jude sucked in a harsh breath as she slid one soapy finger against his anus and then pressed. She stroked in and out slowly with one finger several times before adding a second. Each sweet plunge of her fingers sent a searing wave of heat straight up his back. He was no stranger to such play, but with Kayla everything was new and intoxicating. He spread his legs as his cock, already swollen and aching, jerked in response to the all-too-gentle pleasure of her exploration.

"Enough," he growled, and turned abruptly.

She laughed and stepped back under the jets, tossing the cloth aside as she did so. "Did I rouse your beast?"

"You tempt all of me to near violence," Jude murmured as he joined her under the water.

He closed his eyes briefly as she returned to him and used her hands to help wash the soap away. Pulling another cloth from the tray, he pushed it close and maneuvered her to the end of the stall to the small recessed bench there.

It was difficult to take his time and be gentle, but he gave her body the same thorough washing she'd given his. He allowed his hands to linger over her breasts until her breathing was ragged, and he dipped his fingers between her labia to stroke and tease her clit.

When every inch of her was covered with slick soap, he tossed the cloth aside and cleared his throat. "Rinse."

She stepped away from him, a small smile lingering on her mouth as she turned in slow circles in the water. "Like this?"

He chuckled, pleased with her playfulness and her complete lack of fear. She had to know the wildness she inspired in him. Wrapping one hand around his cock, he watched her as the water slipped down the lush curves of her body. *His woman.* The urge to claim her surfaced again. Clenching his teeth briefly, he forced his body to relax against the wall.

"Come here." She turned and immediately walked to stand in front him. He spread his legs farther apart; his cock jerked and bobbed against his stomach in silent demand as he released it. "Suck me."

The tip of her pink tongue darted out and wet her lips as she knelt in front of him. Her hands drifted over the insides of his thighs, and then upward to grasp his cock. A soft moan escaped her mouth as she lowered and took the head of him between her lips. Conscious that he might hurt her, he remained perfectly still as she worked his sex deep into her mouth until the head bumped against the back of her throat. Then she slowly retreated, her tongue sliding and caressing on the backward stroke.

Jude swallowed hard, overwhelmed by the sight of her soft, full lips stretching over him as she slowly took him back inside her mouth. He'd fantasized about it more than once but the reality was so much more. She moaned again and he lifted his hips slightly. He stilled again, and let her take him inside several more times before he wound one hand into her hair and pulled her gently but firmly off of him.

"Are you wet for me?"

She nodded, her eyes half closed. "Oh yes."

He pulled her from the floor, urged her astride his thighs, and lifted her up onto his cock in one swift motion. Fingernails bit into his shoulder as she arched against the invasion and then shuddered as she slid down onto his cock. The hot, wet heat of her pussy was exactly what he needed.

Kayla let her head fall back as she slowly lowered herself. His cock filled and satisfied her in more ways than she could even begin to consider. His big hands drifted over her hips and then upward to cup and tease her breasts. On some instinctual level, everything about him pleased her and she accepted that without even really considering the ramifications of it. His breath caught and she increased her pace; the need to make him come, to satisfy him, pushed away everything else.

He leaned forward and caught one nipple between his lips. The pull of his mouth and the sweep of his tongue made her whole body clench in response. "More."

Jude lifted his mouth from her breast and cupped the back of her head. "More?"

She moaned softly against his mouth as he pulled her down and kissed her. His tongue swept into her mouth, and a shudder slipped down her back. Gripping his shoulders, she pulled her mouth free. "Yes, more."

He stood from the bench and lowered her to the floor of the bathing unit without another word; the water beat down on his back as he planted two hands on either side of her head. Jude pushed his cock deep into her until her body bowed beneath his and then withdrew. He thrust again and again—his pace so brutal that all she could do was wrap her legs around his waist and hold on.

Orgasm rushed at her like a hard unrelenting fist and she tightened around him until she thought she might break apart. She screamed against his shoulder and clenched her teeth on the muscle she found there. His whole body stilled as he thrust deep and came with her.

Kayla relaxed on the floor beneath him, stunned at the salty taste of blood in her mouth. She glanced at his shoulder; water rushed over the small wound she'd left but the impressions of her teeth marks were evident. She'd broken the skin in one place; with shaking fingers, she touched the spot. "Jude . . . I . . ."

He pulled free of her body and sat back on his knees, his eyes glittering with some emotion she didn't understand but didn't fear. "Relax, little human, I'm the one that has to do the biting around here for our situation to truly change."

She sat up and pulled her legs to her chest, as he stood and retrieved fresh soaping cloths from the tray. "I'm sorry. I've never been so . . ." He held out his hand and she took it with a little sigh. "It seems like you rouse the animal in me."

Jude pulled her to her feet and pressed the cloth into her free hand. "Bathe, and then I believe you need a meal."

"I'm normally not hungry for days after stasis."

"Still, you need to eat." He leaned down and kissed her swollen mouth. "And I find I like the animal in you."

Jude arranged the food on the trencher quietly as he considered what he'd driven her to. *Yaw* women rarely bit their partners, and when they did, it was because they were so turned on both physically and emotionally that they were overwhelmed. Still, with his people, pleasure biting could be dangerous. His little human's blunt teeth had barely broken the surface of his skin, but the pleasure of it still lingered. He'd never come so hard in his life.

"So, do your people go naked?"

He laughed and glanced back at her; she was standing near the bed still wrapped in a drying sheet, the thin gown in which he'd found her in her hands. She was looking at it with displeasure. "No, I've just become somewhat accustomed to it since I've been alone for so long. What's wrong with the gown?"

"Marceau purchased it for me to wear for when I met him."

That was irritating. He picked up the wood tray of fruits that he'd prepared and went to her. "Here, nothing too heavy, but the fruit will help replace some of the water you've lost."

She took the tray and started to toss aside the gown but he caught it with his fingers. "I'd rather never see you in this again." He fisted the material in his hand. "I've a reproduction unit in one of the forward chambers of this cave. I'll have it make you something."

"And something to cover my feet?"

"Yes, of course." He snagged the thin, ridiculous sandals from the floor. "I'll put all of this in the recycle unit."

Kayla nodded. "Thank you."

He left her after watching her settle on the bed with the food. The irrational anger at having another man's things on her was burning in his gut. The large cave he'd made his home in was made up of six chambers; the largest he'd used for his bed and the majority of the things he'd been forced to bring with him. If it had been left to him, his people could have left him here with nothing for the *solace* period. Yet, his uncle insisted that a future king not live so primitively. Hence, the bed, the compu-station, food, and reproduction units had been tucked into his temporary home.

It wasn't all that dissimilar to the suite of chambers he enjoyed in the city. When *Atelier* had been built, the constructionist had used as much of the natural structure as possible, creating a beautiful and unique city for the royal family and those citizens who chose to live in the capital.

He shoved the offending gown and shoes into the recycling unit and walked away as it activated. The gentle hum of the machine working was actually soothing. He went to the reproduction unit to produce the clothes she requested. With a few key strokes, he ordered leggings, boots, a shirt, and a collection of hair paraphernalia he thought she might want. *Yaw* women did not let their hair grow so long after they reached adulthood. He always felt it was a shame.

The reproduction unit finished its cycle and dinged very softly. Jude plucked the entire tray out of the unit and glanced over the stuff he'd chosen for her. Perhaps he should have brought her along to choose, as he really had no idea what sort of thing she preferred. With a sigh, he closed the unit and walked back to the sleeping chamber.

He found her sitting in the middle of the bed, rummaging through her bag with one hand while the other clutched a piece of manga-fruit. It was a rich citrus fruit that was uniquely satisfying. There were chemicals in the fruit that actually induced pleasure in the *Yaw.* He wondered briefly if she would be affected the same way and chuckled when she brought the fruit back to her mouth to suck at the juices. A soft little moan escaped her lips and he had his answer.

"It's not addictive if you are concerned."

She grinned and bit into the fruit again. "It's amazing."

"It causes the release of pleasure endorphins. Humans have such food products, yes?"

"Well, some plant life can cause the pleasure centers in the human brain to respond and one of the few plants to actually thrive on New Earth is the cocoa plant. Chocolate is well known for such properties but it is nowhere near as amazing as this stuff." She set the chunk of fruit down and wiped her hand on the drying sheet with a flush. "Clothes?"

He brought the boxlike tray to the bed and set it in front of her. "What's in your bag?"

Kayla flushed. "Not much, I was only allowed to bring a few things."

"Why?"

"Marceau insisted that he would provide all that I needed in my new life and that I had no need for personal possessions that he did not buy for me."

"He wanted to isolate you from your old life so that you were fully dependent on him."

"Yes." She pulled out a slim metal case and flipped it open. "This is a vid-viewer. It has images of my family in it, but the power cell is dead." Her fingers trembled as she left it on the bed between them. "I brought the memory drive for my compu-station. It has all of my books, personal records, and writings. I doubt there is even a compu-station in use today that could read the contents." Kayla put the heavy silver rodlike case aside as if it didn't matter, but her growing distress was written all over her face. "Can we find out what happened to my sisters and father without alerting them to my location?"

"I can try." He reached out and touched her face. "The average human lives one hundred seventy years without periods of prolonged stasis?"

"Yes." She bit down on her lip. "My sisters would all be in their seventies now and my father one hundred twenty-one."

"And Marceau?"

"He was five years older than my own father." She grimaced. "I hope that he's dead."

"It does not matter if he is dead or not," Jude muttered. "I would sooner cut the man's head off than allow him to have you."

"He was a powerful man forty years ago; there is no telling how far he has come."

"Or how far he has fallen," Jude returned. "Success is not a path that can only be traveled in one direction. It matters little; there isn't a human in this entire sector that would risk displeasing me." He stood from the bed and stretched. "I need to hunt. Do not leave the cave while I am gone, it would not be safe."

"Hunt?"

Laughing at her surprised tone, he leaned down and kissed her full mouth. "Yes, little one, hunt." He ran his fingers through her damp curls. "My beast needs meat."

Her eyes widened.

"Relax, I won't bring the kill back." He kissed her again, his mouth lingering on hers long enough that she reached out for him. "Remember, do not leave the cave."

"I won't."

4

Kayla remained still until he was gone and then leaned forward to inspect the clothing he'd left for her. The pants and boots were gray and appeared to be very nice simulated leather. She touched them and then pulled them out with a soft sigh of pleasure at the luxury of them. His reproduction unit must be very advanced. The shirt was made of a stretchy material and was both gray and a soft shade of pink in alternating rows. It would probably fit like a second skin.

A hairbrush and a series of clips and hairpins were also in there; it was a thoughtful gesture. Who was this man who had plucked her without a thought from the jungle? She knew so little about him, yet in a few short hours, he'd filled her mind and body. Should she return to her family? Would there even be a place for her there after so many years had passed? Had she ever really had a place?

The thought made her uncomfortable but if she were to be honest with herself, the only value she'd ever had for her family was the day she'd been noticed by General Philippe Marceau. What he saw in her, she didn't know and hadn't tried to speculate. She'd been educated because her mother, Dora, wished it and after school, her father had indulged her wishes to have a career, yet again at the pressuring of his wife. And not six months after her mother had died, she'd been sold.

There were other, far more attractive words for it, but in the end, she'd been bartered away from her life and everything she'd worked for without anyone even bothering to ask her what she wanted. Women had few rights in the colonies, life was harsh, and men were in charge. Her sisters, though they had loved her, had all been relieved that Marceau had not set his mind on one of them. That she had escaped all of it was some strange and beautiful twist of fate.

With a sigh, she stood from the bed and pulled off the drying towel Jude had given her. The clothes felt good as she slid them on; the materials didn't abrade or ride against her skin but almost seemed to adhere to her skin in a way that was comfortable and natural. She pulled the boots on and then grabbed the brush from the metal box.

Jude would be able to check and see what had happened to her family. Knowing would be enough and for the time being she was going to force herself not to consider how selfish it was to let them assume she was dead. She had three days to decide what she would do when his people came.

Would the *Yaw* welcome her, or would her presence be so disturbing that they would immediately contact New Earth to have her removed? Politics were politics, no matter the species, and it occurred to her that a newly crowned king would have games to play. Would Jude sacrifice her to keep his people, his uncle happy?

What did he want? Obviously, he was a man used to getting everything he wanted and needed. She's certainly surrendered to his sexual needs without even thinking about it. No! She had surrendered to their *mutual* need. It would be unfair to say otherwise. In the year leading up to her trip to Fourth Colony she had lured man after man into her bed . . . not caring if they found her lacking or were there just because they wanted leverage with her father. Yet, none of them had ever satisfied her the way that Jude did. In fact, none of them had even come close.

With a sigh, she pulled her hair up, pinned it with a binder from the box, and then shoved the rest of the binders and various clips into her bag. After moving the box to his desk, she made quick work of righting the bed and folding the warming blanket she'd slept under. Then she finished off the fruit he'd left for her.

How long would it take him to hunt? The thought of him stalking some animal and killing it for food made her stomach lurch but if he needed that sort of thing to survive, she wasn't going to begrudge him that. Did he enjoy it or was it more of a biological urge? The scientist in her had a couple hundred thousand questions about his species, but so far she'd managed to keep them to herself. Granted, it would have been difficult to question him since he'd been fucking her blind most of the day.

How had his human and *Yaw* genes come together? Was his shifting as smooth and normal as his father's people or did his human traits interfere? What had his mother given him? She sat down on the bed, at a loss as to what to do with herself, and then lay back to stare at the ceiling. He said the city was built in a large cave system; the entire thought boggled the mind, but then what she'd seen of the surface did not speak of an environment easy to live in. Sometimes no technological advancement could prevent nature from running its course.

The click of claws on the stone floor jerked her into a full sitting position; she pulled her legs up onto the bed as the large cat entered the chamber. *Jude.* She relaxed and swallowed hard. She had only seen him briefly in his cat form before and was now enthralled with pure power of the beast that he was. Thick muscle rippled under dense black fur, as he moved toward her. He walked to the edge of the bed, his pitch-black gaze raking over her as if to assure himself that she'd stayed exactly where he'd put her.

As before, the hair started to slip away, and the distinct pop of bones echoed through the silent cave. Her heart thumped against her breastbone as his silky dark skin took dominance, his facial features bled away to a more humanlike appearance, and his body followed. The change was so swift and so seemingly effortless it looked almost like magic.

"You're beautiful."

He ran his tongue along his bottom lip as he stared. "So are you. Thank you for not wandering away from the cave."

"As I said, I'm not really a foolish woman." She reached out with a shaking hand and touched his cheek. "Did your hunt go well?"

"Not as well as my hunt earlier in the day." He crawled up onto the bed and pinned her to the mattress in one swift movement. "But it sated my hunger."

Kayla sucked in a breath as he pressed his cock against her; her legs gave away immediately to allow his body to rest between her thighs. "Not all of your hunger."

"No." Jude grinned. "I brought that appetite back to you."

"I'm so glad." She rubbed her thumb over his mouth and closed her eyes briefly as he rocked against her. "I feel as if you've woken some primitive sexual creature in me that I didn't even know I had."

"Your pleasure is intoxicating, Kayla. I want more. I want you screaming my name, your cunt rushing wet and tight around my cock." He lowered his head and took her mouth in a hard brief kiss. "Tell me I can have you again."

"Yes." She nodded abruptly and clutched at his shoulders. "Always, yes."

Jude sat up, his eyes hard and bright. "As much as I like seeing you in the clothes I've provided, you'll need to undress. Undress very fast."

He watched her through half-closed eyes as she scrambled to her feet and shed the clothes right there in front of him on the bed. Each inch of skin revealed seemed to double the hard need that pulsed through his body. She dropped down to her knees in front of him and he reached up to pull her hair free.

"I love your hair down."

"Then I'll never put it up." She moved her hands up his arms as he brought her close.

"Just for me." He thread his fingers through the heavy blond mass and nuzzled her neck. "And in private."

Kayla nodded her agreement and let her head fall back. "Whatever you want."

He ran the tip of his tongue along the steady thump of her pulse and was pleased when it immediately increased. Her nipples scraped against his chest as he lifted her upward and a soft groan of pleasure broke free from her lips. The sounds he could drag from her woke something unknown in him. Capturing one rigid nipple in his mouth, he sucked hard until the sweet scent of her arousal saturated the air around them.

She wrapped her legs around his waist and pressed her breast against his mouth, her breathing ragged. "More."

He released the nipple as he lifted her and then pulled her down onto his cock. She jerked in his arms, her back arching as she took all of him in. Jude held her close, his hands sliding down her back to soothe the tension that had spread through her as she'd taken all of him inside.

"Sore?"

Lowering her head to his shoulder, she clutched at him. "Just a little, but I can take it."

He turned them, lowered her to the bed, and carefully pulled free. She spread her legs wide and lifted her hands above her head in complete submission as he ran his large hands over her breasts, over her rib cage, and down her thighs to grasp her knees. Lowering his head, he placed a kiss on the soft flesh of her belly before lifting away from her completely.

"No suffering for you, woman, not even a little."

She frowned. "But . . ."

"Relax." He leaned over and kissed her lips gently. "I'll be right back."

Jude ignored her sigh of complaint as he left the bed and went to a large storage trunk near his desk. He pulled the medical container free, flipped it open, and rummaged through it until he located a tin of healing gel. His people healed fast and there had been little cause to use any part of the medical supplies before now.

She was still sprawled on the bed, propped up on her elbows regarding him with those beautiful green eyes of hers. The thought of intentionally causing her harm in the pursuit of his own pleasure had been like a fist in his face. He moved back onto the bed and lay down beside her, placing the tin unopened on her stomach.

"What is this?"

"It's a medical gel. It has several purposes . . . among them helping ease soreness and discomfort in muscles." He opened it with a press of his thumb and looked over her face as he rubbed two fingers across the semisolid surface of the gel. "It will also heal any microtears in the walls of your passage that I might have caused while inside you."

"Oh." She flushed and then spread her legs wide for his hand. "Then you'll fuck me again?"

"Repeatedly," Jude promised, both amused and pleased by her blunt question.

He pushed his fingers into her and bit down on his bottom lip when her body clenched around the invasion. Her hips tilted and her back arched sharply as he slowly spread the gel around inside her. With a sigh, he lowered his head and sucked one rigid nipple into his mouth. Tugging and licking at her breast, he started to stroke his fingers in and out of her, spreading the gel around the edge of her entrance and then back in again.

Jude paused briefly when one of her hands drifted over the hard edge of his cock and then groaned against her flesh as she wrapped her fingers around him. The gentle pull of her hand robbed him of his breath, and then he gave into the urge to thrust against her hand. It wasn't enough, couldn't ever be enough when compared with the wet heat of being inside her body.

He pulled his fingers from her and she sighed, obviously frustrated. With a grin, he pulled her hand from his cock and lifted both of her arms above her head as he closed the tin and tossed it aside.

"What an impatient and lusty creature you are, my little human."

She wrapped her legs around his waist the moment she could and lifted her hips upward as he rubbed the head of his cock upward between her parted labia. "Stop teasing me, please."

"No, do not beg." He kissed her mouth gently as he pushed deeply into her with one heavy thrust. Seated to the hilt, he paused and looked over her face as her body adjusted to his invasion. "My woman does not have to beg for anything."

Her gaze locked with his. "Yours?"

"That's what I said." He tightened his grip on her wrists when she tried to pull free. "Mine."

"No man is going to *own* me." She let her legs drop from his waist, but could find no purchase to push him away.

He rocked against her, and she shuddered with pleasure. "Is that so?"

"It is," she snapped, but her body betrayed her by falling into the gentle rhythm of his thrusting cock.

"You'll say it," he promised softly against her parted lips, pleased with her ragged intake of breath and the way her hips were lifting to meet his.

"No." She bit down on his bottom lip hard and he growled in response.

The taste of blood, even his own, in his mouth was like tossing fuel on a flame. His beast rushed to the surface, but he kept it at bay, preventing the shift from happening. It had been a long time since he'd shifted involuntarily but she pushed so many primitive feelings to the surface that he could barely think straight.

Abruptly, he lifted away from her and hissed as he pulled his cock free of her body. She started to scramble away but he caught her by the ankle and jerked her back to him.

"Don't run." He held her against his chest with one arm as he placed a soft kiss on her shoulder. "If you run, I don't think I'll be able to control myself."

"Jude." She let her head fall back against him as he pressed his cock against her ass.

"You must know I'd never hurt you." His teeth grazed her shoulder, as he placed several soft kisses there before moving to her neck. "That's the second time you've drawn my blood."

"I'm so sorry," she murmured softly, her tone more amused than contrite.

He'd never heard a more insincere apology in his life, and it forced a reluctant laugh from him. "I just bet you are." He cupped both her breasts and pinched her nipples hard enough to make her groan. "What you don't understand, Kayla, is that every time you do it, you make my beast ache with the need to respond."

"What does it want to do?" She stilled completely in his arms, her body tense with fear.

"Bite back."

Excitement. Fear. Need. All of it coursed through her in a

matter of seconds as his lips continued their leisurely path from just underneath her ear to the end of her shoulder. *The Yaw mate for life.* Did this incredible man mean to mate with her? To bind himself to her until he died. Would the passion that moved so easily between them eventually be something more emotional?

He lowered her onto her hands with gentle but firm hands, tilted her hips slightly, and pushed his cock deep into her without another word. Her pussy clenched around him and she fisted her hands in the bedding beneath them. He slammed into her again and again, his hands digging into her hips as the head of his cock met with her womb. The pleasure of it was so much that she could do nothing but rock back against him and demand more.

"I want you to say it."

She gasped as he pressed downward onto the mattress onto her stomach. Still he continued to slide in and out of her, the head of his cock scraping against her G-spot in this new position. "No."

He licked her shoulder, his teeth clenched on her skin but not enough to draw her blood. The thrill of that almost pain made her groan. He pushed one hand beneath them to cup her pussy, his fingers immediately finding her clit. The quick little circles he drew there with the tip of his finger soon matched the steady push of his cock into her. The combination was more than she could stand.

"Say it."

She sucked in a breath as orgasm rushed over her. Her body jerked against his and her vision blurred. The desire to be a part of him for the rest of her life hit her hard as a second orgasm started to build.

"I'm yours."

He slowed his pace, his touch gentled. "Tell me I can have you forever."

"Yes." She nodded.

"You'll stay with me."

"Yes. Yes."

The instant his teeth sank into her shoulder, her entire body reacted. She came hard and screamed at the mixture of pleasure and pain that swept over her. He growled in response, his body jerking roughly against hers as he claimed her completely.

He certainly hadn't played fair, but it wasn't in his nature to. Tending the wound carefully, he used the medical gel to seal the small holes his incisors had made. The chemicals in his bite insured that a scar would remain with her for life. An uncivilized notification to any male that might come upon her that she was taken, mated.

Jude had heard about the effects of the mating bite all of his life; men spoke often of how sweet the blood was in their mouth and how a woman's body would shake with pleasure as they fed from them. He honestly had never really believed it, but Kayla had writhed under him and begged for more even as she'd fainted.

She stirred under his hand and then turned her head so that she could see him. Bright green eyes met his and in that instant, his entire world seemed to shift out of focus. This small human female had become the center of everything he wanted and needed for his future.

Her fear and uncertainty drifted between them and he set aside the gel. Carefully he gathered her into his arms and held her close to his chest. "No fear, little one."

"I don't think I'm prepared for all of this." She rubbed her cheek against him and wrapped her arms around him; her fingers dug into the skin of his back as she clutched at him. "I'm afraid I'm going to wake up in that pod any minute now and be on Fourth Colony."

"This is no dream." He brushed her hair from her forehead. "I'm unsure as to how you will react to the mating bite; it didn't even occur to me to be concerned."

"Your mother survived it."

Yes. But she didn't survive for long.

"It wasn't your father's fault that your mother died. Accidents happen, and staying here to mate with him was her choice." She touched his face. "I'm strong, Jude. I won't die on you."

He pushed down his fear, aware, even if she wasn't, that his fear for her life was making her nervous. Had she heard his thoughts or had she merely responded to the strongest of the emotions he'd projected onto her.

"I'll protect you. There is nothing and no one that can take you from me." His hand fisted in her hair, but his lips were gentle on hers as he kissed her. "When we return to *Atelier*, I'll help you contact your family."

She stiffened. "No."

"Yes." He kissed her again. "Even if General Marceau lives, he is in no position to try to claim the Queen of the *Yaw* as his property. Even voicing such a position would be an act of war. His government would sooner kill him than provoke me. You'll find that very few intelligent people would wish to cross me."

"I can feel your arrogance washing over me like a river."

He laid her back on the bed and pulled the thin blanket over them. "Is that so?"

She let her head rest on his chest with a contented sigh. "Yes. I should be angry with you."

"For pushing you to mate with me?"

"Yes."

"You don't regret it." Jude pushed his fingers through her hair, pleased with how relaxed she was against him. "You don't even resent it."

"It's pretty hard to resent being made a queen," she muttered softly and then lifted her head to meet his gaze. "But just a title right? I won't have to make decisions?"

"You will be on my council of advisors, in fact, you will lead my council of advisors." He rubbed her mouth with his thumb. "Remind me later and I will update your language implant so that you won't have any communication problems once we arrive in the city."

"Language implant?" She frowned.

"Ah." He pressed his fingers to a place behind her right ear. "A small language processor is implanted here with an injection. I've been using the *common* language because I figured your chip would be out of date, it didn't occur to me that you wouldn't have one at all."

"Is this a problem?"

"I don't have one with me in the supplies that I brought. We'll have to wait until we return to the city to get you one. I don't like the thought of you having such a weakness. The ability to communicate is often the best weapon in a new situation."

She smiled and touched his mouth. "Stop frowning, I'm confident that you will protect me."

"I will." The certainty of his agreement drifted between them. "My uncle is likely to be in the retrieval party so you will meet him in the morning."

"You are worried that he will not approve."

Yes, Jude thought and then pulled her closer to him. He had spent most of his adult life listening to his uncle complain about humans. Remus Aroca would have, given a choice, made war with practically everyone after the death of his brother. He wasn't a bad man, but he was a man of strong opinions and a quick temper.

"He's never made any secret of the fact that he resented my mother," he finally said. "He blamed her for my father's eventual death and while he never mistreated me, my mixed blood was a daily reminder."

"Your father was obviously a passionate man who loved his mate deeply. If he had mated a *Yaw* woman, the same situation could have easily occurred." She bit down on her lip and looked away from him.

"Yes, that is certainly a rational thought." He stroked her back as if to ease them both. "You fear that I will never love you."

She sucked in a breath. "Maybe we need to set some boundaries."

Jude laughed. "No such thing among mated couples, little one. Your needs, desires, and emotions will always be with me." He pulled her upward, sucking in a breath at the scrape of her breasts against his chest, so that they were eye to eye. "Tell me what you feel from me."

"You are pleased with yourself." Kayla pressed her hands on his shoulders and sat up. She braced her knees on either side of his body, the heat of her sex flush against his rapidly hardening cock. "You think I'm beautiful." She scraped her nails down his chest and grinned when his breath slipped from his lips in a near hiss. "You want me to be happy."

"Yes." His gaze drifted over her, taking in the hardened tips of her pale pink nipples, the narrow line of her waist, the fullness of her hips. He was very pleased that she was his. "Anything else?"

"Possessive." She dipped one finger into his belly button. "Protective." She moved then, rubbing her dampening sex over the length of his cock, sucking in a breath as she bumped her clit against the head of his cock. "But under all of that there is this wildness inside you."

"Yes." He nodded.

"It's your beast? The animal that lurks under your skin and in your soul?"

"Yes."

"You want to push your cock into me so deep that I never forget, not even for a second, who I belong to."

He turned them over abruptly and thrust deep into her without pause. Her cunt pulsed and clenched around him, and for a few precious seconds he was still, letting her body tighten around his cock again and again. When he could bear it no more, he started to move.

5

Kayla rolled onto her back and stretched; her body was sore in several hundred delicious ways. Jude was dressed and sitting at the desk several feet away from her. Seeing him with clothes on was actually unnerving. Black, heavy soled boots, leather pants, and a fitted shirt that showed off the muscles of his chest and stomach covered him.

He turned to look at her then, his eyes ripping over her in a sweep that reeked of possession and desire. "If only we had time."

She laughed and stretched her arms over her head. "He's going to be furious, right?"

"I don't know."

He was nervous about it though, that much was plain. She slipped from the bed, walked to him, and knelt between his legs. "Do not worry so. If I can win the affection of one crazy panther-man surely I can win over another."

Jude leaned forward and cupped the back of her head. "He doesn't have to like you but he *will* respect you."

"I should shower." She stood reluctantly and smiled when

his hands slid upward over her hips. He placed a soft kiss on her belly and then leaned back in his chair.

"I'll have the reproduction unit make you something to wear back to the city."

"What you've already given me won't work?"

"No, at least the top won't." He looked her over again, and smiled. "You are my queen, and I'll have no one question it."

She showered quickly, his nervousness rubbing off on her. The thought of not being ready when Remus Aroca arrived was enough to make her shake. A queen or not, she had to look put together and ready for whatever was coming. In the bed-chamber, she found a new blouse tossed on top of the gray leggings. It was silky, almost sheer, and would fall off her right shoulder almost completely.

He wanted her mating mark prominently displayed. It was practically the most primitive thing he'd done so far, but she wasn't upset by it. She dressed and put her hair up in an intricate twist with several silver combs that he'd also left on the bed.

Kayla turned as Jude re-entered the chamber followed closely by a large, older near replica of himself. *Remus Aroca.* She swallowed hard, and pressed her lips together. She would not give this man a single reason to think she was weak.

"Forty-one years, you say?" Remus looked her over, his gaze narrow with suspicion. "She could be lying, maybe sent here to spy on behalf of her people."

Jude spared his uncle a brief glance as he gathered up Kayla's bag from the bed and another one that she hadn't noticed before. "Even if I didn't believe her, the mating bond would've told me instantly if she'd been deceptive." He walked to her and placed his hand on the small of her back. "We've discussed this already, uncle. I'm simply not in the mood for your conspiracy theories at present."

"I have led our people for thirty years," he snapped, his gaze focused entirely on Jude.

"You and I both knew that the day I turned thirty-five I would become king. I waited, when I could have taken the throne as a much younger man, because I didn't think either of us was ready for that transition. Now, we have no choice and it is done."

"Yes, it is done."

Kayla stiffened when he shifted his gaze back to her, his eyes hard.

"It would have been better for your people if you had kept this one to fuck and mated with one of our own."

He was speaking the *common* language for her benefit, so that his backhanded insult would be understood.

"As it is, he didn't." She tilted her head when he started to speak. "We are mated and I am, whether you like it or not, your queen. You'll temper your language with respect when you speak to me, or you may not address me at all."

Remus's mouth dropped open briefly and then he clamped it shut with an audible click of teeth. "Your little human has bite."

"Yes," Jude murmured with a laugh. "She does. Did you bring the translation chip?"

"Of course, it's on the transport. Regardless of how I feel about this situation..." His gaze flicked to her again. "I've done exactly as you asked."

Her fear rolled over him in gentle waves and he could do nothing for it. Jude glanced at her as she walked beside him up the ramp and into the transport that would take them back to the city. Her expression was cool and assessing as if there was nothing out of the ordinary about her circumstances. Yet, he knew how sheltered she'd been on New Earth before she'd been crated and shipped off to General Marceau. He was the first alien she'd ever seen outside of a vid-screen.

He led her to a seat and sat down beside her. His uncle sat across from them, his expression somewhat amused. "What?" Jude asked.

"She knows nothing of our species?" Remus asked softly in *Yaw*.

"No. She didn't even know we existed."

His eyes widened and then nodded. "No, of course, she wouldn't have known. The human explorers probably landed here some three years after her pod crashed." His gaze drifted to Kayla. "She is stunning and politically it's almost ideal. Your own human blood made you an attractive leader to deal with the human traders and their demands. A human wife will make you appear more approachable."

"That has occurred to me."

"Yes, but not why you took her and decided to keep her." Remus raised an eyebrow. "I did the research you requested. There is Philippe Marceau on Fourth Colony, a retired Vice Admiral. Her father is dead, and she has two living sisters. The third sister, the youngest of the four children, was killed shortly after your little human was lost."

"Killed?"

"There was no information on how. I was surprised to get any information at all. Our records concerning New Earth are incomplete and often out of date. I believe the connection with Fourth Colony made the search easier."

"What are you talking about?" Kayla leaned against him. "Nothing but the names make sense."

Jude cleared his throat. "You have two living sisters; the youngest has been dead quite some time. Marceau is alive, retired, and living on Fourth Colony."

"Cena is dead?" She bit down on her lip. It was the first time she'd allowed herself to say the name of one of her sisters. In the day since she'd woke, she'd purposely pushed them away from her, not wanting to imagine that they were no longer alive.

"Yes, that is the name. The other two are alive, married, with large families by human standards." Remus leaned forward. "I have no information on how your sister died. I'm sorry."

"It's okay." She looked away from them both. "I didn't expect to know anything at all at this point."

Jude wrapped one arm around her and pulled her close. She tucked her face into the side of his neck and took a deep shuddering breath. He turned to his uncle and asked softly in their language. "You told no one about her?"

"No. Not yet, but frankly it will be a difficult secret to keep."

"I have no intentions of keeping her a secret. I just need a few more days with her before we allow anyone off world to know that I found a human woman in the jungle."

Kayla fisted her hand in his shirt and tugged. He glanced down; her eyes were damp, but no tears fell. "Yes, little one?"

"I want the communication implant. I'm tired of you talking over me in a language I don't understand out of some misguided attempt to shield me. It isn't like I can't see straight into your head, panther-man."

Remus Aroca laughed softly. "Yes, so much bite."

Kayla rubbed the spot behind her ear where the implant had been installed and glanced around the transport. The five men, all tall and thickly muscled, that Remus had brought with him had said nothing and had barely looked at her the entire all-too-brief trip back to the city. The city entrance loomed in the distance, a man-made blight on the otherwise pristine surface of the moon. Large doors slid open as the ship moved into position and started to lower.

"How deep?"

"City development started roughly...." He paused as if he was considering a measurement she would understand. "Sixteen hundred meters and extends to around twenty-five thousand meters."

She swallowed hard. "Is the environment pressurized?"

"Yes. We are going through a series of airlocks now." Jude motioned toward the now-dark windows. "This is the only way in and out of city and there is an energy barrier to shield us from attack."

"As long as they don't try to destroy the entire moon?" Kayla asked softly.

"No one gets that close to Sanctuary without us knowing about it," Remus assured.

"Sanctuary?" Kayla turned to Jude.

"That is our name for this moon. Humans still call it Abundance." He touched her face then. "What will my little human call it?"

"Home." She smiled when his eyes darkened. "I meant to ask earlier, does this queen job come with head gear? Because I'm quite fond of things that sparkle."

"Head gear." He repeated and then laughed. "Actually, it does. I've always considered it somewhat archaic, but I find that I look forward to covering you in things that sparkle." He touched her cheek and then with no regard for their audience pulled her toward him and took her mouth in a hard kiss.

She moaned softly, and opened her mouth for him without even thinking. Her hands moved upward to loop behind his head as the familiar spicy scent of his arousal teased at her senses. Except that it quickly tripled, she stiffened when she realized that he wasn't the only aroused male in the small craft.

Jude lifted his head. "Relax, little one, not a single man on this ship thinks that I'm going to share you."

Kayla flushed and dropped her gaze to his chest. She knew

he would protect her, allow no one to misuse her but still she couldn't quite make herself calm down. Her heart beat wildly in her chest as she settled back down in her seat and pressed her thighs together. It was insane how aroused she was, how the scent of all of them teased at her blood and made her pussy clench around nothingness. The empty feeling was practically a torture.

"You should tell her."

Her gaze jerked to Remus, who was looking at her through half-closed eyes. "Tell me what?"

"It wasn't so much the visual display of your passion that heated the blood of every man on this craft. It was your physical arousal, the scent of you." He raised one eyebrow when she blushed. "Your embarrassment is unnecessary but certainly charming. It reminds us that you are unique to us. Very few of our people have interacted with humans and no human females have been sent to Sanctuary since the treaty was signed."

"I'm the only human female on this moon?"

"Yes," Jude answered softly. "Have trust in me, Kayla."

"I do." She tightened her fingers into a fist and glared at his uncle. "You aren't allowed to find me attractive."

"Too late." He laughed and held up his hands when she started to speak. "You're beautiful. In fact, I'm stunned by how natural your appearance is. The human females I've encountered off world are always enhanced works of . . . they would assume art. They don't even smell natural."

She bit down on her lip. "How do they smell?"

"Practically artificial. It's stunningly unattractive to us." Remus glanced at his nephew. "I suppose Jude can consider himself lucky that he found such a unique human female in his jungle."

Practically artificial. It was an apt description. She liked his arrogant uncle despite herself. Kayla jerked a little as the door to the craft slid open; she hadn't even felt them land. The guardsmen stood as if they were all attached to the same string and left the craft leaving the three of them alone.

"Don't be nervous." Jude rubbed the top of her hand as if to soothe her.

"I can be nervous if I wish," she muttered. "I'm the bloody queen."

He laughed and stood. Carefully, he pulled her to her feet and tucked her hand in the crook of his arm. "And a beautiful queen you are. The docking station will be filled to capacity. They are all here to see me, so you are going to be something of a surprise on several levels."

"Human, small and pale, your mate, queen."

"Yes."

Filled to capacity. The moment she exited, she found out that meant about four thousand people. A narrow path split the eerily silent crowd straight down the middle, and wound its way to a large archway. A thousand meters, at least, from the ship to the exit. If she couldn't make this walk, through just a few thousand of them, how did she expect to be able to act as his queen? She glanced to Jude. His dark gaze was drifting over the crowd in assessment.

He wasn't nervous at all anymore. In fact, pride and contentment seemed to be pouring off of him and onto her. He was proud of the mate he'd brought home, pleased to have finally assumed the role of king, and still somewhat, at least mentally, aroused by the kiss they had shared. Jude led her down the ramp and onto the smooth stone floor. The docking station itself was an intriguing mixture of cave rock and metal. It seemed to blend together in a way that defied that it hadn't always been such. In some places, the metal appeared to almost grow out of the rock.

Four men and a woman stood in front of the path. None of them made the pretense of not staring. She lifted her chin and pressed her lips together to keep from frowning. If her father had taught her anything, it was to keep her head about her and never let a potential enemy see her displeasure. They could stare all they wanted. It would change nothing.

Jude ran his hand along her shoulder, his fingers grazed his mating mark, and it heated under the attention. "They are the current council to the king."

"Appointed by your uncle?"

"Yes."

"You'll keep them?"

"For the time being. I'll be expected to choose my own council within the solar year." Jude remained still until his uncle moved away from them and went to stand with the council. "The woman held some illusions that I might mate with her."

Great. Are all men basically the same? "This is information I could have learned before now, honestly."

He laughed. "It just now crossed my mind."

"Were you lovers?" Kayla asked softly, her gaze drifting over the taller, muscular woman. Her honey-brown skin, full mouth, and statuesque physique made Kayla feel ridiculously unattractive.

"No."

He was being honest; in fact, she could feel the disinterest moving through him. The woman obviously had never once crossed his mind in a sexual way. "Her name?"

"Malaya. The men are from right to left: Borquoa, Garnian, Irisen, and Petrove. Outside my immediate family I am known only has Aroca."

"And your uncle?"

"He is the same."

That was going to get confusing. "And I will be?"

"You are Aroca as well. Most will address you by your title. Only those very close to you and family will be allowed to call you Kayla." He touched her face then, getting her full attention. "A few things before we move forward."

"Okay."

"Never offer your hands in greeting; it is a sign of submission. Always make eye contact with those you speak with and do not be the first to break it. You are Queen of all the *Yaw* and must be dominant over all that you meet. Once we are settled, I will choose men to act as your guards. They will go with you everywhere."

"Okay." She nodded and then smiled for him. "Why are you suddenly so agitated?"

"I don't know what I would do if I lost you." He glanced briefly out over the still-silent crowd and then refocused his attention on her. "Since the moment I met you, I've been at peace. If you were taken from me, I would never know it again."

His fear drifted across her mind, but she let it slip away. Suddenly it was very clear to her why he worried so. "I won't leave you, Jude. Not ever." She touched his face, rose up on her toes, and kissed him. The crowd stirred and the murmur of thousands of voices drifted through the large chamber. "Now, really, I'm starving. Can we leave the docking station?"

"She did very well."

Jude nodded and pressed the panel that closed the bedchamber in his suite. His uncle was ensconced in a chair on the opposite side of the chamber, a glass of targer-wine dangling from his fingertips. Kayla had managed the docking station and a full meal in front of thousands of witnesses without even getting a hair out of place. He wasn't surprised by that in the least.

He poured himself some wine and joined Remus in the grouping of chairs by the large fireplace. The fire, while completely unnecessary, was soothing. "I thought I would linger without a mate for years."

"No, you are like your father. I saw the urge to settle with one woman start in you some time ago. But I never expected you to stumble across your own human in the jungle."

Jude laughed. It wasn't lost on him that he'd met Kayla in much the same way his parents had met. "It isn't like I can help myself."

"No, I see that," Remus admitted. "I see it very well."

"Malaya is out of sorts."

"Malaya is used to getting what she wants." Remus shrugged. "And she wanted to be queen."

Jude frowned, uncomfortable with the thought of his mate having an enemy. He glanced toward the bedchamber and then sunk lower in the chair. "I never made that woman any promises."

"No. You didn't." Remus stood, refilled his wine, and poured another glass for Jude. "Still, she had ambitions that won't be realized and our people have another human queen to deal with."

"My mother was loved."

"Yes," his uncle admitted softly. "Very much so."

"Not by you." Jude took the wine and raised an eyebrow when his uncle started to disagree. "You always resented her."

"I was jealous. Your father was my twin and up until he met her we shared everything, including women." He laughed when Jude jerked. "Don't be surprised, I was very jealous of their relationship and the change it caused in my life. The second worst day of my life was the day my brother took Helena Carsen for his mate."

"And the worst?"

"The day she died." Remus cleared his throat. "Because my brother died with her, at least in all the ways that really mattered. Bastan was never the same after her death. I thought perhaps he would find comfort in you. That he would find a way to live without her for his son. Yet, in the end he merely sought a way to join her."

"My father didn't kill himself!" The denial burst from Jude before he could properly restrain himself, his face tightened and his teeth started to elongate.

"Control your beast, Jude. I did not say that my brother killed himself." He downed the rest of his wine in one swift swallow. "He just didn't fight it, didn't even pretend to want to fight it."

Jude couldn't help but agree. His gaze drifted back to the door that separated him from Kayla. He clenched his jaw as his teeth retreated. "That woman in there fills a hole in me I didn't even know I had. Even now, in sleep, her mind brushes against mine filled with a mixture of panic and the desire to please me. It's absolutely the most amazing thing I've ever experienced. She would do anything; give anything to keep from failing me."

"Yes, it is obvious," Remus murmured. "Human women are unique in their ability to love and sacrifice, Jude. Your mother was physically fragile, compared to us, but in so many ways the strongest woman I've ever known."

"The plant that killed my mother?" It was something he'd never asked about, never wanted to really know. Yet, now, in order to protect Kayla, he had to fully understand.

"Yes?"

"I want to know what it looks like."

"There are records of it in the city database, but it's not necessary. I had the plant eradicated in order to protect you. I couldn't be sure that whatever caused it to react so violently with your mother wasn't present in you. At that point, I'd already lost so much; I wasn't going to let that life-sucking plant take you too. It wrapped around her like nothing we'd ever seen, punctured her repeatedly with barbs, and fed on her. Even with your father and I both there—we couldn't take her from it until she was dead."

Jude swallowed hard. His uncle had never been so blunt about the details of his mother's death. But then they had never really discussed her or her death. "You are sure that not a single one of those plants survived?"

"We bioengineered a virus specific to the plant and seeded the entire atmosphere with it. I'll see that it's released again and that a survey is done to make sure it hasn't rebounded."

"Thank you. I can't stand the thought of something like that being close to her." Of even existing really. His children would be far more human than he . . . children. He looked to the door with a sigh, the image of her full with his child bloomed in his mind. "I don't ever expect you to have affection for her . . . I understand how deeply you dislike humans . . . but she's my world."

"I do understand," Remus murmured gently. "You've spent your whole life among *Yaw* and now there is another in your life that is similar to you. You are just as much human as you are *Yaw* and now through your mate you can fully explore that."

"Yes."

"She is what you want and I will see her protected, just as I've always protected you." Remus stood and put his glass down. "She is my family and I'm looking forward to some kits to play with."

"Ah." Jude chuckled. "I wonder when I should discuss children with her."

"Her main concern will be the form she'll give birth to." Remus chuckled. "It was your mother's. She was quite relieved to find that we don't enter life on four legs."

His eyes widened and he chuckled. "I'll address that first."

"Good." Remus walked to the exit and then paused. "And Jude?"

"Yes, Uncle?"

"I loved your mother as much as your father did." He glanced away as if he were ashamed of it and sighed. "If I had found her first, I never would have shared her either."

Jude remained where he was as the door swished shut at his uncle's exit. The shock of his final words drifted over him and he was suddenly very relieved. His uncle's potential disfavor had weighed on him; had even worried him on some deep level he hadn't addressed.

He stood and sighed when the visitor signal rang gently throughout the suite. All he wanted to do was go roust his mate from sleep and bury his cock in her, yet now there was someone at his door. He went and pushed the control on the view panel. *Malaya*. Disgruntled, he opened the door and stared at her.

"Jude, may I enter?"

"No."

"No?" She raised an eyebrow.

"No, and you're to address me as Your Grace." He pressed his lips together to keep from snarling at her as the perfume of her sex secretions filled the air between them.

"I've served on the King's Council for two years." She crossed her arms over her breasts. "I was chosen by your uncle."

"Yes, I'm aware."

"He chose me so that you and I could spend time together and mate."

"My uncle has never once presumed to make such plans for me." Jude stiffened when he heard the bedroom door open. Kayla's scent hit him scant seconds before her hostility bloomed between them.

Kayla came to a stop beside him, her hand moved up his back and settled on his shoulder just where her teeth had sunk into his shoulder as if she meant to clarify her claim. "What is the punishment for thrusting oneself between a mated pair?"

Malaya gasped and took a step back. "What? No!"

"Do you think I can't smell you?" Kayla asked softly. "Perhaps it's because you are entirely alien to me, but I smelled your pheromones before I even entered the room. Male *Yaw* release theirs unconsciously, but that isn't true of the female of your species is it?"

"No." Jude grimaced at her perceptiveness. "It's not. Females release when they seek to entice a male into intercourse."

"Leave and do not ever presume to approach him in such a way again. If and when we chose to add another to our bed, you can be assured that it would not be you."

"Or?" Malaya asked softly.

"I couldn't fight you and win. But if you learn nothing else your entire life about humans, it should be this: We do not fight fair, we give no quarter to the inferior, and I would just as soon put a pulse-round in your forehead as look at you."

Malaya glanced at Jude in shock.

"It's a projectile weapon cartridge. It's a metal rod filled with an explosive compound that explodes within its target." He watched her digest that information, turn abruptly on her booted heel, and stalk away. With a sigh, he reached out to secure the door. The panel dinged gently as the door slid close. "That was probably the most uncivilized thing I've heard you say, little one."

"How long were you going to stand there and let her spread her sex hormones around our home?" She glared at him. "Am I to learn to deal with such disrespect?"

"No." Jude cleared his throat, surprised by the level of her anger but not entirely displeased. Women of his species did not tolerate an uninvited female's sexual advance; he just hadn't anticipated it in Kayla. "You'll have to forgive me; this is a new situation for me." He held out both hands when she opened her mouth. "No, listen. You do realize that I couldn't have been less interested in her?"

"I do." She glared.

"It won't happen again." He chuckled when she raised an eyebrow. "She's afraid of your primitive human ways."

"She'd better be."

He felt the anger drain away from her and he relaxed. Returning to the entryway, he programmed it for privacy and walked back to Kayla. She hair was mussed from sleep, but still captured by combs. Her bright green eyes were clear and focused.

He held out his hand for her, she paused, staring at him for a long moment, and then a smile drifted across her full mouth.

"Are you submitting to me, Jude Aroca?"

"Absolutely, my Queen."

Kayla slowly slid her fingers against his palm, and sucked in a breath when he sank to his knees in front of her. He brought her hand to his mouth and kissed the palm before pulling her to him and wrapping his arms around her. His big hands slid up her back and then down to her ass as he maneuvered her so that her back was to the wall. Heat slipped over her body as he ran his fingers over her thighs and then downward to flick across the top of her bare feet.

"Take down your hair."

She lifted shaking hands to her hair and pulled the combs free one at a time, dropping them on the floor without a thought as his fingers hooked into the waist of her leggings and carefully pulled them down.

"What are you doing?"

"It is my duty to see to all the needs of my Queen." He tossed the leggings aside and looked upward as he ran his hands from her hips to her knees.

She pulled her blouse over her head quickly and tossed it in the direction he'd thrown her pants. "And how does my King plan to serve me?"

He lifted one of her legs onto his shoulder, effectively spreading her sex open. She gasped softly as cool air drifted over her already heated flesh before he scraped his tongue upward from her entrance to her clit in one sweeping motion. Kayla pressed back against the solid metal wall and groaned when he lifted her other leg up as well. She ran her hands over the back of his head as he pressed one hand to her stomach to keep her in place.

His tongue flicked over her clit several times before he drew it into his mouth to suck. She jerked against him, her womb clenching around nothing and her body arching against him. Her heels digging into his shoulder blades, she could do nothing but push forward against the wet pull of his lips and breathe. The hard edge of orgasm slid into her sharp, quick like a knife, and she screamed with the intense pleasure of it.

"All hail the king," she gasped as he lowered her shaking legs to the ground.

Jude chuckled as he came to his feet, his hand still pressed against her stomach to keep her from falling. "I love you."

Kayla jerked at the softness in his tone, she hadn't thought to hear the words so soon, but she'd felt the emotion brewing between them since they had mated. He pulled her close against his chest and ran his fingers through her hair; the hard press of his cock against her stomach told her that she had a long night ahead of her.

"I never thought I'd have this." She clutched at his back, desperate to be as close as possible. "I never thought I would love a man."

He picked her up carefully and kissed her brow. "You certainly weren't given any reason to believe that it would be possible." Jude carried her to the bed and laid her out there. "And do you love me, little one?"

She watched him as he shed his clothes with ease, relief evident in his every movement. Her panther-man was never going to be truly comfortable in clothes. "You don't know?"

He walked to the edge of the bed, his predator gaze flicking over her. "Of course I do."

"So arrogant." She laughed softly and held out her hand.

"Are you submitting to me Kayla Aroca, Queen of the *Yaw*?"

She spread her legs wide as he crawled onto the bed. "It is my duty to serve my King."

He took both of her hands in his, pinned her arms above her head, and thrust his cock deep, hard, and without pause into her. Her legs snaked around his waist immediately.

"Say it," he demanded through clenched teeth.

"I love you." She lifted against him and moaned softly when he moved.

Kayla turned in the pitch darkness, her ocular implants allowing her to see the faint outline of her mate's face. The air of their bedchamber was scented with the spicy remnants of his sexual release. Cool silken sheets covered them. Even in sleep, he had one hand on her, as if he feared she might be snatched from him during the night. Never would she have thought that she'd find such a man and that he would want her for exactly what she was.

Abundance. Jungle moon. Sanctuary.

What will my little human call it?

Home.

She'd slept forty-one years away to find a place to call home. With a sigh, she turned and curled around Jude. He was all the home she'd ever need.

Passion of the Cat

Dawn Thompson

1

The Hindu Kush, Winter, 1810

Captain Lyle Clarridge, Earl of Blackmoor, groaned awake. It wasn't the ache in his shoulder where the beast had wounded him that wrenched the sound from his parched lips. The pain had been dulled somewhat, since the animal tore his flesh despite the bulk of his uniform and greatcoat. It was the soft, small hands kneading his bare chest the way a cat pads upon its mother's belly extracting milk, that caused another groan to rise, and something else besides. His cock rose with it, hard and thick against the woman's naked thigh.

The exotic scent of strong herbs ghosted past his nostrils from a poultice strapped to his wound; aloes and adder's tongue, boiled in olive oil from the smell of it, fanned by the heat of the hearth fire. As near as he could tell, the herbs had been spread on dried adder's tongue leaves and bound in place with cotton strips. But it wasn't the woman's doctoring that held him in awe, it was the throaty purring sound she made, and the tiny wrists working fisted fingers that kneaded and pressed and massaged his pectoral muscles coming closer and closer to his right nipple. Swooping down, she took the nipple in her mouth and began to lave it with her soft, skilled tongue, while continuing to knead the other. His nipples had always been sensitive, but never like this.

Lyle tried to blink away the dregs of sleep, but the evocative smells in the dwelling were making him dizzy, and the strange taste in his mouth suggested opium. Then there was the woman herself. What was he doing lying naked in the arms of such an exquisite creature? He would have thought it was a dream but for the heady scent of patchouli and myrrh drifting from her skin, and the way her long dark hair teased his sweat-glazed skin. Her body felt like hot silk in his arms as he embraced her. Sharp, stabbing pain soon restricted the wounded arm, but the other snaked its way around her narrow waist, and pulled her closer still.

"W-who are you?" he murmured. "What am I doing naked with you in this bed?" His aching head spun dizzily, like that of a lord in his cups. His tongue felt thick and dry, and his words were slurred. Yes, he had been drugged with something. Whatever it was had not only dulled the pain, it had heightened his sexual awareness. His loins were on fire.

"Shh," she soothed. "You need my body heat, my lord. You were nearly frozen. I must awaken your blood . . ."

That wasn't all she was awakening, but she was right. While his sex burned with the flames of raw, ruttish passion, his hands and feet were suffering another sort of burning, the kind that comes from exposure to extreme cold. The pain in those extremities was almost beyond bearing, yet they felt numb. He'd known the feeling many times before on other campaigns. He was on the verge of chilblains from exposure to the bitter cold in the windswept mountain passes of the Hindu Kush, the northwestern curl of the orogenic arc of the Greater Himalayan complex.

It was a snow leopard that felled him. The great cat had sailed through the blizzard-whitened night sky from an invisible ledge above and driven him out of the saddle into the drifts. He could still see its golden yellow eyes nearly dilated black in the darkness. They'd had a silvery iridescent glow about them that he wouldn't soon forget. He saw death in them. Those eyes almost hadn't seemed real, for it had been a long, hard journey and he'd begun to nod in the saddle when the huge cat slammed into him. But that desperate fiction was soon dispelled. He could still feel the animal's hot breath puffing against his face, and its curved, razor-sharp fangs clamping upon the shoulder of his greatcoat. He could still hear the beast's terrible growls as it tore the fabric away, driven by bloodlust to reach his flesh beneath. He could still see those deadly jaws flinging bits of superfine and braid into the wind as if the cloth were made of paper and the heavy braid nothing more substantial than string. He felt again the stabbing agony as those deadly fangs sank into his shoulder, draining blood and consciousness with them.

Lyle shuddered in the woman's arms as the recollection drifted across his mind, and she pressed him closer still, her tawny olive skin tinted golden in the firelight, her perfect breasts flattened against his chest, the tall, dark nipples, like two nut-brown acorns, boring into his warming flesh.

"M-my horse?" he asked, fearful that the leopard had savaged it as well. Lyle Clarridge was many things, but above all he was a soldier. He had to complete his mission, and traveling afoot in the Kush in winter would be suicide. The snow and wind never ceased to howl through the passes, and even in spring and sultry summer, the uppermost peaks wore caps of pristine white, a grim reminder that Mother Nature's reprieve would be brief.

"The animal is safe," she said. "You must calm yourself and let me minister to you."

"You haven't said your name," he responded. "I have never

lain with a woman when I didn't at least know that much about her."

"I am called Ihita," she purred, sliding her leg over both of his until she straddled him, aligning the root of his shaft with her slit. "Shh now, my lord . . . Lie still and let me save you."

How beautiful she was, with the firelight gleaming in her dark, shiny hair. It fell about her like a silken shower, as she continued to knead his chest with the heels of her hands and her fisted fingers. It was a strange caress that riddled him with waves of erotic desire, numbing the dull, nagging ache in his shoulder. All that mattered was that golden body undulating against him, those skilled wrists and hands and fingers kneading, pressing, padding like a cat, igniting his loins and his blood, the blood she'd said she must awaken. He felt it coursing through his veins now, pumping, thrumming, keeping time with the runaway heart hammering against her fisted fingers as his cock, swelling against her mound, nestled in the soft thatch of her moist pubic curls.

Enraptured, he groaned. Her undulations were drenching him in achy fire. He'd heard tales of the sexual skills of Asian women, but this . . . oh, *this* was something he had never imagined. Not even Lydia March, his skilled courtesan at home, possessed such a talent. Ihita's fire was feral, deeply rooted in primeval mystery, which she only let him glimpse. What would it be like to lose himself in the deep, dark depths of her psyche, to learn the secrets of such a passion?

Just when he thought he could bear no more, she broke her strange kneading rhythm and raised herself enough to let his anxious cock penetrate her. Lyle's breath caught as she took him deeply, and he leaked a guttural groan as her sex gripped his shaft, squeezing it in a steady rhythm. Emboldened by raw, libidinous need, he reached with his good arm to embrace her, but she slipped her arms around him instead and raised him to a sitting position. Pain shot through his shoulder with the sudden motion, but what delicious pain it was, as she wrapped her slender legs about his waist, bracing her heels against his buttocks to support him upright in her arms.

Grinding her vulva against his shaft, she rocked him gently, as they sat coupled face to face. The hardened nub of her clitoris felt like steel as she undulated against him. His cock had never felt so huge, so hard, so captured. Gradually, her undulations slowed then stopped altogether. He could feel the muscles at the epicenter of her sex expand and contract in a steady involuntary flow not unlike the kneading rhythm of her hands upon his chest earlier. He could feel the pulse in his shaft strike a steady tempo also, without moving a muscle. The feeling was intense, like nothing he had ever felt before, as they sat conjoined thus.

"Do not move," she murmured. "Sit perfectly still, my lord."

Lyle did not dare move, for to do so even a hair's breadth would bring him to a shuddering climax. He gazed into her eyes; they held him utterly, pulsating with glints of gold from the fire in a rhythm that matched the pulse beat pounding through her sex. His cock responded until their two pulses beat as one, until he could feel the shuddering waves, and warm wetness of her release.

His chilblains forgotten, he sat perfectly still and let the contractions of her climax bring him to orgasm, milking him of every pearly drop of his seed. He felt it rush into her until it overflowed. Never had he known a release as intense. Their gazes never shifted as the climax took them. His eyes, dilated with desire and the mindless oblivion of orgasm, never left her lovely face. Were those tears he saw misting her shuttered gaze? Was her dimpled chin quivering? Yes. She neither spoke, nor did the tears flow. No sound but a low, throaty purr leaked through her parted lips. It resonated through his body, and his sex responded, leaping to life inside her again, answering some primeval call in that raw feral sound that riddled him like cannon fire so totally he grew hard again.

Ihita slipped one hand behind his neck, and with the other firmly planted over his pounding heart, she eased him back down on the pallet. Then, crouching over him, she lowered her wrists to his chest, fisted her fingers, and began the padding rhythm again. But this time she moved her hips as she kneaded him, grinding her pelvis against the thick root of his penis to the same shuddering meter her tiny fist had reached.

Lyle's skin was running with sweat. The burning had subsided in his hands and feet, though the numbness and tingling remained. The same pulse that throbbed in his cock and vibrated through Ihita's loins was pounding in his shoulder wound. Whatever power linked them spoke with the same voice. Whatever energy it was that quivered in the sexual stream that joined them echoed in his savaged flesh and whispered through his body, igniting every pore with sultry fire.

Groaning, Ihita threw her head back until her long black hair cascaded over her buttocks teasing his rigid thighs. It felt like spun silk, and his pelvis jerked forward, driving his shaft deeper into her. Reaching behind, she gripped the rock-hard thighs. His muscles responded to her touch, and to the sight of her firm round breasts displayed in their perfect fullness by the arch of her slender spine. Lyle sucked in his breath as she began to rock from side to side, undulating in mindless oblivion, her throaty purr striking chords deep inside him, awakening ancestral memories rooted in another lifetime. Something seemed to be calling him, something stirring in his soul that he should recognize, but he couldn't quite part the veil that cloaked the memories. He was foxed on her passion, drunk on her desire. His wound forgotten, but for the pulse beat that now echoed through his whole body, he abandoned himself to her insatiable appetite.

How beautiful she was, with her tawny skin burnished to a golden patina in the hearth light. It picked out the shine in her hair, and the golden gleam in her eyes. It pulsated in the auburn shadows collecting beneath her cheekbones, and outlined the curve of her full bowed lips. He had never seen anything so exquisite. That it was happening seemed the most natural thing in the world, the perfect outcome to a journey back from the brink of the abyss in this cold and unwelcoming place—a celebration of life, ritualistic and fine. He would not question why Divine Providence had literally yanked him from the jaws of death, or why it had awarded him such an exquisite prize. He took the gift. He shut his eyes and let her possess him as no woman had ever possessed him before, totally, claiming his seed, his mortality—his very soul as her own.

Tossing her long mane of dark hair, Ihita crouched over him again, kneading his chest, slippery with sweat, meanwhile nestling her clitoris in the dark thatch of pubic hair at the base of his penis. Grinding it against his sex while she rode the length of his engorged shaft, she raised and lowered herself, keeping time with the padding motion of her hands. Lyle watched the intricacy of her movements, his eyes drawn to the globes of her breasts shuddering with the vibration of her thrusts. It was like watching an exotic harem dancer the way her moves were coordinated.

The tall hardened nipples caught his eyes and held them, inviting his fingers to touch. Working the dark buds between his thumbs and forefingers, he wrenched a high-pitched cry from her throat that resonated in his loins until he could hold back no longer. Once again he felt her sex grip his cock, though this time, she took him like a wild beast, swaying and grinding and thrashing about in carnal abandon, flaying him with her long dark mane, and he cried aloud as the mind-altering climax she wrenched from him drained him of every drop.

Slowly, like a mechanical toy winding down, she lowered

her body over his, though her hands still pawed, and her throat still manufactured spasmodic moans. She crouched steadily lower, until her breasts grazed his chest then finally dropped her head to his shoulder, though her hands continued to knead the broad span of his pectoral muscles. Her gyrations had nearly lulled him to sleep when her cool hand swept across his scorching brow feeling for fever. He was burning up. There was no question that she had "awakened his blood." He could feel it pumping though his veins in a way he never had before. It was as if all his senses had been heightened in the arms of this exquisite creature. He could smell and taste her essence of patchouli and myrrh, laced with the evocative musk of raw sex. It was dizzying, infused with a host of herbs that permeated the steamy air in her cavelike mountain dwelling carved from the exposed strata that walled the pass. He could see the strange golden aura that surrounded her like a mantle, a glittering halo, backlit by the hearth fire. He could feel every pulse in her body, every beat of her heart, every vibration in her breathing as she slid back easing his cock out of her and left the pallet with a serpentine motion that was breathtaking to watch.

Despite the hearth fire, cold rushed at him with her body heat removed. He shivered, and she covered him with a thick quilt that felt weightless and cool against his hot skin, though it warmed him. Padding to a chest beside the door, she snaked out a sheer kirtle that lay folded inside. It was golden in color, embellished with spangles that looked like mirrors to Lyle as he lay in sated bliss devouring the sight of her as she slipped the garment over her head and began to sway before the hearth. He had never seen such a rhythmic creature. She seemed to find the pulse in everything she touched.

The hot blood of fever pounded in his ears as he lay watching her move before the fire. Her swaying became whirling. Her ankle bells rang through the quiet. When had she slipped them on? She seemed to be dancing to the strains of some music she alone could hear, pivoting on her tiny feet as she twirled and spun and slid her hands the length of her body. They lingered on her breasts, her open palms caressing the dusky nipples clearly visible through the fine transparent gauze. Lyle watched beguiled as she thrust her hips and her hands slid lower to stroke the shadow of dark hair showing through over her pubic mound. Her performance seemed like some sort of triumph to Lyle, a glorious celebration. Fascinated, he watched her twirl faster then drop to her knees resting upon her forearms, her fisted fingers padding against the floor the way they had padded his chest as she swayed to the silent music that moved her. Something pinged in his loins reliving the strange sensation those tiny hands had left behind like an indelible mark upon his memory, for it was as if she was doing the same to him even from the distance.

She rose then, like a wisp of smoke rising from the hearth fire, and began to whirl again. Faster and faster she spun, pivoting gracefully on her tiny feet. The motion was making him dizzy, drawing his eyelids down heavy with sleep. Mesmerized, he could almost hear the music she heard. He felt himself spin as she was spinning. It was as if he had risen out of himself and joined the dance as vertigo starred his vision. The last thing he saw was the shimmer of the spangles on her kirtle, glimmering like faerie light as she twirled like a whirling dervish. The last thing he heard was the tinkling of her ankle bells, until suddenly, on the brink of oblivion, the deep, throaty, blood-chilling roar of the snow leopard that had felled him echoed across his memory, and then he saw and heard no more.

2

Dreams came, dark, frightening visions dredged from the shadowy recesses of Lyle's subconscious mind. They had to be; some of what he saw in the nightmares could only be induced by fever, and by pain, to say nothing of the opiate Ihita dosed him with. Juice of the poppy; he could taste it in the bitter dregs of the draught she'd forced through his fever-parched lips. He could smell it on her hand when her cool fingers flitted across his brow feeling for fever now and then. The scent brought visions of a vast red sea of poppy flowers swaying in the wind, just as Ihita had swayed when she danced before the hearth fire. He had seen such a sea of blooms, blood red and golden, for in summer, poppies grew in great profusion in the valleys.

Time was passing; time that he could ill afford to lose. He had suffered worse than the mauling of the snow leopard in battle many times. It was nice to lay nestled warm by the fire and be tended by a beautiful enchantress, but he needed to complete his mission and return to his regiment. Lives could well depend upon it.

Again and again, he relived the attack in his dreams. His

mission was a grave one, too vital to trust to a courier. He was to rendezvous with the captain of the Twelfth Regiment, who was camped on the other side of the mountain pass, and deliver information vital to the campaign. He was carrying critical documents, orders that the two regiments join or face defeat, for an uprising was imminent.

He recalled noting the changing weather pattern when he entered the pass. He'd seen the clouds hanging heavily over the mountaintops, watched them slip steadily lower until the tallest peaks speared the white tufts through. It was a bad sign. Dirty weather was on the way, but he'd thought he could outrun it until the wind picked up and the snow began to swirl down. It came softly at first, but that soon changed.

He'd heard tales of the deadly winters in the Hindu Kush, of the bitter cold and flesh-tearing winds, of the blinding snow that could make a man lose his way, or worse yet, his life. But he was a soldier. Soldiers did their duty, regardless of the weather. How lost could a person get traveling a pass carved out between the mountain peaks?

He could still feel the sting of the bitter, wind-driven snow. It had bitten him sore before the sun set. It was then that he'd realized how easy it was to lose one's way, even cradled in the belly of the great mountains. It had been impossible to continue heading into the blizzard, and he was seeking an unoccupied cave large enough to accommodate him and his horse. There were many such caves formed in the stratum by the elements in that sector, and he was well aware of the possibility that wild animals might have already laid claim to some of them.

The eyes of the great snow leopard were even more vivid in the dream than they had been when the attack actually occurred; large and yellow, glowing with an eerie iridescence in the darkness. There hadn't been time to react before the animal sailed though the whorls of blowing snow and impacted him, driving him out of the saddle into the mounting snowdrifts.

One great paw planted in the middle of his chest, the leopard began to gnaw upon his greatcoat until it had torn a gaping hole in the superfine then the uniform beneath until it reached his flesh. He cried out as, despite his struggling, the creature's enormous fangs sank deep into his shoulder, the pain ripping through his body shockingly sexual. He cried out again as the huge cat let him go then moved in for a second strike, both paws planted on his chest now, kneading what remained of his garments into a hopeless mass of bloody tattered cloth.

Cold stabbed at the bare flesh of his savaged shoulder as the leopard moved back taking fresh aim. Its hot breath puffed in his face as it made its death lunge moving in for the kill and he cried out yet again, bringing Ihita, who was instantly at his side. Lyle's eyes came open to soft semidarkness and her serene face looming over him, no deadly fangs dripping blood—*his* blood, only Ihita gazing down.

Her cool, skilled hands gently probed his wound. The touch of those deft fingers was like a lightning strike, a direct hit to his loins, drenching him with waves of blistering fire, making him hard. He shifted beneath the quilts with the arousal, and she moved back and slipped out of her kirtle. When she threw off the covers and started to climb in beside him, Lyle resisted, attempting to raise himself on the elbow of his good arm.

"No," he murmured. "I have to go. I am behindhand already. You must fetch my clothes and help me to my horse."

Ihita eased him back against the pillows. "The storm still rages," she said. "Your horse fares well in my shelter."

"You do not understand . . . I must away," he insisted, struggling against the tiny hands holding him down. "I am on a mission of great importance. My regiment—"

"Your regiment is just as hindered by the storm," she interrupted. "It will soon pass, and then you will continue on your journey . . . when you have mended, when you have rested enough to sit a horse."

"By then it may be too late."

"There is naught to be done, my lord. There are many predators abroad, and food is scarce in winter. Attempt to continue, smelling of blood as you are, and you invite the ravenous. All is at a standstill until the storm passes, and no one will fault you for the delay. You must let me tend you. Your blood now wakes, but fever still comes and goes. You must let me cool the leopard's fire. Shhh now, you are infected with the passion of the cat. You must let me minister to you . . ."

Lyle groaned as she climbed in alongside and straddled him. Her scent rushed at him. His senses were heightened. Was it the opiate, the intoxicating aroma of herbs permeating the room, or something else, some magic of her own making? Her hands were roaming over his body and he was too enraptured by her touch to care. *Passion of the cat*, what did she mean? He couldn't concentrate on that now, not when those hands were riding up and down his engorged cock in a twisting motion that drove him mad. Stroking him thus from the thick root of his shaft to the mushroom head leaking pre-come, she had set his loins on fire.

What sorcery did this woman possess that she could make his body obey her so completely? It was almost as if they were one entity the way he responded to her every touch. Need and desire went hand in hand in her embrace, as she played him like a fine musical instrument, extracting melodic harmonies from his sex that no one else could hear, and he had never known. But there was music in her ministrations, just as there had been music in her strange erotic dance. He couldn't hear it then, but he could hear it now, in his mind, just as he heard the blood-chilling roar of the great cat. Both were thrumming through his veins as she worked her magic on his sex, and he shut his eyes, for they stung in the herbal infused air, and let her have her way with him.

It was like a dream dredged from the fringes of his opiate

haze, but he knew it was not. She was real enough. Dreams did not have a pulse that beat to the rhythm of his own, nor did they possess juices that flowed, like those laving his shaft now, nor did their sweet breath fan his hot face. And dreams did not knead his chest like a cat padding its mother's belly. This time, her abandon brought out fingernails like claws that scratched, leaving marks on his moist skin. No, this was no dream. Dreams did not draw blood.

Seizing her waist, he raised and lowered her on his shaft as her sex gripped it. His wound forgotten, he rolled her on her back and wrapped her legs around his waist, filling her totally. She felt like liquid silk sheathing his cock. How perfectly they fit together, like two halves of a whole, her essence laving him as he plunged in and out of her in hammering thrusts. The sounds of their coupling alone was driving him to the brink of ecstasy.

Ihita arched her slender body against him, taking him deeper still. His breath caught as she raked her fingernails over his torso, tracing the scratches she'd made there earlier, dragging the long nails lower and going deeper. The old wounds still bled, as did the new, and she rolled him on his back again and laved the blood away with her tongue.

Lyle's hips jolted forward. The soft scraping of her tongue on the scratches resonated in his sex, causing wave upon wave of orgasmic fire loose in his loins. His cock tensed brick hard, the distended veins bulging. He could feel them tighten against the walls of her vagina as she gripped him with it in rhythm with his thrusts. Then the humming began. It was a strange monotone sound from deep in her throat, like the purring of a cat. A glowing iridescence overcame her dilated eyes as she licked him clean of the blood, though the angry scratches remained. Beguiled, he let her take him as she had before, tossing her long dark mane from side to side as she undulated against the root of his sex, taking all of him. Swaying from side to side as she had when she'd danced, she found the secret place inside, and cried aloud grinding her clitoris into the dark hair curling between his thighs until the friction igniting both erogenous spots brought release.

Lyle reached for her breasts, grown taut; the nipples, tall and hard, responded to his touch. He felt her juices as she came— hot silk mingled with the lava flow of his seed as he climaxed with her. It felt as if his bones were melting as she pumped him dry and sat perfectly still so he could feel the palpitating rhythm of their orgasm. It was as if not only their bodies, but their souls had joined.

Lyle drew a ragged breath, embracing her as she eased off his shaft and curled on her side against him. Exertion had made his scratches bleed again, and she raised herself, leaning over him, and sucked the blood clean from them one by one. All the while, the heels of her tiny fisted hands kneaded his side, the throaty purring sound keeping time with his runaway heart.

"Ihita . . ." he murmured, "such a beautiful name. All Hindu names have meanings, so I'm told. What does yours mean?"

She hesitated. "Ihita means *desire*," she said.

Cupping her dimpled chin in his good hand, Lyle reached for her lips. "It suits you," he murmured.

She lowered her mouth to his and closed her eyes. How long her lashes were, sweeping the shadows at the edge of her cheekbones. What color were those exquisite eyes? Why couldn't he remember? All he could recall were the golden eyes of the leopard bearing down upon him.

Plunging her tongue into his mouth, she probed him deeply. She tasted sweet, of honey and herbs, and savory with the salty metallic taste of blood. It aroused him, and he took her again and again as the night wore on, like a man possessed, until dawn lightened the sky and the fire grew cold in the hearth.

There was almost a facet of desperation in her passion. It demanded much under the guise of ministrations. Something primitive, almost bestial lived beneath the surface of her ardor, and yet, she was possessed of a strange childlike quality that defied all else about her. She was a complex creature to be sure, and she had so captivated him that he took a totally unnatural circumstance as perfectly natural, which wasn't like him at all. But nothing mattered then, nothing but her soft supple body, so malleable in his hands, her sweet breath against his skin, and her unflagging stamina in his arms. Never had he known such in the arms of a woman. They moved as one entity.

It was three days before the snow stopped falling. By day, Ihita hovered, nursing his wounds with poultices and unguents, and fighting his fever with herbal draughts and tinctures. By night, she came to his bed. Her strange mountain dwelling, artfully carved out of the side of one of the august peaks, had many chambers. One, he learned, was outfitted as a herbarium. That she lived there alone only piqued his curiosity marginally. She was a woman of few words, but she did tell him she had lived there with her father until he passed, and that she was the healer of her tribe. It was not unusual that such a one live alone, separated from the others; her mystique demanded it.

Lyle had grown steadily stronger by the third day. Though his wound was still bound with an herbal dressing, her doctoring had reduced the angry redness, and her stitches had held despite their vigorous lovemaking.

It was their last night together, and Lyle was loath to leave her, though he knew he must. When she climbed into bed beside him, he took her in his arms.

"You know I must leave in the morning," he said. "They will send a search party after me if I do not return in a timely manner. It would not do for them to catch me out here with you."

"I know," she murmured.

"I don't want to leave you," he confessed. "When I return—"

Her finger across his lips silenced him. "Make no promises

that cannot be kept," she said. "I have taken you inside me. I have tasted your blood. This is a greater bond than you know, my lord. Will you taste mine?"

Lyle stared. What did she mean? He wasn't left long to wonder, for in a blink, she bit down on her lower lip until it bled.

"Taste," she purred. Fisting her hand in his hair, she brought his head down until their mouths met, and groaned as he laved the blood from her lips. "Now, you will carry me wherever you go, and I you, my lord," she said. "In the Gypsy world, we are wed. Roma began here in the east, and such mysteries are known to us since time out of mind. There is much power in the blood, for it is the only truth."

She had not mentioned her heritage before. There was something final in her speaking of it now. It struck a chord deep inside that left a nagging ache behind, and he took her lips again in a deep, searching kiss as if to banish whatever ill omen she had put between them. There was deep sorrow in it.

Ihita melted against him, dissolving into his kiss. Twining her limbs about his naked body she spiraled into another trance-like state of carnal oblivion. Sliding her hand along his shaft, she pumped it with a circular motion, avoiding the rim of the sensitive mushroom tip, only casually grazing it as she stroked him. The neglect was deliberate, causing him to reach toward her flitting fingers. Forcing him to arch his back and thrust his pelvis, anything to call her attention to the head of his throbbing penis as she continued her long, languid caresses.

Just when he could bear no more, Ihita swooped down and took the rock-hard head of his cock in her mouth, laving the ridge with the tip of her tongue. Lyle's heartbeat pounded in his ears in rhythm with the pulsating madness thumping in his rigid member. She had taken him to the point of no return. One swift plunge of those skilled lips along his shaft to the thick root and his loins exploded sooner than he'd wanted, but oh, what ecstasy.

It was deliberate. His cock was slow to go flaccid just as it always was in the arms of this enigmatic sorceress. She knew how to keep him hard. Her fingers roamed over his moist skin. As if they possessed a mind of their own, they sought out every recess, every orifice, driving him to the brink of another orgasm.

Straddling him with her long, shapely legs, she took him deep inside her in painfully slow increments so tantalizing he feared he really would go mad. How he longed to seize her waist, thrust his pelvis and plunge into her in an unstoppable frenzy, but he restrained himself. It was all part of the libidinous ritual their coupling had become. She knew exactly how to make his member live, and he gritted his teeth as the kneading began, the strange feline massaging of his pectoral muscles that drove him wild. Never had he experienced anything as intense as he did in this woman's arms. Her release was more powerful than any thus far. He could feel every orgasmic contraction that seemed to take her out of herself as she took him deeper still.

Lyle held back. He was too stunned by her breathtaking abandon to come. He wanted to savor the sight of her in the throes of climax. How beautiful she was with her head thrown back until her long, lustrous hair swept his thighs. How desirable she was with her pleasure moans coming in the shape of the growl of a contented cat. She shuddered with the last contraction, her sex gripping his cock, and Lyle sucked in his breath as she eased his shaft out of her and slithered along his body, kneading as she went until she reached his hot, hard member. He was on fire for her, his very bones aching for release, and as she began to grind the heels of her hands into his groin beside the root of his sex, his own groans joined the provocative music of their joining.

Leaning forward to watch her, he buried his hands in her hair and massaged her head, holding it down as she took his member in her mouth again, sucking fiercely. The orgasm was riveting as she lightly stroked his sac and ran her fingertips along the inside of his thighs as he came. It wasn't until he fell back exhausted that he realized she'd scratched him again.

He drifted off to sleep then, holding her in his arms. Sated at last, his heartbeat slowed and his breathing sought a calmer level. The desperation in her lovemaking was troublesome, but he was too tired to address it then. She was curled in his arms in her childlike mode. Her hair, spread out wide on the pillow and smelling of patchouli and myrrh, numbed his senses. How could he leave her? But he knew he must.

Morning came all too quickly. Lyle was alone when he woke. Calling Ihita's name at the top of his voice, he struggled to rise. Leaving the nice warm bed that smelled of her, of their lovemaking, was the last thing he wanted to do, but somehow he rose to find his clothes neatly folded on a chest beside the chamber door. They had been artfully mended. He dressed hurriedly, and called her again, but there was no answer. Perhaps she couldn't bear to say good-bye; perhaps it was best. He needed time to think.

Outside, his mount was waiting saddled in the snow, standing bridle down pawing the sugary frosted ground as he approached. Lyle glanced about. There was no sign of Ihita. He didn't call out again. He knew she would not answer. Heaving a ragged sigh, he mounted the horse, and, taking a last look behind him to fix the location, marked by two tall boulders that edged the mountain path, in his mind, he set out to complete his mission.

But to his horror, when he reached the position of the Twelfth Regiment on the other side of the mountain pass, it was to find, by the looks of the tracks in the snow, that they had already left the region. He estimated that they had decamped as soon as the storm stopped. The trail of their departure was hurried, and carried south, no doubt to avoid new weather coming in, for another storm was on the way judging by the heavy slate-colored clouds dusting the mountaintops. That being the case, they were well out of range to be of help, and out of danger. His regiment was on its own. What was needed now was that he make haste and return with that news hoping that the storms had deterred the thugs ready to attack from the foothills long enough for them to come up with a different strategy.

He'd been in the saddle all day. Soon it would be dark, and the new storm was imminent. Turning back, he was heading right into it. His fever was returning, and his shoulder began to pain him, the weight of the fine woolen greatcoat being too heavy rubbing against the wound with the horse's motion. He longed for sight of the mountain dwelling, and the prospect of lying warm and dry in Ihita's welcoming arms until the storm passed as the other had done. When he rounded the bend that showed him the two boulders that marked the rise to her cliff-side dwelling, it wasn't a moment too soon. Fresh snow had begun to sift down, and the wind had picked up. Bending his head into the gusts, he drove the horse relentlessly, but his euphoria was short lived, for though the boulders were there, the mountainside dwelling was not. The ridge rose sheer-faced to the summit, and was glazed over with snow. There was no sign of the dwelling or the path leading to it carved in the side of the mountain, and no sign of Ihita, only the distant echo of a great cat screeching its lament in the darkness riding the wind. It was the last sound Lyle heard as vertigo blurred his vision and he slipped from the saddle, landing hard in the drifted snow.

3

Lyle had the sensation of being dragged through heaps of glacial tundra. Something large and lumbering, white like the snow, peppered with spots of gold and tawny olive brown, had clamped its deadly jaws down upon the hem of his caped great-coat. It was hauling him along in the darkness beneath the full winter moon, its progress making a trench through the drifts of newly fallen snow. *The leopard.* He heard its deep throaty growl, but he couldn't see it. His eyes wouldn't come open more than a crack, no matter how he tried to force them.

The icy stuff beneath his face should have revived him, but it didn't. He groaned, and the sound echoed back in his ears, seeming far away. Still, the great cat lumbered on relentless in its mission, just as Lyle had been in his, until horses loomed up before them. Then, the leopard spat out the tattered remnants of his greatcoat and sprang through the air, a high-pitched screech spilling from its throat. A shot rang out, but the leopard didn't fall. The pistol ball ripped through Lyle's shoulder in-stead, wrenching his eyes open. He vaulted upright in the bed, his broad chest heaving, his skin running with cold sweat.

But it wasn't cold. It wasn't even winter. Across the way the sweet breath of a balmy spring night puffed in at the open bed-chamber window of Lyle's London townhouse. He shook himself like a dog to chase the nightmares that always seemed more urgent when the moon was full and round, and silver-white, like it was now. The scent of patchouli and myrrh lingered in the air, just as it always did after the dreams. They were never exactly the same. This time he had confused his rescue by the scouting party with the leopard attack. Two things in the visions, however, always remained constant: the pain and the beautiful peasant girl who had saved his life.

Absently, he soothed his shoulder wound. It had healed, though the savaged flesh still remained tender for all of Ihita's doctoring. Ihita. She was ever with him, in his thoughts, in his waking and sleeping, in every breath he drew . . . Ihita the exotic enchantress, whose Hindi name meant *desire*.

Lyle climbed out of the bed. He was naked, though he didn't remember stripping. He padded to the window. A shaft of silvery light beaming in from the full moon blasted him like cannon fire. He stared up at the indigo vault. It was early yet, and he was aroused. His thick hardness called his hand to soothe his rigid cock. No. This would not do. He needed the warm, welcoming flesh of a woman to bury his needful member in.

He dressed in haste, collected his horse from the mews, and within the hour found himself upon the East End doorstep of his long time mistress, Lydia March. One rap on the door with the head of his riding crop gained him nothing. He rapped again, more urgently now, and after a moment the door came open in the hand of a bleary-eyed manservant, his green and gold livery and white wig askew. The servant was wearing an odd nonplussed expression as he gaped through the partially open door.

"Well, Phibes, aren't you going to let me in?" Lyle said, impatiently.

"Th-the mistress has retired," the man said. "Did you forget something, my lord?"

"Come, come, man, let me in," Lyle grumbled, pushing past the servant.

"But, my lord . . ."

"Never mind," Lyle said, halfway up the staircase. "No need to announce me. I know the way. Go back to bed, man. I'll see myself out."

Lyle rapped at the first chamber door on the west side of the narrow corridor. He didn't wait for an invitation to enter. He burst into the room to find Lydia in bed. Gazing at him groggily, she raised herself on one elbow, brushing her long coppery mane back from her face. Her voile nightdress had slipped off one shoulder nearly exposing the nipple on one firm, round breast. For a moment, she froze in place as her eyes focused.

"What on earth?" she breathed. "What did you forget, my lord?"

"What are you talking about?" Lyle wondered out loud. "Phibes just asked me the same thing."

"My lord, you just left here little more than an hour ago," she informed him.

Lyle's mind reeled back through recent memory, but he had no recollection of visiting his mistress that night. Strange lapses like this had been occurring since he'd been mustered out. It only seemed to happen during the full moon, but this was the worst. He dared not let on that something untoward was afoot, and he certainly didn't want to look the fool by admitting the obvious. Instead, he removed his beaver hat with a flourish, set it aside on the drum table beside the door along with his riding crop, and strolled toward the bed to embrace the willing flesh he'd evidently just left.

He smiled his most winsome smile, the one that brought out the provocative dimples in his cheeks. "How many times have I told you I'd gotten halfway home and almost returned to you?"

he asked, sinking down on the bed beside her—clothes, boots and all. "I warned you one day this would happen, Lydia; now it has . . ." Sliding her nightshift down the rest of the way, he exposed the nipple fighting the lacy edge to be freed and ran his thumb over the turgid bud. Swooping down, he laved it with his tongue, and she lay back, freeing the other breast to take his kiss, and fisted her hands in his hair to direct his lips there.

"Well, well, you are a caution, my lord," she warbled. "But you could have spared wear and tear on your horse, not to mention poor Phibes, had you just stayed on earlier."

"I could have," Lyle said through a guttural chuckle, "but it wouldn't have been half as exciting, now would it? Why, the whole East End will be buzzing once the servants spread this tale tomorrow. You shall be the envy of all and sundry for having lured the Earl of Blackmoor back to your home and hearth when he'd only just left it. Your powers of seduction will be the stuff of legend. Take care they do not brand you for a witch."

She giggled. He'd pulled it off. A ragged breath of relief relaxed his posture, and he gathered her closer in his arms seeking her lips.

She held him at bay with a firm hand planted on his chest. "Do you mean to have me in your top boots and tails?" she said.

Lyle let her go and surged to his feet, peeling off his togs layer after layer until he stood naked before her, arms akimbo, his hard shaft picked out in bold relief in the moonlight streaming in through the window.

Lydia scrambled to her knees in the bed and raised the nightshift over her head. "Come, my lord," she murmured, reaching toward him. "Ravish me . . . again . . ."

Plunging into carnal escape, Lyle embraced her. Spreading her thighs wide, he sidled between them and urged her legs around his waist, while he palmed her breasts, concentrating upon the tall, rosy nipples. Silken fire raced through his loins as she raised her hips undulating against him.

Lifting her legs until they rested upon his shoulders, Lyle reached beneath her, cupping the globes of her buttocks in his hands, and rocked her back and forth as he filled her. Why didn't she smell of patchouli and myrrh? Why couldn't he feel her release? Courtesans didn't always climax, since they catered to their patron's needs whenever those needs arose, even when they were not so inclined. That was their primary function.

Lydia was a skilled lover. She knew how to please a man. He was the envy of the *ton* for having snared the much sought after Lydia March long before he went off to India with the ill-fated regiment. He'd found her waiting when he was mustered out due to the wound the snow leopard had left in his shoulder, though he'd released her before he left for the Asian tour of duty. Whether or not she'd been chaste in his absence didn't matter. That she welcomed him back with open arms did. Their arrangement was an amiable one. She was discreet and he was respectful. Everyone knew of their alliance, and proprieties for such arrangements demanded a code of ethics that was immutable. The East End house, where she stayed during the Seasons, was hers. Lyle had given her a cottage in Brighton, a handsome carriage, and a generous yearly stipend. There was no question of marriage. That was not a courtesan's role. While they were well suited, they were not in love. They were in lust, and that arrangement suited them both.

All at once Lyle felt ridiculous. What was happening to him? He'd blundered badly, and covered the blunder, but this was not where he wanted to be. He could never go again to that magical place he'd longed for since his return. Now, his cock was submerged in willing flesh, but there was no passion in it, only mechanical moves that stimulated carnal satisfaction. He would come—was on the verge of coming even now—but it was mechanical, nothing more. There was no fire, not spark, no ecstasy, only a plunge into lascivious lust.

Her leg against his shoulder wound had begun to irritate the slow-to-heal tissue, and he shifted position. Rolling with her on his back, he let her control his climax. It was what she did best. Riding him as if he were a thoroughbred stallion in mindless oblivion, she took all of him, her hands splayed out upon his chest. Why weren't they kneading him in rhythm with her motion? Why wasn't she purring like a contented cat? Was he really here earlier, making love to her as he was now? Why couldn't he remember?

The climax came quickly, riddling him with waves of orgasmic fire. Yes, Lydia was a skilled lover, but he'd had more. He wanted more. Would he never again be able to find the sort of passion he'd felt in Ihita's arms? Did she even exist? How could she have existed, and yet . . .

Breathless and spent, Lyle eased Lydia off him and gathered her into his arms. "Thank you, my dear, for indulging my silly whim," he said. "You are gracious as always."

Lydia gazed up at him, her green eyes glazed with what he took to be want of sleep, for he'd interrupted her at that. It had to be. She hadn't climaxed, though she seemed content enough without. "Do you want to talk about it?" she murmured.

Adrenaline surged through him. "Talk about what?" he said, lightly.

"About why you really came back here tonight, my lord," she replied.

He gave her a playful squeeze. "I came back because I simply cannot get enough of you, my dear."

"You are a poor liar."

"All right, the truth," he said buoyantly. "I'm going into my dotage and totally forgot I'd been here earlier. Does that suit?"

She laughed outright. "That, my lord, is insulting," she tittered.

"You wanted truth."

"Could it be that you were checking up on me, my lord?" she asked.

Lyle stiffened against her. Here was a new wrinkle. The thought never entered his mind. That it had entered hers was telling. Could she be cheating on him? Why would such a thing occur to her if she wasn't?

"If I needed to check up on you, I would not be here at all," he returned. "Why would you even ask such a thing?"

She shrugged in his arms. "You haven't been the same since your return, Lyle," she said. "I sense something . . . different in you. It's almost as if you haven't returned at all. You seem so far away, like you are still *there*. Forgive me, but you certainly are not here, no matter how you try to be. What happened to you in India, my lord?"

"I lost my way in the mountains, in a blizzard on the border. I was bloody near devoured by a ferocious snow leopard. I failed in my mission, and in failing cost my regiment bitter defeat and many deaths at the hands of barbarous thugs, not to mention what happened to the search party that came looking for me."

"What did happen to them, my lord?" she probed. "Sometimes the pain of these things is best healed when we talk about them."

Yes, she was the perfect companion. She knew how to soothe and placate and heal and coddle. But she could not relieve the hollow emptiness that losing Ihita had left behind nor could she relieve the guilt over his failure in the Hindu Kush. These were things he would take to his grave. And he could not explain the strangeness that had come over him since his return, either. He could not share what he did not understand himself.

He rubbed his shoulder absently, for it pained him severely of a sudden. The throbbing pulse beat thrumming through the wound had returned. That always seemed to happen at the full moon as well.

"The men who came searching for me were savaged by what could well have been the same leopard that felled me," he said. "One was killed, another lost his leg, and the third was mauled but not so severely that he couldn't get me back to camp. Afterward, he collapsed, but he lived. We were both mustered out together, once the ragtag band we had become finally reached a safe haven."

"What happened to the leopard?"

"I do not know," he said. "They drove it off I think. Shots were fired. The man who saved me swore he hit the beast. Perhaps he did. I never saw it again, though I heard it many times, but that may have been my imagination. I still hear its strange shrill cry in my dreams."

Lydia sighed. "I'm sorry, my lord," she said. "It must have been dreadful for you."

"Why have you never broached the subject before?" he wondered.

"It is hardly my place—even now," she said. "But I see you falling further and further away where I cannot reach you. I thought perhaps if you were to talk about it, it might help to bring you back to me. I miss you, my lord."

"My poor Lydia," he murmured, soothing her gently. Why wasn't her skin burnished to a golden patina? Why weren't the nipples he toyed with as they spoke dusky and dark? Why wasn't her hair like black spun silk? He'd been neglecting his mistress with it all, and it was going to get worse. "I can only beg you to forgive me," he said.

"Will you stay the night?" she murmured seductively, her fingers stroking the length of his shaft.

When those deft fingers approached the head of his cock, and she began tracing the rim with her forefinger, he captured her hand and raised it to his lips. "No, my dear," he said. "I have kept you from your slumber long enough."

"Will you come again tomorrow night, my lord?"

Lyle shook his head. "Not tomorrow, no," he said. "I have an engagement at Astley's Amphitheatre."

"Ah, yes, the Reynolds girl," said Lydia. "I'd almost forgotten."

Though she tried to hide it, there was a touch of pain in her voice, and he gave her a hug before rising. "You knew this would come," he said. "I'm thirty-six years old, Lydia. It's time I get an heir. Our arrangement will not change."

She was silent a pace. "You are contemplating marriage with the Reynolds girl, then," she said at last, answering her own question.

"I've joined the marriage mart, yes," he said, stepping into his breeches. "Whether it is to be Lady Rose Reynolds or another, I cannot say. I've only seen her twice in company. She's pleasant enough, not the argumentative sort, though no raving beauty, but that hardly signifies."

"I've heard the lady is quite well to pass," Lydia said. "I wish you well, my lord."

Lyle straightened up from tugging on his top boots, and took up his superfine frock coat. "She is," he said, "quite well to pass. Lady Jersey made the introduction herself, and you know what a stickler she is."

"Half the *ton* has set their caps at you my lord," Lydia said. Sliding her legs over the side of the bed, she reached for her wrapper.

"Only half?" he said playfully, attempting to make her smile. She obliged him, rising. "No, no, do not get up, my dear, stay," he said. "I shall see myself out. I shall visit you again Thursday week. Meanwhile, you might give some thought to what you will wear to the Cyprian's Ball. It is soon upon us, you know." She brightened at that, and he felt relieved somewhat for having given her something to look forward to before he bowed out for what had evidently been the second time.

He left her then, and rode back in the moonlight through the all but deserted streets to Clarridge House in Mayfair. He

202 / Dawn Thompson

was exhausted, but he would not sleep. The wound in his shoulder was still thrumming an achy steady rhythm that resonated in his sex. Somehow he had no recollection of being at Lydia's earlier. How could that be? What other lapses had occurred that he had no recollection of, and whatever next? He would have no answers tonight, and he dragged himself back to the townhouse to make ready for another day.

4

─────────

Lyle called at the Reynolds's townhouse in Hanover Square in the Clarridge brougham to collect Lady Rose and her Aunt, Lady Cecelia Moore, the following evening. It was balmy and fair under the full, round moon beaming down from the indigo vault studded with stars. So why did the night, so totally opposite, remind him of the snow-swept mountain passes of the Hindu Kush, and Ihita? The answer was simple, everything did. There was no explanation for it. Ihita had possessed the depths of his soul.

Across the way, another dark-haired, brown-eyed lady sat beside her pinch-faced aunt. Rose Reynolds was the picture of innocence ripe for the plucking, demurely avoiding his gaze as was right and proper. Lyle took note of her short-cropped curls styled in the fashion of choice amongst the ladies that Season. It was threaded through with a length of periwinkle blue satin ribbon that matched her embroidered muslin frock. There was no doubt that one could get an heir quite pleasantly upon her, but where was the long silky mane of hair to tease his thighs as she straddled him? Would she even allow such a scandalous position? He doubted it. Would those rosebud lips suck his cock? Not likely. Here sat a woman who would come clothed to her marriage bed, and every bed thereafter, buttoned to the neck in dense homespun stuff. He shuddered imagining it. Yes, one could get an heir upon her, but where would be the pleasure in it? This was why men had mistresses, why he had Lydia, but even his Cyprian's lusty skills paled before the talents of the bewitching Ihita. For Ihita had done more than ignite his loins, she had set fire to his heart, something that no woman before had ever been able to do.

Astley's, the famed London amphitheatre, just east of the Westminster Bridge, was packed with spectators. Lyle had purchased choice, arena-level seats for the performance. Seating Lady Rose and her aunt, he took his place between them, flipping the tails of his superfine frock coat with a flourish.

Lady Rose raised her handkerchief to her nose. "It smells like a stable," she remarked through the fine, lace-edged linen.

Lyle ground out a bemused chuckle. "Well, it is animal acts that we've come to see, my dear," he said.

"Perhaps we should have taken seats in one of the upper levels, my lord," Lady Cecelia said. "We are rather close to the arena. Suppose one of the horses bolts."

Lyle surged to his feet. "If you wish to move, certainly," he said. "But I fear that odors, like heat, rise, my lady . . . and then, I was only being mindful of your rheumatism. There are the stairs to consider . . ."

"No, no," the woman said, waving her fan. "Sit, my lord. It's too late now in any case. Here come the clowns."

Lyle resumed his seat. He was sorry he'd come. Between the insipid Lady Rose and her petulant aunt, it had all the earmarks of being a very dull evening. But he had heard that new animal acts had been engaged. A year ago that wouldn't have interested him, but now, the anticipation of something wild, something primal, set his heart racing.

The clowns were amusing, as were the jugglers that followed the tightrope act. Then came Astley's main attraction, the horses, and the bareback riders with their tall feather plumes and scandalous costumes. Lyle glanced in Lady Rose's direction. She seemed to be having a good time, though she hadn't removed the handkerchief from her nose since they'd taken their seats. It was worse now that the horses were stirring the stale air, spreading their musky odor as they pranced and reared and performed their dressage routines. There was something very erotic about the sleek, shapely animals that set Lyle's heart racing.

He glanced at Lady Rose. No, she was no raving beauty, but her attractiveness was undeniable. The rise and fall of those milk-white breasts challenging her décolleté invited his eyes. His fingers itched to touch, to slip down the low-cut bodice that barely concealed the areola surrounding the nipples he saw straining the muslin, exposing those buds to his gaze. Now and then he caught a glimpse of the puckered rosy flesh. It made him hard.

What was happening to him? He had never lacked control before. A pulse had begun to throb deep inside him—something unstoppable. He didn't want this woman. It wasn't about her. Something feral had risen at his very core. Cold sweat was running over his brow. He'd begun to shake, and he ran his finger inside the edge of his neckcloth. It felt as if it was about to strangle him. Stretching his neck didn't help. His heart had begun to race. Patchouli and myrrh rushed up his nostrils, spreading waves of drenching fire through his loins. He was tight against the seam of his white silk dress pantaloons.

"Is something wrong, my lord?" came Lady Rose's voice muffled behind her handkerchief. "You've gone ghost white of a sudden!"

Lyle opened his mouth to reply, but the horses had left the arena. A team of workmen had swarmed in. They had begun setting up platforms and portable steps, and a ringmaster had strolled to the center of the arena and begun addressing the gathering. When had the horses trotted off? Where was the applause? How could he have missed the applause at their exit? His field of vision was closing in around him. He wanted to surge to his feet and stalk from the amphitheatre, but he dared not rise. The bulge of his thick, curved shaft was clearly visible through the tight-fitting silk pantaloons.

"And so tonight, you have the privilege of seeing something never before seen within these walls," the ringmaster was saying. He swept his arm wide. "I must ask for complete silence, so please no applause. We would not want to frighten the animal. Ladies and gentlemen, it is with great pleasure that I present Trader Alex and his magnificent she-cat!"

All eyes were trained upon the entrance to the arena, where a tall man decked out in top hat and tails was leading a large cat into the circle on a leash. Lyle's scalp drew back. Absently, he reached to soothe his shoulder that had begun to pulse and pain of a sudden. It was a *snow leopard*, its high-pitched cry desperate and shrill.

The she-cat had her back to them as the man led her around the arena counterclockwise. In spite of the ringmaster's warning, an unruly murmur rose from the crowd as Trader Alex paraded the magnificent animal around the perimeter. Many spectators had risen and were scrambling back from the low retaining wall that separated the seating area from the arena floor. Lyle rose also and froze spine-rigid as the leopard came closer, slinking along on the short legs that identified its gender, its long thick tail dragging on the ground. It hadn't seen him yet, but that was short lived. His heart nearly stopped when their gazes met. How beautiful she was, her snowy white coat peppered with tawny olive and cream-colored spots, just like the golden-eyed leopard that had savaged him. Instantly, her tail shot skyward flagging danger.

Her roar was even more riveting as she padded closer, but it
wasn't the acoustics in the arena that heightened the sound.
Ancestral voices were calling. Lyle felt her terror, and her pain.
It was all he could do to keep himself from answering her heart-
wrenching lament.

Lady Rose and her aunt were on their feet now, scrambling
out of the way, while Lyle remained rooted to the spot, unable
to break contact with the golden iridescent eyes that seemed so
human bearing down upon him.

"My lord, come away!" Lady Rose screeched, as the leopard
bared its fangs. She took hold of Lyle's forearm, gripping with
pinching fingers, for, mesmerized by the great cat, he barely
heard.

Lady Cecelia, meanwhile, was pulling the girl in the opposite direction. "Rose!" the woman shrilled. "Left to him we
shall all be savaged. Get back from there. The beast looks about
to spring!"

Lyle glanced down nonplussed at Lady Rose's small soft
hand fisted in his superfine sleeve, as if he had no idea what it
was, or why it was gripping his arm so fiercely. But it was only
a brief glance. Another ear-splitting growl from the leopard
called his eyes back to the animal as it sailed through the air,
over the retaining wall, knocking the unprepared Trader Alex
to the arena floor as it leaped, not toward Lyle, but with dead
aim upon Lady Rose.

Roaring like a leopard himself, Lyle sprang between, slam-
ming into the great cat just in time to spare Lady Rose its powerful jaws, and fell to the floor locked in mortal combat with
the animal, knocking over chairs and tables, and scattering spectators in all directions as pandemonium broke loose in the amphitheatre.

Two gentlemen Lyle did not know were leading Lady Rose
and her aunt away. Lyle could hear the two women's shrieks

above the rest. Lady Rose dug in her heels resisting, and Lyle's strained voice boomed like thunder, as he wrestled with the snarling cat.

"Go!" he charged. "You are in grave danger—graver than you know . . . *Go*, I say! I cannot hold her much longer . . . !"

Sobbing, Lady Rose and her aunt disappeared in the fleeing crowd, as Lyle struggled with the leopard in a desperate attempt to keep it from following. It had all happened so quickly, in just seconds, but it seemed like hours as he wrestled with the leopard. There was a wound in the cat's shoulder. It appeared to have healed fairly recently the way it favored its left side. It had straddled him. Its right paw was planted firmly in the middle of his chest. He could feel its hot breath puffing against his moist skin. Déjà vu hit him like cannon fire, and his mind reeled back to what seemed like another lifetime. Somehow, Lyle felt joined in some way to the great cat. Out of the corner of his eye, he glimpsed several patrons with pistols drawn. They were jigging about trying to get a clear shot at the cat from their distance.

"*No!*" he thundered. "Don't shoot!" As if she'd understood, the leopard leaped off him and bounded over upturned chairs and urns and tables to disappear through an alcove that led to one of the exits.

Shots rang out from behind, and the cry of the cat pierced Lyle's heart. He staggered to his feet and spun toward the sound. "Hold your fire, you gudgeons!" he thundered, bounding over the debris toward the direction of the sound of yet another snarl and breaking glass. He'd nearly reached the alcove, when he stumbled over Trader Alex, cowering under an upturned table. Hauling the man to his feet, he seized him by the front of his frockcoat and shook him none too gently.

"Get up out of there, you nodcock!" he seethed. "Where did you get that cat? Answer me!"

"Lemme go, gov'nor, I ain't done nothin' wrong!"

"The cat, man!" Lyle seethed. "Where did you get it?"

"It come from Asia," the man responded, "from the Hindu Kush mountains. We just come back. Old Astley and that young Mister Ducrow he's thinkin' o' makin' a partner wanted some animals nobody had ever seen for a new act this summer."

"She's got a recent shoulder wound. Did you shoot her? Answer me!" he demanded, shaking the man.

"N-no, gov'nor. Somebody else done that. She was half dead when we found her. We fixed her up and brought her back is all . . . I swear it! Lemme go!"

Lyle shoved him away then, and ran out into the street. Some patrons were still milling about, but most had fled. He ran to the brougham. As he'd hoped, Lady Rose and Lady Cecelia were waiting inside.

"Thank God you're safe," Lady Rose sobbed. "The animal . . . they shot at it, but it got away."

Lyle's shoulder wound was throbbing wildly. His head was reeling, and he was aroused as he had never been before. Was it excitement over what had just occurred, or was it something more, something metaphysical, of an occult nature that had taken hold of his body and his mind? Something bestial and wild had taken possession of his cock—of his thoughts before he'd had a chance to think them—of his very soul. Contemplating that mystery, he could only stand and stare. Whatever it was, he was at its mercy.

Overhead, there wasn't a cloud in the sky, and the full moon shone down upon the chaos, like a paper cutout. Nothing seemed real. Who were these people? What were they doing in his carriage? Why could he feel nothing but the great cat's paw pressing down upon his chest? Why had it aroused him? Why did the touch of that great paw drench him in shocking waves of achy fire?

He could pull no answers from the balmy spring night air. Whatever the strangeness was that had come over him, it was growing steadily worse with each full moon. He would resist.

He would fight it, whatever it was, with his dying breath if needs must, but oh, how he longed to embrace it—to feel such fire as he had never felt except in Ihita's arms. Through the haze of his narrowed vision, Lady Rose's comely face came clear. What could he be thinking?

He dared not trust himself in the young lady's company. Something terrible was roiling inside him, something beyond his control, a strange upheaval in the blood that was shockingly sexual. The physical evidence of that was so pronounced he dared not climb into the coach with the two horrified simpering women for fear of what he might do!

"My ladies, f-forgive me," he faltered. "I . . . I cannot leave as yet. I am . . . detained. I must give account of what has just occurred to the constables, and it is not safe for you to remain here with that animal on the loose. My driver will see you safely home, and I will call upon you tomorrow."

"You are bleeding!" Lady Rose shrilled, nodding toward his hand.

Lyle glanced down. Blood was running over his wrist and down his fingers. He wasn't aware until then that the great cat had scratched him with its long, hooked claws. "It's nothing," he said. "Just a scratch. You had best away." He leaned back addressing his driver. "Take the ladies back to Hanover Square, Benjamin, and see them safely inside."

The coachman nodded, and Lyle stood back as the carriage whip snapped overhead, slicing through the still night air, and the brougham lurched forward, tooling off into the moonlit darkness.

It was a lie, of course. Lyle wasn't detained. The strangeness that had come over him was worsening. What he needed was proof that he wasn't running mad, and warm, welcoming flesh to relieve the throbbing ache in his loins that had him hard against the seam. The lovely Lady Rose Reynolds offered neither of those comforts. It was much too soon in their relationship for thoughts of bed sport. Even if it wasn't, proprieties demanded marriage first, and it was certainly way too soon for that. This was why gentlemen had mistresses, to keep them satisfied and in so doing preserve young ladies chastity until said proprieties eased at the altar, and such intimacies were allowed. Madness.

Right now, Lyle needed proof of his own sanity, and carnal oblivion. There was only one place where he could fulfill those needs, and he waited until the brougham was out of sight to hail a hackney cab and order the driver to take him to the East End, and the modest home of Lydia March.

When the door came open, Lyle pushed past Phibes, all but knocking the servant down, and bounded up the staircase to Lydia's chamber. A brisk knock was all the warning he gave before bursting inside to find Lydia dressed only in a thin voile nightshift pouring water from a pitcher into a basin in preparation for her evening toilette. At sight of him the pitcher slipped from her hands and smashed on the floor in a shower of water and porcelain shards that wrenched a cry from her throat.

"My lord!" she gasped, her eyes snapping between whatever horror he knew must be visible in his gaze, his bulging crotch, and his bloodied hand. "What has happened to you?"

"One of the acts got loose, a snow leopard. It came over the retaining wall. I grappled with it and it . . . scratched me. It's nothing."

She gestured toward the obvious bulge in his pantaloons, her handsome eyebrow raised. "*She* is responsible for that . . . your Lady Rose?" she asked. "Whatever are you doing here, then?"

What could he tell her, that Lady Rose Reynolds had precious little to do with his being tight against the seam, but that wrestling with a magnificent she-cat had made him hard? She would send for the equipage from Bedlam.

"No, not Lady Rose," he gritted out through clenched teeth.

Something was happening deep inside at his very core, something unstoppable building at the epicenter of his sex that would not be denied. "Let us call it circumstance," he added, seizing her in strong arms.

"My lord, your hand!" Lydia cried. "Let me see to it. You are bleeding!"

"The devil take my hand!" he growled, sliding the nightshift down to expose her breasts to the moon glow streaming in through the mullioned panes.

He was like a man possessed, trying to beat back a strangeness that was rapidly taking control of him. It was carnal in nature and there was no doubt that it was somehow linked to the great cat.

Lyle divested Lydia of her nightshift in one sweep. It floated to the floor and puddled at her feet, leaving her naked in his arms. His sense of touch was heightened. The tactile feel of her skin washed him with waves of riveting sensation.

"How masterful we are this evening, my lord," she purred.

"I am not myself this evening," Lyle said. Scooping her up in his arms, he carried her to the four-poster and dropped her in the middle of the feather bed.

"Well, whoever you are, my lord, I am glad to make your acquaintance," she replied.

Lyle pulled off his boots, struggled out of his elegant toilette, and dove in beside her. It was to be a libidinous dive into the carnal oblivion he so desperately needed to prove to himself that the strangeness was all in his imagination.

Panting like a wild beast, he seized her in an unstoppable frenzy, his hands roaming over every inch of her in mindless abandon. Driven by lust and longing, he plunged into her, his passion fueled by her pleasure moans as she matched him thrust for shuddering thrust. Raw need drove him then. There would be no foreplay, no long, drawn out savoring of the moment. She didn't seem to mind as she gripped his cock with the muscles of her vagina in rhythm with his pistoning thrusts.

Climax came quickly, but it brought no relief from the strangeness that had come over him, if anything the phenomenon had heightened. Nor did it leave him sated. No sooner had Lyle collapsed spent and breathless beside Lydia, than the urges began afresh. His cock had scarcely begun to go flaccid, when it grew hard again, inviting her fingers to fondle him. The erection enticed his hand to cup her breast, directing his thumbs to graze her taut nipples. Desire compelled him to tweak, to lightly pinch and nip the rosy buds with his teeth as he took first one and then the other into his mouth.

Lydia twined her arms around his neck and arched her spine, drawing him closer between her spread legs, flattening her breasts against his chest. She was aroused, but she hadn't climaxed, and her hardened nipples, wet from his kisses, were boring into him as he moved against her, grinding his hard shaft along her slit, riding her juices until her breath caught in anticipation of penetration.

He could feel the flutter of her heartbeat through his skin. Why wasn't it racing, thumping, pounding as Ihita's had done? Why wasn't she purring like a contented cat? Lydia's passion was palpable, but it was benign by comparison to what he'd felt in the arms of the Gypsy sorceress of the Hindu Kush. Ihita . . . Was she but a dream, a fever vision brought on by the attack of the leopard that had savaged him? How could she have been? He could still feel her fisted hands kneading his chest, arousing him as he had never been aroused before. He could still feel her pulse beating in rhythm with his own, and hear her low, throaty purr. No, Ihita was no phantom dredged from the depths of his ordeal in the Kush. She was real, and she had spoiled him for any other.

He was about to plunge into Lydia a second time, when a

strange rumbling began deep inside that seemed to claw at his very soul. His skin was running with cold sweat. He'd begun to shake, and searing pain ripped through his shoulder wound, for somehow it held a memory of the flesh-tearing jaws of the great snow leopard that had clamped down upon it, tearing cloth and flesh with its savage jaws.

Moonbeams streaming in through the window lit the bed, shining upon Lydia's flushed face. She was arching herself against him, every pore in her skin, every cell in her body begging for him to seize her raised hips and thrust into her in mindless oblivion. He could feel her anticipation. He could read the urgency for release in her closed eyes and parted lips murmuring expectantly, and hear her frustration in the sound of his name coming from those trembling lips. How they shone in the moonlight.

His rock-hard shaft was grinding against her nether lips, wet with the dew of her juices, its thick root undulating against the hard bud of her clitoris, making her writhe in his arms, groaning, reaching, her whole body begging him to enter her.

Tearing pain ripped through Lyle's body, twisting flesh and expanding tissue in a silver-white streak of blinding light that somehow seemed to take him out of himself. The transformation was so violent that he reached to steady himself with a hand planted firmly between Lydia's trembling breasts. But when he looked down, it wasn't his hand resting there, it was the great paw of a huge cat, and he saw it through the glaring iridescent eyes of a snow leopard.

A high-pitched, ear-piercing roar left his throat in concert with Lydia's blood-chilling scream as she opened her eyes, not to the sight of her handsome lover, but to the hulking shape of a regal snow leopard looming over her, its curved fangs bared and leaking drool.

Strangely Lyle maintained enough of his human intellect in the body of the cat to know he had to flee, and he backed away from Lydia, still screaming beneath him. He was just as aroused as the cat as he had been in his human incarnation, which accounted for much of Lydia's hysteria. The pendulous erection was gargantuan looming over her, thick and red and slick with pre-come; her eyes were riveted to it. The veins in her neck were so distended he feared they would burst. The instincts of cat and man were warring inside him. The bestial dictates of the leopard demanded that he attack with the fangs he'd bared, just as the great cat had attacked him in the Hindu Kush. The last semblance of Lyle Clarridge, meanwhile, was fighting the feral instincts of the beast he'd become whose heart beat in a different rhythm, a savage rhythm unknown to him. Somehow it was exhilarating, which shocked him almost as much as the unexpected transformation from man to beast. Moving in the skin of the great snow leopard charged his body and his mind with unstoppable passion, the like of which he had never known. But he had to get away before Lydia's screams brought the servants, before the cat he had become possessed him completely, before he hurt or killed the hysterical woman, who mercifully seemed about to faint beneath him.

The pain and the trauma and the sheer horror that he'd become a shapeshifter brought a surge of strength unlike anything he could have imagined, and he leaped off the bed, jumped up on the window seat, and crashed through the mullioned panes. In a streak of silvery misplaced energy, he soared through the air, hit the ground running on all fours, and disappeared in the moonlit darkness.

5

In the back of his mind, Lyle recalled that snow leopards only mated in winter. Why then, was he still aroused and on the prowl? Evidently, shapeshifting cats retained some of their human incarnation while in their creature form. He had read of such in a tome that had raised the librarian's eyebrow at the lending library in Bath, but never credited it as being anything more than fantasy. Since his return from the Hindu Kush, he'd gleaned every bit of knowledge available about the snow leopard. This was one bit he wished was myth.

How long would he stay this way? His clothes were in a rumpled heap on the floor in Lydia March's bedchamber. However would he explain that? Her eyes were closed when the transformation occurred. She knew an animal had escaped the amphitheatre and that he'd tangled with it. The best explanation would be that somehow it had followed him, gotten into her cottage and that he'd fled, leading it away. Considering his ordeal in the Hindu Kush, no one could blame him for fleeing. Why, they'd probably brand him a hero for drawing the animal's attention away from Lydia. The worst explanation was too grim to contemplate. Either way, there was no time to dwell on that now. Lydia hadn't been harmed, and she did pass out at the last. He would think of something. It was only beginning to sink in that he was a hunted animal prowling about on all fours as he was.

Pistols were raised against the cat at Astley's. They would surely be hunting it now, a deadly predator loose in the streets of London at the height of the Season. He shuddered, recalling the great cat that had mauled and bitten him in the snow-swept mountain pass of the Hindu Kush. Though the snow leopard was a smaller species than a lion or a tiger, it was certainly as dangerous. He was living proof of that.

All he could think of was reaching Mayfair, and the sanctuary of his townhouse. It never occurred to him that he wouldn't be any safer there than he would be anywhere else in his present incarnation. All of London would be in an uproar hunting the cat. But now there were *two*.

It was still hours before dawn. Keeping to the lesser traveled network of alleys and muses, Lyle padded trough the deserted streets he knew so well, slinking from shadow to shadow. Once, he thought he heard the cry of a cat close by, and once he stopped, certain he'd seen the silhouette of one projected on the façade of a shop front in the moonlight, but it was gone in a blink and he dismissed it as his heightened imagination playing tricks upon him.

Somehow, he reached Hyde Park, but so had the silhouette of his supposed imagination. He stopped in his tracks and raised his head, sniffing the still night air, startled at how his sense of smell was heightened in the body of the cat. His vision was heightened, as well, and his heart skipped its rhythm as he saw the silhouette move, and the she-cat emerge onto the moon-struck mall at the edge of a little copse, where she had evidently been hiding.

A low guttural growl lived in Lyle's throat as the leopard coyly moved toward the wood. It was an invitation. How did he know that? *He* didn't; the cat he had become did. His thickening cock, emerged from its sheath, was on fire, red and moist and at the ready. He could feel the pulse throbbing in it as he padded after the female snow leopard. Would she let him mount her? He was compelled to try.

Fractured shafts of moonlight stabbing through the trees showed her clearly. She had paused, one paw raised, looking over her shoulder, as he approached. It was her injured shoulder, the healed wound indenting her otherwise perfect fur. She was slightly smaller in build than he was, her female legs being shorter, but that by no means diminished her stature. How utterly magnificent she was with her creamy white coat peppered with tawny rosettes, her golden eyes beckoning. The courtship was unmistakable. She was baiting him, teasing, seducing. The female psyche of the cat seemed no different to him that that of the human species. Nor was his prowling maleness any different than the mating ritual of the elite *ton*, when stripped bare of its slavish veneer. How very superfluous all that pomp and protocol, all the fastidious dictates of fashion and the rigors of stiff-necked propriety seemed now, when reduced to the naked passion of two lovers in the moonlight. Animal or human mattered not. The elemental drive, the very chemistry was the same; the universal call of a male to his mate, and the female's headlong plunge toward her completion.

Déjà vu riddled Lyle with gooseflesh again. These strange memory episodes were occurring more frequently with every passing hour. The sight of her took him back to winter in the Hindu Kush and another leopard, the great cat that had savaged him. Was that creature a female as well? He wasn't sure. There hadn't been time to determine its sex as it mauled and clawed and mangled his shoulder. But gazing at the she-cat before him, it was like looking at the selfsame animal, just as it had been when their eyes met at the amphitheatre. Could she know she was looking at the same entity that she'd wrestled with at the arena? It didn't matter; nothing did but that he prowl closer and accept her invitation to join the mating dance.

How odd that he knew the moves, that he knew the ritual. She beckoned, he followed, as she padded deeper into the little grove, her throaty purr guiding him, until at last she stopped and reclined in a little secluded spot on the far side of a bridle path that sidled through the trees. A favorite haunt of horsemen and women during the day, the spot was deserted now, with only the full moon looking down upon them.

Slinking cautiously, for that is how it was done, Lyle circled the she-cat once. Circling again, closer now, he nudged her rump with his broad hind quarters. She roared, changing position to raise her behind, flicking her long, thick tail to tease him with a glimpse of her slit.

Lyle smelled her mating musk. Darkly mysterious, it set his pulse racing as her regal tail spread the scent stirring the air. It was faintly tinged with patchouli and myrrh, but that had to be conjured of his longing. Still, it heightened his lust and drew him nearer, but just when he was set to mount her, she lowered her bottom, denying him entrance. It was all part of the dance, but the cat Lyle had become was impatient. His cock was bursting. He would not be denied for long. Sidling close, he leaned into her, one great paw upon her silky rump and thrust his shaft under her tail.

The she-cat flashed her fangs and growled. *Not yet!* her mind spoke to his. Taken by surprise, Lyle rocked back on his hind legs without penetration, her words echoing across his mind, wrenching a low, throaty warning snarl from his throat. Her voice replied in a similar growl. He watched the cords in her thick, muscular neck expand and the sleek fur ripple and vibrate with the sound. It thrilled him to the core, and his cock extended further still from the white furred skin of its sheath, wet and hard against her side. Could he speak to her thus? If he could and she responded . . .

You tease me? he said, testing the theory.

She purred seductively. *I heighten your pleasure*, she said.

Lyle loosed a bestial roar at that. His cock was ready to explode. He had no patience for games, sexual or otherwise. His throbbing member was engorged to the point of pain, his balls so swollen he could barely walk. He'd been too long aroused, and he had no hands to relieve himself. The female of the species may be the seductress when it came to mating, but it was the male whose rock-hard member ruled the dance.

The she-cat loosed another sound that he likened to a sigh, and raised her rump again ever so slightly. She would concede, but she would make him work for his pleasure in her. Lyle's jaguarlike roar announced his intentions, and he seized her hips with his massive paws, nudged her tail aside and thrust into her. How tight and soft she was inside, like hot silk gripping his cock as she backed into his thrusts. Deep, shuddering plunges filled her as his paws clutched her velvety soft sides. It didn't take much to bring the release his lust demanded, and he roared as his seed rushed out of him filling her to overflowing.

Lyle backed out of her sated at last, though there was another urge he needed to satisfy. There was something strangely familiar about her essence. It was like something remembered from another lifetime, something darkly primeval, like the ancestral voices calling that he'd long suspected. Lyle wasn't sure. This was all so new to him, but he did know he needed to probe it.

I want to taste you, he said, trying the peculiar mind speech again. Was it a strange erotic instinct carried over from his human incarnation, or was it strictly a trait of the cat? Lyle didn't know. Everything was so strange. He could scarcely believe he was prowling the streets and byways of London in the body of a wild snow leopard, mating with another such beast, or that he'd just left his hysterical mistress's bed, where he'd nearly ravished, or ravaged her, depending upon the dictates of the creature he'd become. It was madness, but there it was! Somehow he was *two* entities now. Was the transformation triggered by the full moon? That was when all the strangeness in him seemed to occur of late. Why was it happening? Was it because of the slow-to-heal wound the snow leopard had left behind in his shoulder? Would he return to himself with the dawn? Would he change back and run naked through the streets of London in a mad dash to reach the safety of his Mayfair townhouse unseen?

The one shocking thing was that he actually enjoyed being in the body of the great sleek cat. He thrilled at the power, at the heightened senses. He marveled at the enhanced sexual prowess that let him perform with the raw, bestial maleness and unbridled instincts that had lived dormant inside him, buried beneath the strictures that separated man from beast until now. It was lethal and dangerous, unpredictable and forbidden, a plunge into the mystery of unfettered carnal abandon unknown to man, but commonplace in animals, and he would keep it, no matter the cost.

She hadn't responded to his request, except to purr, and coyly monitor his advances with her humanlike golden eyes. How her gaze thrilled him. His heart had begun to race all over again at her attitude alone.

Well? he spoke up, knowing she'd heard by the tremor in her iridescent gaze. *I want to savor your sweet essence . . .*

The she-cat loosed a guttural snarl. *If you can catch me*, she responded, surging to her feet. Before he could blink, she was off and running deep into the little grove, her huge paw pads dredging up mulch and dead leaves carpeting the forest floor that the caretakers hadn't yet removed. The smell of fresh, sweet earth mingled with the musky residue of death and decay, rushed up Lyle's nostrils exciting him, making him one with nature in a sensual way that he had never experienced before. It was all part of the awakening—an explosion of the senses that played to his repressed primitive nature.

He was after her in a flash, scrambling through the grove, bounding over the bridle path, splashing through the little brook winding among the trees, flinging droplets into the air that sparkled in the moonlight like diamonds raining down.

His legs being longer, he had the advantage, though she was more agile in her sleek, female body, able to fit into places that he could barely scrape through. Lyle's heart was hammering in his chest, thudding against his ribs like the echo of a primeval jungle drum. The thrill of the hunt had charged him with energy he never knew he possessed and something more. It had aroused him again. He'd all but forgotten that half of London was doubtless armed and combing the area for the she-cat that had escaped Astley's Amphitheatre. Nothing mattered but the hunt, the chase, and the prize at the end of it, his gargantuan leopard cock immersed in the warm, tight and welcoming flesh of the she-cat seducing him.

What a sight she was streaking through the night, her sleek coat silvered in the moon glow. She slowed her pace, and he knew it was time. He tackled her, and they rolled playfully among the sculptured hedges along the path. Lyle washed her face with his long, pink tongue, swallowing the contented sound of her low, throaty purring. What a seductress she was. Rolling him over, she began to knead his broad barrel chest with her paws. Déjà vu riveted him again. He welcomed it, anxious to lift the veil that would not part. One thing was clear. The rhythmic pressure of those paws was a direct link to his sex, drenching him in achy heat, blazing a fiery trail that dulled all but the primal tug at his loins that brought his cock free of its sheath.

Rolling her over again, Lyle pinned her on her back and nuzzled her soft, white belly, sliding the length of her until he reached her slit, and began laving it with his tongue. Beneath him, the she-cat turned her head to the side in true feline indifference, though the deep rumble of her heightened purring betrayed her, as her posture did, for she spread her legs wide to his tongue, in a gesture more human than animal.

Lapping at her entrance, Lyle tasted her essence, savoring

her juices. He could not drink his fill. He'd tasted it before, the dusky sweet flavor of her feral musk. This was no ancestral memory, it was much more recent. Her essence was already in him. But how could that be? Was it the same with all cats? Did they all have the same scent? Adrenaline surged through his body, pumping the blood fiercely through his veins. Every sinew in him tightened like fiddle strings.

Are you like me, his mind murmured, *or are you a real cat, knowing no other body?*

All at once she stiffened, then in a blink scrambled out from underneath him and froze, listening, her head raised, her nostrils flared, sniffing the still pre-dawn air. It was nearly first light. Had they frolicked together that long?

Quickly, someone comes! she responded, crashing through the foliage in the direction of the sound he hadn't yet heard. *Stay! I will lead them away . . .*

Lyle regained his balance. *No!* his mind screamed after her. *They will be armed! You will be killed!*

But the she-cat didn't answer. All that met his ears was the shrill, piercing echo of the roar she'd loosed to draw their attention, and he bounded out of the hedges only to freeze before men on horseback carrying torches. A closed horse-drawn wagon followed. There were bars on its sides. His eyes snapping between the horsemen and the sinister looking equipage rolling to a halt just yards away, Lyle started and stopped, trying to gauge his best escape route, but it was no use. It was the torches. His instinctive feline fear of fire ruled him now. He was surrounded, roaring ferociously, swatting at the torches with his great paw. Some of the men had raised their weapons, everything from clubs to pistols to antiquated blunderbusses menaced him, but still his flashing eyes desperately sought a means of escape.

"Hold your fire!" one of the men called out. "Don't shoot! You heard what old Astley said. He wants us to take 'er alive if we can."

"Yeah, well, it ain't his hide bein' put to the hazard, now, is it?" someone else chimed in.

"She's gonna spring, gov'nor!" another man shouted, and a chorus of like-minded opinions followed.

"She's afraid o' the torches," the first man observed. "Close in on 'er." Then to one of the men in the box of the wagon, "Quick, man! Bring the net!"

All at once in his feral haze, Lyle realized they thought he was the she-cat. Praying that she would not cry out and put paid to his efforts to give her time to get away, he stood his ground and let two men cautiously approaching with the net toss it over him. It was stiff and it stung. Instinctively, he resisted, but the men were swarming now. Some had tossed down their torches, and many hands were controlling the net, cinching it tightly around him so that he could not move a muscle as they dragged him along to the waiting wagon. There, several more men waited inside the vehicle to haul him up and lock him inside.

Lyle felt the wagon lurch as the man who had come with the net climbed back up in the box, and the driver's whip set it in motion. They were leaving Hyde Park, and Lyle strained his eyes hoping for some sign of the she-cat, but all was still in the park. She had disappeared, and he drew a ragged breath and lay back in the net. There was no use to struggle. He would only become hopelessly tangled in the mesh. He knew the London streets well. They were taking him back to Astley's. They would put him in a cage, and hopefully not discover that he was a male snow leopard, and not the she-cat they hunted before he had a chance to escape.

The inky midnight sky had just begun to lighten when the wagon rolled to a halt in the mews behind the amphitheatre. Lyle held his breath in anticipation of the barred door falling open and rough hands hauling him out onto the cobblestone street where they would be sure to see that he was no female.

He wasn't sated from his encounter with the she-cat, and his cock was hard and very visible. A low throaty growl rumbled up from deep inside as he waited, but neither happened. The men had begun to argue, and he fell silent to listen.

"You hear that?" one said. "I ain't goin' near that beast till it's dosed with somethin'."

"Well, we can't just leave it here," another responded.

"Why not?" the first man said. "It ain't going nowhere all trussed up like a Christmas goose behind them bars. I ain't riskin' life and limb to haul 'er arse inta that theatre. She can stay right where she is 'till mornin'. Let old Astley sort 'er out. We done our job."

"Still," the other said. "Suppose it gets loose again?"

"How is it goin' ta get loose, you nodcock?" the first man said. "Only a cretin would go near that wagon with the beast inside. Enough! I've got a bottle of Blue Ruin stashed inside. I'd say we all earned a little nip. Leave it! Astley wanted that she-devil. Let him tend her. They don't pay me enough ta mess with no beasties. What say . . . are ya up for getting castaway, or what?"

They said more then, and others chimed in as they moved off toward the rear of the amphitheatre, but Lyle didn't listen. He couldn't believe his good fortune, until the first bleak rays of a foggy dawn broke over the mews, and the pain began again. Searing, blinding pain ripped through his body, twisting him every which way inside the net, as his skin began to stretch. His hard penis felt as if it were about to burst. Bones and muscles, sinew and flesh expanded in a streak of silvery displaced energy. The tender wound in his shoulder was the worst of it, for it had begun to throb and burn as if a thousand torches had ignited the slow-to-heal flesh. And he reached to soothe the scars not with the great paw of the leopard, but with his own trembling human hand instead.

The leopard had vanished, taking the pain with it. It was as if the beast had clawed its way out of him from the inside, wounding more flesh than his shoulder in the process, as if it had rent a tear in his soul. The transformation was shockingly sexual. Every pore in his body tingled, crying for release of the pent-up pressure of randy lust that had made his cock as hard as granite. He was himself again, whoever that was. He did not recognize this Lyle Clarridge. Making matters worse, he remembered all that had happened to him in the body of the great cat. He remembered transforming from man to beast in a mad erotic burst of bestial passion. His mind's eye saw him leaping from Lydia March's bed in the body of the snow leopard. He saw himself crash through her bedchamber window and slink through the shadows of London to the soft, green sanctuary of Hyde Park, and release in the body of the she-cat. She was still out there somewhere. Would they find her? Would they kill her? He had to get free. He had to find her—hide her. He had to do *something*.

It was only then that his fogged brain registered that he was naked, bound in a net in a caged wagon in the amphitheatre muse.

Naked.

How would he explain all this to Lydia? How would he reach the townhouse in broad daylight with no clothes on his back? What would he say to the staff if he did? First, he had to get out of the net and that wagon before the men returned. And now that he had hands instead of paws, he needed to relieve the ache in his bursting penis so he could think clearly again. His erection had not diminished with the transformation. If anything, his hard, throbbing need had become more urgent.

Lyle clawed at the cinched-in net like a man possessed. It was knotted underneath him and it took some maneuvering, but he finally got his hands on the cinch and freed himself in seconds. Scrambling out of the tangled mesh, he surged to his feet and grabbed the barred wagon door, pulling on it with all his strength, but it was locked and he groaned, raking his hair back ruthlessly.

As he reached to soothe his rigid penis, his hips jerked forward. What had been a nagging need had become an unstoppable demand. His fingers tightened around the sensitive circumference of his shaft. He could feel the distended veins and the hot blood pounding through them. His loins ached for release, and he leaned into the hand pumping him with a twisting motion from the thick root of his erection to the rim of the mushroom tip, leaking pre-come.

Soft, low moans spilled from his throat in orgasmic spasms. There was something powerfully erotic about standing naked in the first light of day in a public place, where folk were already stirring. That alone brought him to the brink. Out of the corner of his eye, he saw someone moving across the mews; a woman. She was robed from head to foot in a garment that resembled the saris the Hindu women wore; hardly an uncommon sight in Town. She was carrying a bundle of what appeared to be her morning washing. Sight of her only hastened his need. Glancing down through eyes hooded with the undeniable urgency of carnal abandon, he watched his member release his seed in long, shuddering spurts as his body stiffened against the quick deep thrusts.

He cursed and gave thanks for his heightened carnal prowess in one breath. It had been thus since the winter, and the leopard attack, his need growing steadily more urgent with each full moon. *Whatever next?* he wondered. He was fast becoming a sexual glutton. But release brought no relief for the condition. He had just come, and he was growing hard again. Memories of Ihita had tugged at the sexual stream roiling in him like a tempestuous sea since the Hindu Kush, but now—oh, *now*, those images were all tangled into memories of a different kind, visions of the rock-hard penis of his leopard incarnation plunging into the hot, musky sex of the she-cat. He had entered the forbidden realm of the animal kingdom and learned of pleasures unknown to mankind. He had become the beast, become one with its psyche, and taken the raw, feral pleasures of its genus. As scandalous as that was, he would know again those pleasures no matter the cost.

The sound of a key turning in the lock at his back dissolved those thoughts, and he spun to face the barred door falling open with a grinding rasp that set his teeth on edge. It was the woman in Hindu garb he'd just seen crossing the mews that had set him free, and he quickly covered his risen penis with both hands as she thrust her bundle toward him.

"Take these and go quickly," she murmured huskily, her words muffled behind a veil of aubergine silk flecked with threads of gold that covered all but her golden brown eyes. They were nearly dilated black and glowing with an iridescent shimmer in the misty sunlight. "Do not dress here. There is a little mall with foliage in the square just south of Westminister Bridge. Hurry, before others come."

Lyle knew it well. He took the bundle. It held a pair of buckskin breeches, a cambric shirt, and a pair of worn top boots.

"Who are you, my lady?" Lyle asked, fingering the clothes still warm with someone's body heat. "Where did you get these?"

"*Go* I say!" she charged. "Before the drunkards I stole those things from come seeking them."

She moved off then, and Lyle climbed out of the wagon and started to follow her. "Wait!" he called. "What is your name? Why are you doing this?"

"Come to the park an hour before the sun sets, and all will be made clear to you," she called, disappearing around the corner where the muse met the thoroughfare.

"Wait!" Lyle called out. "What park, my lady?"

You know what park, a soft voice said ghosting across his mind. And then it said no more.

6

Phibes hesitated before admitting Lyle at the March cottage. Even at that, it took Lydia's frosty voice drifting down the staircase charging him to stand aside before the rattled servant let Lyle enter. Saying no more, Lydia turned her back and floated into her bedchamber, her diaphanous peach voile night-dress and wrapper spread wide. Lyle squared his posture and followed. In that moment he would rather have faced the ravenous snow leopard that had savaged him and begun it all, than suffer an interview with Lydia March after what had gone before. But he would do what needs must to set things to rights with his longtime mistress. Here was what separated man from beast, Lyle thought, and never more than now did he wish he was in his other body, where passion ruled and such protocols held no sway.

The broken glass had been cleared away inside Lydia's chamber, and Lyle's clothes had been rescued from the debris and folded neatly on a chaise lounge. Lydia nodded toward them. "You'd best put those on," she said. "You can hardly go about as you are. Wherever did you get such shabby togs?"

"I stole them," Lyle said. "It was better than going about naked."

"What happened here last night, Lyle?" she asked. "How did that cat get in here, and how could you leave me alone with it?" He reached to embrace her and she sidestepped his advance. "Oh, no," she said. "That won't do this time. You owe me an explanation. Well? I'm waiting . . ."

Lyle hesitated. He wasn't a good liar, and it took a moment to pick out some truths to base the lies upon. He had no choice. He couldn't tell her the truth entire. She would never believe it. Evidently, she wasn't sure what had happened, and that was to his advantage.

"That is why I am here," Lyle said. "I'd have come sooner, but I could hardly parade through the streets of London in the altogether."

"Hardly."

"Um, well, at any rate, I told you an animal escaped from Astley's. I tangled with it and it scratched my hand. You saw the blood. It must have followed me here. The scent of blood drives such beasts mad. I do not know how it got in. All at once it came charging into the room. You fainted, and when I tried to lead it away it drove me through that window and chased me clear to Hyde Park before men from Astley's bearing torches captured it." It was as close to the truth as he was prepared to go, and he held his breath hoping she would accept it.

"Why didn't you return afterward? You left me unconscious, Lyle! How could you have?"

"You would have preferred that I present myself naked upon your doorstep in the light of day?" Lyle said, indignant. "You screamed the house down before you fainted. I was confident that your servants would see to your needs. My concern was leading that beast away, and togs do not grow on trees, m'dear. Believe me when I say that I have seen the seamy side of every alley in Town looking for a castaway gudgeon willing to part with his finery. Now, enough! Will you let me make it up to you? Though I do not for the life of me know why I should be apologizing for saving your life. I did lead the beast away, after all. We have unfinished business between us, as I recall. Will you let me finish what I started before this unfortunate situation interrupted us?"

"Not like that," she said, yanking the bell pull. "You'll have a bath first. I draw the line at having the 'seamy side of every alley in Town' in my bed, sir."

The prospect of submerging himself in the French porcelain tub in the privacy of Lydia's dressing room was more than he deserved, but he eagerly accepted, sinking to his neck in water fragranced with rosemary and lavender. He'd thought Phibes would play valet as he always had done in the past, but that was not the case. It was Lydia who entered bearing his favorite coconut soap, several vials of precious oils, and sea sponges on a silver salver.

She was wearing her peach voile wrapper, but now she wore no nightshift underneath. It gapped in front, barely covering her nipples, which she had rouged like a tart to enhance their color just as she always did when they played out their fantasies in bed. His eyes slid the length of her. She had shaved off her pubic hair, and her slit was clearly visible. So this was how it was to be.

She sauntered closer. "I don't know what you've gotten up to romping about naked through the London streets, my lord," she said, "but when I'm through with your toilette this morning, you will know you need not venture past my bedroom door to seek your pleasures."

"Is that what you think?" he ground out through a dry chuckle. "Lydia, you know me better than that."

She dropped the sponges into the tub, opened one of the oil bottles, and began lightly massaging the fragrant oil into his shoulders. It had a woodsy scent that smelled of rosemary and pine.

"I do not know you at all of late," she said, working the oil into his muscles. "You are like a different person since you've come home from India. Your . . . appetites have changed. It is as if you cannot get your fill of carnal pleasure." That was certainly true, but she didn't give him a chance to defend himself, as she rubbed the oil into his neck. "You scarcely come before you are ready to come again, and I find myself competing with whatever ghost has possessed you in a mad rush to be the one who satisfies you. I certainly have not been that person since you are come home, and quite frankly I am feeling . . . unsatisfactory."

"That is ridiculous," he said at last. Arresting her hand, he pulled her close and kissed her tenderly. "Lydia, I *am* different since India, I shan't deny it. What man wouldn't be after being savaged as I was out there, and I apologize if you've thought my strangeness was your fault in any way; it is most definitely not. You are an excellent lover."

"What is it, then?"

"I think what has occurred in me is that the ordeal made me face my mortality. It is as if I must drink in every last drop of life in order to beat back the death I nearly suffered in the Kush. When one comes that close . . . well one wants to live one's life to the fullest, if that makes any sense to you. It in no way reflects upon you, and I am happy that we are having this conversation. I had no idea such daft thoughts were knocking around in that pretty head of yours."

She laid a finger across his lips then, and wriggled out of her wrapper until it puddled at her feet. "You need to find yourself, I think," she murmured. "I would like to help you do that, but I cannot. It is something you must do on your own, and so I am going to make love to you in ways that I have not ever done before . . . to give you something to remember me by. No! Do not speak," she quickly said, for he had opened his mouth to do just that. "Let me finish, Lyle. Afterward, you will leave, and I do not want you to return until you can do so without this mad rush to carnal lust that makes me feel inadequate. I want my old Lyle back or no Lyle at all."

He held his piece. She was right, of course. Love and future were never part of their bargain, but in his present state, he was robbing her of what little remained of their relationship. He owed her more of himself than he was able to give. Silence was the only answer to that.

Lydia didn't seem to expect an answer. She set the vial of oil aside on the drop leaf table alongside the tub, and took up the other bottle. Lyle looked on as she poured several drops of oil on her fingertips, and he sucked in his breath as she plunged her hands into the warm soapy water and massaged the oil into his penis, bringing him to a hot full arousal. It had a light floral scent unfamiliar to him, evocative enough to pique his curiosity.

"What is that?" he breathed. "I do not know its scent."

"It is what the Turkish people call *salep*, an oil made of the roots and flowers of the early purple orchid. The Persians grind the root and mix it with honey and milk to be drunk for enhanced sexual prowess, but we have no time for that. The light-skirts use it thus"—she gave his penis a long, swirling tug, while working the oil into his shaft—"to get its benefits more quickly."

Lyle's cock was on fire, but then it had been since the moon waxed full, come to that. "We hardly need the stuff," he observed, thinking out loud.

Lydia smiled, handing him the bottle. His hands were trembling and he almost spilled it. "Be careful!" she cried, shooting her hand out underneath the threatened vial. "It comes too dear to squander, my lord. Now then, put some on your fingers and massage me as I have massaged you."

Lyle did as she bade him and rubbed the oil along the curve of her slit.

"Deeper," she purred, parting her legs a little.

Lyle slipped two fingers inside her, mixing the oil on his fingers with the cream of her juices. How wonderfully soft she was inside. She felt like hot silk against his roughened skin. He could feel the walls of her vagina contract, squeezing his fingers, and he shifted in the tub as his loins responded, soothing his penis with his free hand. It was an autoerotic response. The oil she had massaged into his shaft had made it tingle and burn with a pleasant throbbing heat. It had intensified his arousal tenfold.

A soft smile lifted the corners of Lydia's lips. "Slowly, my lord," she murmured. "Or you will come too soon. *Salep* is a powerful sexual stimulant."

"Have we not just established that my not needing such a stimulant is at the root of our difficulty?" Lyle queried. "Why would you want to make matters worse?"

"Not worse, my lord," Lydia purred. "I want you to remember this . . . and me. *I* wish to be your stimulant this time, not some outside influence. Indulge me, my lord, this one last time . . ."

Was this their swan song? Evidently, though she'd veiled it nicely. Lydia was no fool. She had pinpointed when the change in him had begun, and sensed that somehow there was another woman involved, maybe no longer in the physical sense, but she, too, was a woman and a woman always knows, he'd learned from experience. It was part of the feminine mystique. She was competing with a ghost of the Hindu Kush, and she knew she had lost the fight. So she would give him her all at the last in hopes that one day *her* ghost would haunt him as well.

Taking up a sea sponge, Lydia worked up a rich, creamy lather with the cocoanut soap and began slathering it over his shoulders, his arms, and chest in slow, concentric circles, lingering upon his nipples. The velvety soft lather spread by the rough-textured pores of the sea sponge set his loins on fire, wrenching another moan from his lips. She had learned well how to please him over time, but that was just it, Lydia had to learn. Ihita *knew*. Instinctively, his little Hindu sorceress had pleasured him beyond his wildest expectations. Why had she left him? Why had she ignited passions in him that he didn't know existed—spoiled him for any other, and then abandoned him?

"Stand, my lord," Lydia murmured, jolting him out of his reverie.

Lyle surged to his feet. Steamy water and soapsuds slid down his body like a waterfall, the droplets tinkling musically as they rushed back into the tub. He glanced down at his erect cock. Rivulets of soapy water were running over the distended veins and mushroom tip, collecting along the rim, and in his pubic hair. The soft caress of the soapy water rushing over sensitive flesh riddled him with drenching fire. As if she knew, Lydia loaded the sponge with more water and cocoanut soap and squeezed it over his shaft. The woman was diabolical!

Lyle's loins clenched and his hips bucked forward. His hand itched to seize his throbbing penis and relieve himself. It was all he could do to keep his fingers from acting upon the fantasy that had gripped his brain. He longed to feel the rough surface of the sponge grinding into his groin, scraping against the tender skin of his shaft, but she stroked him with it in the maddening circular rhythm just short of touching the thick, curved length of his cock. Excruciating ecstasy.

When she soaped the sponge again and began to massage his buttocks, they tightened and he groaned. "You are driving me mad!" he said.

"Shhh," she cautioned. "Soon you will have a chance to do the same to me." A long, agonized groan poured from his throat at that prospect, and she laughed, soaping his rigid thighs.

Lyle had avoided looking at her in all her naked glory as she lathered him. The way her breasts trembled when she worked the sponge made him long to cup the globes in his soapy hands and feed upon the hard rosy nipples. The rouge she'd applied picked out the large puckered areola. His hands worked in and out of fists at his sides at the prospect of acting upon the urges riddling him then. Try as he would to ignore it, her shaved pubic mound and hairless slit glistening with the oil he'd spread there drew his eyes and held them despite his resolve.

Something began to rumble deep inside him, something feral. A raw serge of bestial energy threatened to bring out the animal that lived just under the surface of the skin she was caressing. Could it happen in the daytime? He prayed not as he fought to suppress a deep, feline roar.

Lydia handed him the soap, climbed into the tub, and stood before him. Releasing the lather from the sponge, she plunged it beneath the surface frosted with soapsuds into the clear water beneath and began squeezing it over his body from the neck down, rinsing all the soap away, until his flushed skin gleamed, burnished to a slick patina.

She handed him the sponge. "Now then," she said, holding her hair up out of the way, "do the same to me."

Lyle soaped the sponge and began massaging her shoulders, paying particular attention to the provocative notch at the base of her throat that defined her collarbone. Taking the circular revolutions lower, he approached her breasts, concentrating upon their fullness, while avoiding the nipples that had grown tall and hard as the sponge approached. Two could play at this game. She was an excellent teacher.

When she began to writhe closer to the sponge, Lyle shook his head, what he hoped was his most fiendish leer fixed in place. "Ah, ah, my lady," he said. "It is my turn to torture now."

Lyle wondered if she was contemplating how the rough-textured sponge would feel rubbing against her hardened nubbins just as he had fantasized it scraping against his penis. No. Aside from squeezing rivulets of soapy water over those rosy buds, he would not make this any easier on her than she was making it on him. He would make her wait, just as she made him wait, and then the climax would be all the sweeter.

Leaving her breasts, Lyle soaped the sponge again and took her measure. She was still holding her long hair up with both hands, and he began soaping her sides in long, languishing strokes that made her moan. Then bringing the sponge in front, he concentrated upon her navel, and slowly lowered the sponge to her hips and belly, avoiding the hairless slit that leaned toward him begging to be touched. Instead he soaped her thighs then spun her facing away to do her back.

Lydia's breath caught as he turned her from him and began inching down her back with the loaded sponge. He watched the soapsuds trickle down her spine, welling in the dimples at the base of it, watched it run into the fissure that separated the rounds of her buttocks, watched her shudder as the little soapy rivers dripped down underneath her clenched behind and cascaded over the back of her legs.

Lyle could bear no more. The physical pain in his penis aching for release was driving him mad. Rinsing the sponge deep in the tub, he squeezed clear water the length of her again and again, until all the soapsuds had floated away from the pink skin beneath. Raking her with eyes dilated with desire, he tossed down the sponge and climbed out of the tub. Then, seizing her about the waist, he lifted her out and onto his erection in one swift motion that wrenched a cry from her lips.

Wrapping her legs around his middle, he danced over the towels she had laid beside the tub with her impaled upon his member in an unstoppable frenzy. Slip sliding over the parquetry to the chaise lounge across the way, he fell upon her, raising her legs as he hammered into her in the total aberration of mindless oblivion.

Lydia matched him thrust for thrust, grinding her body against his, the heat of their coupling enhanced by the oil riddling him with pulsating spurts of searing fire. It was as if she had engulfed him in flames, and like the proverbial moth he could not resist those flames, though they threatened to consume him.

The climax was riveting. He could feel her release through the friction and the pain and the throbbing rush of his seed. He swallowed her moan with a hungry mouth, his tongue tasting her deeply, and she arched herself against him, milking him of every last drop of his come.

Lyle's heart was shuddering in his breast. It seemed like two hearts beating inside him instead of one, for the heart of the great cat lived just under the surface of his human incarnation waiting for the moon to set it free.

Panting heavily, Lyle leaned back and looked Lydia in the eyes. Why weren't they darkly golden? Why didn't she smell of patchouli and myrrh? Yes, they were well matched, but in lust, not love. Still he smiled, and said playfully, "Am I now fit for the forbidden sanctuary of your bed, my lady?"

Lydia smiled sadly. "No, my lord," she said. "Now, we say good-bye."

7

_____

It was still some time before his assignation with the strange woman who had freed him from the wagon in the mews. The evening had ended badly all around, and he'd decided not to pursue a relationship with the milk-and-water miss, Rose Reynolds, after all. He had no control over the strangeness that had come over him. He had no idea where it would take him. He'd seen Lady Rose's reaction to the snow leopard at Astley's. He couldn't imagine her reaction if he were to transform into the cat before her very eyes. He wouldn't subject her to such as that, or any woman. Besides, even if the transformations could be controlled, it would take years to get the shy little mouse anywhere near the level of sensuality he'd enjoyed with Lydia March. And he couldn't imagine the prim and proper Lady Rose ever being able to compare with Ihita in his bed, nor was he willing to put his patience to the test chancing it. There was no substitute for love, or the passion of the soul that went with it.

The winds of change were blowing him every which way now. Was he man, or beast, or was he both, and how long would it last? Only time would tell. Meanwhile, he knew what he had to do to put things to rights if such a thing were possible. He needed to take his dilemma back to the place where it had all begun to find his answers. No matter the outcome, the fact remained that above all else he was still a gentleman. He at least owed a courtesy call at the Reynolds's townhouse in Hanover Square, and he had Benjamin drive him around in the brougham just after nuncheon.

One of the Reynolds's footmen took his beaver hat and walking stick and showed him into the parlor to wait. Lyle felt awkward sitting. He began to pace, his hands clasped beneath the tails of his indigo superfine frock coat. His skin had begun to crawl with impatience. He was going to make an end to something that had really never even begun, and he feared he'd do it badly, because he could hardly tell the truth. He wasn't even sure what the truth was anymore.

He wasn't left long to agonize over it. Presently, Lady Rose entered with her aunt, Lady Cecelia, and they took their seats. Lady Rose, though cordial in her greeting, seemed aloof, her face as gray and dour as the demure dove-gray muslin frock she wore buttoned up to her chin. Lady Cecelia's demeanor was not so benign. Traces of anger and annoyance creased her wrinkled lips and flashed in her dull gray eyes. Yes, he'd made the right decision. They were not right for each other. It would be cruel to mislead the girl with false hope.

"Thank you for receiving me, ladies," Lyle began, still standing. "I needed to see how you fare after the shocking events of last evening. I am relieved that you are both unharmed."

Lady Rose opened her mouth to speak, but it was her aunt's voice that broke the awkward silence. "My lord, I have to say I find your conduct of last evening quite shocking," Lady Cecelia said. "Sending us home in your carriage unescorted, with that animal loose in the streets, indeed! And when the beast attacked, allowing perfect strangers to remove us to safety while you engaged that cat. One would have thought your exhibition was part of the entertainment, it was that bizarre. We were quite scandalized."

"I am sorry to have offended your ladyships," Lyle returned. "But you weren't unescorted. You had Benjamin, my most trusted servant, at your disposal. I put myself between you two and the cat to spare you a mauling. The creature sprang at Lady Rose, and would have savaged her just as one like it savaged me in the Hindu Kush last winter if I hadn't intervened. I didn't see anyone else willing to rise to the occasion. If you felt my actions too cavalier, I do apologize." That was the second apology he'd made for saving a woman's life in the space of a day. *Whatever next?* he thought.

"No," Lady Rose spoke up, casting daggers in Lady Cecelia's direction. "You must excuse my aunt. The excitement was too much for her. John Esterbrooke, one of the young gentlemen who saw us to safety, called earlier with news that the cat had been captured, only to escape again. It is all most unsettling." She rose to her feet. "But enough about that. Please make yourself comfortable. I shall ring for refreshments."

"No, my lady," Lyle spoke up. It was the most initiative she'd shown since he made her acquaintance, and that relieved him somewhat, since he'd evidently had a hand in bringing that spirit to the fore. "Please don't trouble yourself. I haven't time. I am called away, you see. I'll be going abroad, and I have much to do beforehand. I just wanted to pay my respects and see that you fare well before I sail."

"A sea voyage?" Lady Rose cried. "Is that safe in wartime?"

"It is necessary, my lady," Lyle replied, the sober tone of his voice implying lines to be read between. "I shall be gone for some time, I'm afraid."

"But you *will* return?" Lady Rose urged.

"For pity sake, Rose, don't grovel!" Lady Cecelia spoke up. "Can you not see what the man is saying? Do not abase yourself. Let him go."

"My lady," Lyle said, presuming to raise Lady Rose's hand to his lips, for she hadn't offered it. "If my situation were different, if I could give you a promise . . . but since circumstances beyond my control are such that I cannot, I must take my leave. Please accept my sincere good wishes for you and yours in future. And now, I'm afraid you must excuse me."

He concluded with a heel-clicking bow, and left them, though Lady's Rose's sobs echoed after him along the narrow corridor outside. "Now look what you've done, Aunt Cecelia!" she wailed. "I hope you're satisfied. I've lost him!"

Lyle felt freer than he had since India as he rode into Hyde Park an hour before sunset. He'd almost decided not to come, since he'd already made up his mind as to what he must do, but curiosity got the better of him, and he reached the little secluded spot among the trees on the far side of the bridle path to wait.

The park was all but deserted. He imagined it would be, with the cat still on the loose. By the time he reached what he presumed to be the trysting place, since it was familiar ground and the most secluded option, there wasn't a soul in sight.

Tethering his mount to a young sapling, he reclined on a moss-covered spot in much the same attitude as he had in the body of the snow leopard the night before. He didn't have long to wait. He had scarcely settled himself resting on one elbow amid the ferns, when the sound of soft footfalls disturbing the brush called him to his feet again, his eyes peeled in the direction of the sound.

When she stepped out from behind the trees his heart skipped its rhythm. She was robed as she had been that morning, from head to toe in aubergine silk spangled with gold, her eyes—the only part of her visible—dilated black in the eerie green darkness of the little copse. She looked like a specter risen from the mist that had begun ghosting over the ground as night approached after the heat of the day.

She floated closer in a cloud of patchouli and myrrh, her feet making no sound. Lyle couldn't speak. His eyes had to be playing tricks on him. She was near enough to touch, and he reached with trembling fingers and removed the veil concealing her face.

For a moment he froze where he stood, gazing into the golden eyes of his fantasy come to life, for he had lived this moment waking and sleeping a thousand times over since his return from the Hindu Kush.

"Y-you," he murmured. "How is this possible? Are you spirit? So many times I have dreamed this moment. Tell me this is not just another of those dreams."

Ihita smiled sadly. "Before this night is done, my lord, you may well believe it is a nightmare."

Lyle slid the rest of her headdress down, exposing her long dark hair. He fingered it, appraising its texture. Raising a lock of it to his nose, he breathed in its exotic fragrance. "You *are* real!" he cried, seizing her in such a powerful embrace that her knees buckled and she melted against him, her parted lips eager for his kiss.

How warm and soft she was in his arms, clinging to him as if her very life depended upon it. He deepened the kiss and tasted her deeply, swallowing the moan rumbling in her throat as he crushed her closer still.

After a moment, he leaned back and met her gaze, her honey sweetness living on his tongue, his hooded eyes devouring her. "How have you come here?" he asked. "I returned to your dwelling after I completed my mission, but it wasn't there. It had . . . vanished. And now I find you here. What kind of sorcery is this?"

"You call it sorcery. Perhaps it is," she responded. "My dwelling did not vanish, my lord. I have the power to cloak, and to cloud men's minds from seeing what I do not wish them to see. The Orient is full of mysteries. You have happened upon one of them."

"Why did you hide yourself from me?"

She shrugged. "I had no right to you, my lord. It was best to let you go."

"And now?" he urged. "Why have you helped me? Why have you let me see you *now*?"

"Because now, my lord, we are equals, and you have the right to choose."

"I do not understand," Lyle said, nonplussed.

"Before the night is out, you will," she said, meeting his gaze as she slid the sari cloth down, exposing the midriff-bearing bodice underneath.

"But how are you here?" Lyle persisted. "How is it possible?"

"Patience, my lord," she said. "You will soon have your answers."

Handing him the loose length of the sari, she pivoted upon her dainty toes and spun away unwinding the silk. Lyle gathered the cloth as her spiral dance shed it until she stood before him wearing only the bodice and long underslip into which the sari had been tucked. He set the silk on a clump of bracken, but when she reached to open the bodice, he rushed to her side.

"We cannot. Not here," he said. "Someone might see us."

Ihita smiled. "No one will see," she said. "We are quite alone in the park, my lord. Everyone has fled, anxious to be away before dark. They fear the cat, for it is still at large."

"And what of those that hunt the cat?" Lyle said, taking her in his arms. It was a valid question, but her answer didn't matter. He was hard against the seam and the possibility that they might be caught naked in the act of coitus only heaped fuel on the fire already burning in his loins.

She laid a finger across his lips. "Shhh," she purred. "There are two cats, and neither will be caught this night. You must trust me, my lord. There isn't much time. Soon the sun will set, and all will be made clear to you."

Lyle needed no persuasion. He helped her shed her bodice and underslip, and pulled down the flap of his breeches, exposing his thick, hard shaft. But when he pulled her to him, she resisted.

"You must strip naked, my lord," she said.

Lyle stared. "I have waited so long for this moment," he said. "I still do not know if you are real, or a figment of my imagination, for I have conjured you to my bed on many a lonely night, Ihita. I fear that if I let you go—even to shed my clothes—you will disappear again."

"I give you my word that I will not," she assured him. "Please, my lord, I have my reasons. Humor me."

Lyle stripped of his boots, and then the rest of his clothes, his eyes riveted to her as he tore the garments away and tossed them down like a madman, for he half expected her to vanish before his very eyes despite her promise.

Shed of all restraints, they came together in a volatile embrace as charged with pent-up power as a lightning strike. Energy arced and spat about them in a shower of crackling cosmic fire that spread its aura far and wide as they clung to each other in a paroxysm of carnal abandon.

Trailing ropes of mist tethered them. Gentle breezes spreading the scents of spring whispered against their moist skin. Clasping her arms around his neck, Ihita pulled herself up until his penis parted her slit. Without hesitation, he plunged deep inside her, gliding on the wetness of her liquid fire, matching her rhythm thrust for thrust as she took all of him to the root of his bursting cock.

Lyle seized her waist, his shuttered gaze riveted to the curved length of his shaft as it plunged in and out of her, each shuddering motion riveting him with heart-stopping waves of achy heat. Her passion was inexhaustible as she clung to him, each thrust wrenching a deep throaty groan from her that drove him wild.

All his questions dissolved in the heat of their passion. This was no dream like the rest. She was real. All his doubts and fear disappeared with the low-sliding sun. He was in the arms of the woman he loved, the woman he never thought he would ever set eyes upon again, the woman whose name meant *desire*. Nothing else mattered.

His senses were exploding. Every nuance of tactile pleasure

was taking him to heights he'd never climbed. Her dusky olive skin glistened with sweat as she clung to him. Her firm round breasts were flattened against his chest. The hardened buds of her nipples boring into him reminded him of another time, a time of passion and of pain in her arms while a blizzard raged outside. He would not lose her again, no matter the cost. How could he live without the perfect sheath for his shaft? How could he die separated from the soul mate he'd found at the top of the world?

Gripping the globes of her behind, he sank to his knees and fell upon her in the soft, cool moss bed. The heady musk of her arousal struck a feral chord in him that rang with resonance throughout his body and soul. He was on the brink of climax, and he slowed his rhythm, wanting to make the ecstasy last, but Ihita had other plans. Rolling, she took him with her, straddling him as she undulated against his shaft, spreading her nether lips to expose the hard dark bud of her clitoris to the base of his penis.

Ihita's breath caught as she undulated against him, the deep, voluptuous swells of her heartbeat triggering a troop of orgasmic sobs as her release came, mellow and full. He could feel the muscles in her vagina contract and throb and pulsate as her tight walls gripped his cock in the involuntary contractions of orgasm. Reaching behind, she gripped his legs, her head bent back until the silken fall of her hair brushed his thighs. Their bodies spoke a language all their own. How could he ever have thought to settle for less than this mysterious phantom lover?

Lyle had not come. He had been holding back to satisfy Ihita and his penis felt as if it would combust imbedded in her silken heat. She began moving her hips in a circular motion as she leaned over him, kneading his pectoral muscles with the heels of her fisted hands, coming closer and closer but not touching his hard nipples. Just when he feared he could stand no more, she swooped down, her silky hair teasing his chest, and laved first one rigid nub and then the other as she ground her clitoris into the thick, hard base of his shaft.

The orgasm was mind-numbing. It was as if he were transported out of his body and hovered somewhere in the treetops gazing down at their coupling in the moonlight streaming through the branches.

Moonlight!

When had the sun set? When had darkness fallen around them like a thick, indigo blanket spangled with stars? Lyle groaned, seeing her through an iridescent golden haze. Her eyes shone with golden fire as well. Where had he seen eyes like that before? His hooded gaze fell upon a dark puckered blemish on her shoulder that he'd overlooked until now in the heat of passion. It was strangely like the wound on the she-cat's shoulder.

He groaned again as she withdrew from him and rose to her feet. How exquisite she was with dappled moonlight spilling down over her, bathing her in a silvery sheen. So absorbed in her beauty, he didn't feel the transformation begin until the pain doubled him over on the ground. He gritted out a guttural moan that became a high-pitched roar as flesh and muscle, sinew and skin stretched and expanded making way for the great snow leopard inside him as it clawed its way into existence in a silvery streak of displaced energy.

But no sooner had he leapt erect on all fours, than across the way, a similar streak of light, like a lightning strike more graceful than his lumbering shapeshift had been, gave birth to another cat—a female, standing in the very spot where seconds before his beautiful Ihita had stood like a marble statue in the moonlight.

Lyle's leopard heart lurched inside, and he froze stock-still as another deep-throated roar spilled from his throat. Just as she had predicted, he had, indeed, come face to face with his worst nightmare.

It was you! His mind cried out. *Last night at Astley's . . . it was you I grappled with, and afterward here in the park!*

The she-cat began to pace and purr, her golden eyes flashing in the moonlight. *Now do you begin to understand?* she said.

248 / Dawn Thompson

Lyle did not understand, except that somehow they were both shapeshifters, something he had never believed to be real. Could she have been savaged by the same cat that attacked him last winter? Whatever the phenomenon, it had originated in the Hindu Kush, and it had tainted them both.

No, I do not understand, Lyle's mind said. *What has happened to us?*

The she-cat padded closer, slinking along the edge of the trees. *You asked how I came here*, she said. *Not of my own free will, my lord. I was captured as you see me when the moon was full, and brought to entertain your people in that arena.*

Lyle rocked back on his haunches. His strong feline legs would no longer support him. *How is it that you did not change back on such a journey as I did in that wagon?*

Ihita's cat ground out another roar. *I have been a were-cat for many eons, my lord. I have learned to control my urges; so will you. Believe me it was to my advantage to remain in the body of the cat, wounded, aboard that stinking vessel with those lecherous men. They never would have taken me but for the bullet wound.*

Lyle snorted. *You would have killed Lady Rose last night if I hadn't intervened*, he realized.

She was not for you! The she-cat roared. *Make no mistake. We are savage beasts in this body, with passions and appetites of the species that has possessed us as well as our human ones. Not the least of these emotions is jealousy.*

Lyle could not take his eyes from her magnificence. The sight of her alone in the body of the cat had aroused him. *So this is what you meant when you said that we are equals*, he knew.

Yes, my lord.

Lyle snorted again, padding in circles, the cool evening breeze ruffling his sleek fur, as he tried to absorb what she was saying. *You said that I had the right to choose. Choose how? I see no choice in this. That cat bit me, and now I am as you see me, as I see you! Where is my choice, Ihita?*

There was a long silence. It could be tasted, like fear, strong and metallic building at the back of his throat, and when she finally spoke to his addled brain, a high-pitched roar preceded her words. *Your choice is, now that you know what I am, whether or not you wish to remain with me, my lord.*

Lyle stopped in his tracks and faced her. *Why wouldn't I want to stay with you?*

Again, she hesitated. *Because, my lord,* she said at last, *it was I who made you what you have become.*

As though she'd struck him, Lyle swayed while he absorbed what she was saying. Of course, how had he not seen it? Was his mind so obsessed with the delights of the flesh that he failed to see that his mysterious lover was also his attacker? It was almost more than he could take in as he stood before her in the little glade beneath the full moon.

If ever a cat could heave a sigh, he was that cat. *Then there is no choice,* he said, sidling closer to her. *We are one in body and soul. We wed by Gypsy rite when we tasted each other's blood, remember? You were the one who told me this, and it must be so, because when your fangs sank into my shoulder, it was as if they sank into my soul. I have been lost in hell without you.*

Ihita allowed him to nuzzle her. *When the cat comes upon us, we are what we are,* she cautioned. *In snow leopard form, we are slaves to the psyche of the cat, and the cat can be a ravenous beast.*

Lyle snarled, his great paw raised in a playful swat. *As well I know firsthand,* he said.

We are also possessed of carnal pleasures unknown to man, she purred. *Last night here in this park was only a taste of the power of the passion of the cat. And there is one more thing our union has granted you, but that will keep 'till later. Come! We have the park all to ourselves.*

She leaped into the air and hit the ground running on all fours, inviting him to chase her through the trees, over the bridle paths, and into the sculptured hedges, over the malls and drives and gardens. Her speed was unmatched as she bounded over the walks and brooks, under the band boxes, over the benches and into the fountains. It was a glorious romp, a celebration of their union. It would culminate in a mating of mind, body, and spirit, a violent, volatile joining of woman, man, and beast, a carnal explosion like no other.

It ended in the little grove where they had shed their clothes, for they would need them come the dawn. They scrambled into the little copse in a blur of fur, muscle, and sinew, their great claws gouging clumps of mulch and winter's leavings from the ground, flinging them into the air as Lyle's great cat brought the she-cat down mounted, his massive paws clasped fast to her hips as he thrust his unsheathed penis, thick and red and slick with pre-come, into the musky depths of her.

The she-cat roared as she raised her hind quarters, inviting him to plunge deeper, her regal tail swept aside to welcome him. Their pelts, wet from the fountains, glistened in the moonlight spilling down over them. She was still in a playful mood, and she clawed the ground in a vain attempt to break free just as the climax hit him like cannon fire. But Lyle was ready for her. Gripping her sides with his claws retracted, for he did not want to hurt her, he made it plain that she wouldn't get away from him that easily. He wanted a taste of the passion she'd promised.

Laving her ear with his tongue, he nuzzled her and growled into the little shell-like protrusion, causing her to shudder and purr. The night was young, and the golden gleam in her eye promised mysteries untold. Dark, deep, sultry mysteries eons old were coming to life in as unlikely a place as England's Hyde Park, under the full round moon.

8

The Hindu Kush, winter, 1811

Lyle yawned and stretched and pulled Ihita close in his arms. Across the way, the hearth fire blazed, bathing them with incandescent heat. It pulsated toward them in erotic waves of radiance, spreading the sultry aroma of herbs, of patchouli and myrrh.

They were naked beneath the quilts, Lyle on his side, Ihita backed up against him as he pulled her close in his arms. He was aroused, his penis resting between the firm round buttocks leaning against him.

Outside, the wind whistled down the mountain pass, driving clouds of swirling snow. It hissed against the cliffside dwelling, tapping upon the windows like a thousand fingertips in the inky darkness, for there was no moon or stars. The dense cloud cover speared by the mountain peaks had swallowed them.

Ihita stirred in his arms and he pulled her closer still. How lovely she was, how soft and fragrant; he couldn't get enough of her. In two days time, the moon would be full again and they would prowl the snow-swept mountain passes from dawn until dusk. They would frolic and romp and couple in their crystalline world until the moon waned once more, for they were were-cats, whose sexual appetites knew no bounds.

They had returned to where it all began. There was no other way. It was not safe to remain in England as they were. Now nights were long, for there were only six or seven hours of sunlight in the Greater Himalayan complex in bitter winter. In summer, just the opposite was true. Then, the hot sun beat down upon the Kush for twelve or thirteen hours a day, warming burgeoning land rich and lush, whose thawed rivers made the place a paradise. All in all, it was good, a sanctuary for snow leopards, and a haven for were-cats whatever the season.

Ihita stirred again, and Lyle began to move his shaft between her legs, riding the tight fissure along her slit from the base of her buttocks to the hardened bud of her clitoris. She was also aroused, and awake, though she played the game as if she weren't, for there was no end to their fantasies, and their passion was limitless.

This time, Lyle raised her to her knees and entered her vagina from behind, in the manner of the cat, though the leopard would not surface in the flesh for two more days at least. Some things carried over from human to animal now, just as some animal traits bled into their human forms. They were one with their creature, and with their passions.

The silken sheath of her vagina gripped his penis as he moved inside her, driving deeper with each shuddering spiral thrust that buried him in her to the thick root of his sex. Hands upon her narrow waist, he plunged faster, deeper, filling her totally as he exploded inside her.

The climax was so riveting, white pinpoints of light starred his vision and his breath was coming short. His pleasure moans more closely resembled the throaty purr of the cat that resided just under the surface of his human skin, ready to erupt into being when the moon waxed full. Then, they would mate out of doors in the snow. They would race through the drifts, over the crude footbridges swaying in the wind that spanned the gap between peaks in desolate places. There, they would savor the thrill of the chase, the exhilaration of the capture, and the ecstasy of release in the wilds of nature. There, as the cats, not even the frozen spires, the stinging snow, or the bitter gusts that drove it could cool the fever in their blood and quell the heat of their desire.

Lyle withdrew himself and lay back, while Ihita straddled him. Backlit by the fire in the hearth, a coppery halo rested upon her long dark hair. She had never looked as beautiful as she did then, like a goddess come to life, and she was his—all his. It was still so hard to believe, but there it was.

Raking her fingernails playfully over his chest she grazed his nipples. His pelvis jerked forward in response. She knew just where to touch him, just how much pressure to use to drive him mad, like now, as she slid her skilled fingers the length of his shaft from root to tip, tracing the distended veins, and circling the rim that wreathed the burled head.

Raising her up, he lowered her upon his penis and cupped her breasts, strumming her tall, dark nipples with his thumbs as she undulated against him, grinding the hard bud of her clitoris into his groin. Lyle felt the deep pulsating contractions of her climax. He felt the warmth of her juices lubricate him as she came, and the shiver that rippled along her spine at the last. It was that little shiver that made him come again riding the contractions that milked him of every drop.

Folding her in his arms, he gathered her against him, and grazed her moist brow with his lips as she crowded close. "Don't ever leave me," he murmured against her hair. How soft it was, like spun silk, its fragrance like an aphrodisiac, casting its mysterious spell.

"Leave you?" she murmured. "I *chose* you, my lord. There

were many soldiers on both sides of the border pass that I could have taken for my mate, but I chose *you*. We are one. You need not fear that I will ever leave you."

"But then you let me go."

"For your own good," she added. "But fate had other plans."

"Back in Hyde Park, you said that there was one more thing I had gained," he said. "But you never told me what it is."

Ihita smiled. "Immortality, my love," she murmured. "Were-cats do not age. You will stay just as you are, wherever you go, whatever you do—leopard and man together as one, just as I am one with my leopard . . . and you will be with me forever."

Lyle pulled her close. Her throaty purring meant something now. Rich and mysterious, it was filled with forbidden promise. There was no need of words. She had said it all. Fisting her hand in his thick, dark hair, she took his lips in a fiery kiss that made him hard again, and said no more.

Turn the page
for a preview of
ANIMAL LUST!
On sale now!

1

Cumberland, England, 1800

Sweet mother! What a blunder she'd made! Jane's hand shot to her mouth, and she bit the skin of her palm.

Jonathan had never loved her. He lied.

Tears blurred her vision and streamed down her cheeks. She tripped and stumbled, barely seeing the wooded trail before her. The flesh of her sex burned, and her legs ached. How she needed a nice long soak in a tub and time to sort this out. Dash it!

When had she misunderstood his intentions? They had been secretly touching and kissing behind his tavern for months. The whole town thought they would marry. Then, today at the fair, they'd snuck into the woods.

"Lovely, lovely Jane, ye give me a tickle, won't ye, love?" The smell of the ale from his breath wafted about her.

She shouldn't, but how she fancied him. What could it matter?

"You will marry me?" she breathed into his hair, her head spinning in aroused bliss.

He grunted as her touch ran down his muscled back.

He'd grunted! Her teeth ground together as she ran without seeing the trail before her. Sweet mother! He had never said he would wed her. She had craved his touch and the feelings he created in her so madly she'd mistook the grunt as an affirmation of his designs.

She'd given her innocence to a man who had no intentions of wedding her. Her fingers clutched her stomach. She could be with child, and she had no way to take care of a babe nor herself. Daft, truly daft.

Her head spun. She gasped for air as her legs tangled in her skirts, and she tripped, landing, limbs spread wide on the hard, damp earth. Oh. She lay, lungs burning, unable to breathe, and closed her eyes. Her entire life had changed in one act of wanton misdeed. She would pull herself together. She would find a way if she carried a child, but for now ... she would grieve while no one could see her.

"Lovely Jane." He buttoned up his trousers as he inhaled a deep breath, the crisp air clouding as he exhaled. "Not bad for a green tickle, and no worries about the clap."

The clap. He'd rutted with her like she was no better than a tavern wench. He loved her. He said he loved her. Her eyes closed as tears welled.

"'Twas a lovely, Jane. Ye have a sweet little honeypot. Take good care of it and we'll come out here again sometime." He turned and headed off into the trees.

By God. What had she done?

With her face down in the dirt, tears silently ran down her face. Her limbs trembled, and her head spun. She hadn't cried in an age. The act depleted and exhausted her. *Pull yourself together, Jane.* With a sob, she straightened and got to her feet on shaking legs. She was a wealthy merchant's daughter. He was friends with her pa. How dare he treat her ill?

Panic grabbed at her heart.

This act ruined her prospects of a normal life and brought

shame on her family name. Her father's business would suffer. How could she be so selfish? Her family, she held dear.

Frantic, her gaze darted around the forest. Nothing but trees. *Think, think, you fool....*

Her fingers pinched the bridge of her nose. She would go to Jonathan and beg him not to say a word. Dash it all. Her eyes squeezed shut.

If she could only figure a way out of the woods. She held her breath, listening for any sounds from the fair. Nothing. What is the rule? Follow the sun and it will lead you to the north.... No.... Sweet mother, she should have listened to her father when he talked about directions.

She stepped toward the setting sun; pain spread through her ankle and up her leg, and her temples throbbed. Ouch! She put weight on her leg and swayed. She could limp but not far.

The forest grew darker. Where was she? She hobbled up the path. Dash it all. Lost, that's where. She picked up her pace. Frost eased up around her heart, and she pushed aching dreams down. Just ahead, a road loomed, and the sun dipped below the horizon. The lane, rutted and ill used, surely led somewhere....

Thunder cracked in the distance as she stared up at the large wooden door. Darkness brewed, and she passed not a soul on the road to this place. The house stood four stories tall, with huge spires that reached to the sky. She had resided in Cumberland for five years, and not once had she heard of an estate such as this. Lifting her hand, she knocked as rain plummeted to the earth in large wet thunks behind her.

She knocked again; shivers raced over her skin. The door creaked open.

"May I help you, ma'am?"

"Oh, indeed." She practically jumped at the man sticking his head out of the small crack. "I'm lost and injured." She pointed to her ankle. "And, well, you see, it is beginning to rain. Would it be possible for me to stay here this night? I could sleep in the kitchen or . . . or . . . the barn. I shan't be any trouble."

The man's eyes went wide behind his round spectacles, and his face twisted in what looked like horror.

"I . . . I . . . know this is highly irregular, but please?"

He schooled his features back to a serious line. "I'm sorry, ma'am. There is no safe way for you to stay here."

Safe? "Pardon?" *Oh, please just let me in.*

The wind whipped up and blew down the last of her pinned-up hair. A shiver racked her body, and her teeth chattered.

"Oh . . . Oh . . ." He glanced into the house. "Very well, ma'am. You will do as I say, do my bidding exclusively. Without fail. Women should not be in this house."

He was concerned about propriety? What a jest! She was ruined. Tears touched her eyes in shame, and she shook them away. What silliness! This man possessed no way of knowing that.

"I will do as you wish, sir." She had no choice. Either she stepped into this house and escaped drowning in one of Cumberland's deluges, or she would try to find her way back in the dark and probably die. She cringed. That was a bit too pessimistic, but she just couldn't go another step this night.

He hesitated and then opened the door just enough to admit her. She slid into the darkened hall and glanced around. A grand staircase stood twisting up to the roof. Dim light shone through a window above the door and illuminated the entry and the paintings that covered the walls. Where did the stair lead? An eerie chill raced up her spine, and she stepped forward, eager to see what lay at their end.

"This way, miss."

Startled, she spun around and followed the servant down a hall that went off to the left of the entry.

"I will put you in the east wing. You will lock your door. Every bolt. I will bring you warm water to wash. After, admit no one to your room."

A bit protective for a servant, but then again, maybe his master was a real curmudgeon. The last thing she wanted was to end up back out in the rain now. "Very well, sir. I have no wish for you to lose your post. I can surely sleep in the kitchen."

"No!" His voice was a sharp shrill.

Her brows drew together as her eyes adjusted to the dim light in the hall they trod down. Why was he so nervous?

"Until I tell Lord Tremarctos you are staying with us, you will stay out of sight." The man swallowed hard. His hand moved upward as though to tweak his collar and then stopped midair as he glanced at her from the corner of his eye.

Odd! Surely she had nothing to fear. Besides, tiredness ruled her, and the events from the day shook her so terribly it would be no problem to stay locked behind a door in this house.

This house. . . . Her gaze darted around the hall, and she almost stopped and spun on the spot. What a beautiful house! The floors shone of a dark, polished marble. The doors stood floor to ceiling with massive iron hinges bigger than anything she had ever seen.

In the dim light she could tell that the house shone with delights she would never see again. Truly a pity. She wished she could see every detail. They turned a corner, and she followed the man up three flights of narrow servants' stairs. At the top of the hall another male servant approached, and the man who let her in waved his hand, calling him to them.

"Bring me hot water, a pitcher, and have Jack send up tea with cheese and biscuits."

"Sir." The man inclined his head and stared at her as she passed.

Her attire was a mess! Nevertheless, politeness dictated that he shouldn't stare. Her fingers picked at the mud that covered her dress, and her gaze settled on her dirt-splattered hands. She rolled her eyes. Just her luck! Finally she saw the inside of a fancy house, and she looked as if she'd spent the day gathering greens from the garden.

Halfway down the hall, they stopped and he pushed open a door. She stepped across the threshold and stopped. Her eyes widened, settling on the well-appointed room. "Oh, sir, a servant's room will suffice."

"No, ma'am. None of the servants' rooms have doors. And . . . well, you promised to lock yourself in."

She turned as he bent to light the fire in the grate. The sputtering flame cast more light into the dark room. Oh, how she wanted to get warm, wash the filth from her body, and curl up in that huge, heavenly bed. Her mouth dropped open. My goodness, the mattress was enormous; the posters were carved but with such dim light she couldn't see the design.

The linens looked a scrumptious deep shade, too dark to discern in the glow from the fire. The image of her lying on deep scarlet silk, naked, flashed before her. Her hair spread across the pillows as a lover caressed her thighs, his head between her legs, licking the entrance to her womb. Her knees wobbled as tingles scorched through her sex. Oh, my! Her hand shot to her mouth in shock, and she shook herself, trying to erase the image from her mind.

Never in her life had such thoughts entered her head. When she imagined the act with Jonathan, loving never involved a bed, and never with his mouth there. Her hand smoothed down the front of her dress to the apex of her thighs. Would kissing there be pleasurable? Her cheeks flushed warm, and she snatched her hand away. Thank goodness no one could see her thoughts!

She was tired; that was all. The man who had passed them brought up water and filled a tub for her to wash in; he was followed by a gentleman with a tea tray. She waited until they left, bolted the door as requested, and then sat down on the chair by the fire. Tears trickled down her face; they were the last she would allow because of Jonathan. Tomorrow would be a new day, and she would find a way out of this mess. But tonight . . . she let herself cry once more.

* * *

A noise pierced her slumber. What was that?

The sound increased as her eyes fluttered open to darkness. The fire in the fireplace burned no more, and the rain outside fell in a deafening pour.

Crack.

Lightning lit the edges of the curtain as a scratching from the other side of the door grew louder. Her heart increased to a fast beat. What was that? A dog?

She pushed back the covers, scrambled to her feet, and crossed the icy room to the door.

She shivered as she stood before the white painted wood. Her gaze scanned the line of eight locks the servant had requested she bolt. She had felt silly when she listened to him, but his nervousness about letting a woman stay here made her wonder what lay beyond that door. Leaning toward the door she placed her ear to the crack.

Sniff, sniff. A low rumble of a growl came from the opposite side. "I can smell you." *Sniff.* "The virgin's blood, the semen, dripping from you."

She jumped and scrambled back, an arm's reach from the door in outrage. How . . . how could anyone know what she did today? She had washed . . . thoroughly. There was no possible way anyone could smell her folly. Was this a dream?

"Who . . . who is there?" Her voice wavered as she reached out and touched the bolts she had thrown that night.

"Let me in." The growl, so low and throaty, made the hairs on her neck stand. "Let me taste what you have so freely given to another."

She continued to stare at the door; shame and panic boiled through her body until her body shook. The scratching increased. The sniffs echoed as if the person outside her door stood beside her. "Let me in. . . . Let me in. . . ." the raspy growl rang, and sweat slid down her back.

264 / Lacy Danes

It would not give up. Somehow she sensed it.

The sound of something dragging widened her eyes, and with a bang, the door shook on its hinges. "Let me in, damn you!" It howled in outrage. "I will have you. There will be no denying me."

"No. . . . go. Leave me be!" She yelled into the blackness and stepped back from the door as the wood once again shook and creaked with the weight of the pounding.

This surely was a dream. Nothing like this could be real.

Her body shook, her gaze stuck on the door. *Please let the locks hold firm.*

A sharp cry of pain came from the other side of the door, and a breath tickled her neck. Her hand shot to that spot as she spun, expecting to see someone there. Nothing. The curtains blew, and the window snapped open with a crack.

Dash it all! She jumped and hurried for the window. The wind howled, blowing her hair back from her face in a gust. She grasped the sodden wood in her hands and tugged; she stared out at the night. Rain came down in sheets, and as the wood frame clicked shut, lightning lit up the gardens below.

A figure clung to the wall at the base of the building. Crimson eyes stared up at her. She gasped, bolted the window, and pushed away from the glass, the curtain falling back as—she swore— the eyes emerged above the edge of the sill.

The cry rang in her head once more. Her heart pounding, she spun and stared at the door.

Nothing. Not a sound except the pounding in her heart. Her body shook uncontrollably as every shadow in the room moved, alive and coming for her.

This is just a dream.

Close your eyes and things will all get better.

She jumped, nerves taut as she stumbled back to the bed and crawled up on the mattress. Her eyes darted back and forth between the window and the door, searching for anything she could make out in the black, but all stayed still.

Just close your eyes and things will be well. In the morning you can leave this place for home.

As she forced her lids shut, quiet met her.